Core Classics Plus™

Little Women

By Louisa May Alcott

Core Knowledge® Foundation

Core Classics Plus™

Editors
Victoria Fortune
Amy Miller

Assistant Editor
Amy Tucker

Senior Editor
Michael L. Ford

Typesetting & Design
James K. Lee

Illustrations
May Alcott
Kazuko Ashizawa
Katy Cummings
Steve Morrison

Copyright © 2007 Core Knowledge Foundation
All Rights Reserved.

ISBN: 978-1-933486-01-7

First Edition
1 2 3 4 5 6 7 8 9 10   11 10 09 08 07

Cover: March Family Portrait,
Kazuko Ashizawa, 2005

Trademarks and trade names are shown in this book strictly for illustrative and educational purposes and are the property of their respective owners. References herein should not be regarded as affecting the validity of said trademarks and trade names.

No part of this work may be photocopied or recorded, added to an information storage or retrieval system, posted to the Web, or otherwise reproduced or transmitted in any form or by any means, electronic or mechanical, without prior written permission of the Core Knowledge Foundation, unless said reproduction or transmission is expressly permitted by federal copyright law. Inquiries regarding permissions should be addressed to the Core Knowledge Foundation, 801 E. High Street, Charlottesville, VA 22902. 1-800-238-3233.

Printed in Canada

Contents

Introduction: Life and Times of Louisa May Alcott v

• Little Women •

1	Playing Pilgrims	1
2	A Merry Christmas.	13
3	The Laurence Boy	26
4	Burdens.	38
5	Being Neighborly	53
6	Beth Finds the Palace Beautiful	63
7	Amy's Valley of Humiliation	73
8	Jo Meets Apollyon	82
9	Meg Goes to Vanity Fair.	96
10	The P.C. and the P.O..	110
11	Experiments	122
12	Camp Laurence.	132
13	Castles in the Air	145
14	Secrets.	153
15	A Telegram	165
16	Letters.	173
17	Little Faithful	183
18	Dark Days	191
19	Amy's Will	205
20	Confidential	212
21	Laurie Makes Mischief, and Jo Makes Peace . . .	222
22	Pleasant Meadows.	234
23	Aunt March Settles the Question	241

• Appendices •

A Final Look 251
Resources for Writers
    Revision Checklist 253
    Proofreading Checklist 255
Glossary 257

Illustrations by May Alcott, from the original 1868 edition of *Little Women*, appear on pages 9, 86, 154, and in the "A Closer Look" icon.

• Introduction •

Louisa May Alcott was born in Germantown, Pennsylvania, on November 29, 1832, during a period known as the Victorian era. At that time, moral standards were very strict. There was a strong belief that men and women were obligated, for the good of society, to embrace separate roles. Women were expected to devote themselves to taking care of their families and doing charitable work. Those who were prim, pious, modest, and self-sacrificing were often called good "little women." Louis May Alcott used this common phrase as the title of her novel about the four March sisters, who strive to live up to this societal ideal. The novel is semi-autobiographical: In many respects, it is based on Louisa May Alcott's life. The striking similarities between the author and her main character, Jo, have led many readers to assume that the two are one and the same. But Alcott was always irritated by this assumption and insisted that she was a very different person than Jo.

One of the main similarities between author and heroine is that Louisa was the second of four sisters, the daughters of Abigail and Bronson Alcott. Louisa's sisters were very much like Jo's. Anna, the eldest, was the most domestic and motherly of the sisters, like Meg in the book. Lizzie, the third sister, was like Beth, fragile and forever sick; and May, the youngest, was a talented artist and seemed to be blessed with good fortune, much like Amy. Of course, Louisa, like Jo, was a writer and the tomboy of the family.

When Louisa was still a young child, the Alcotts moved to Boston, Massachusetts, where Abigail's family lived. Bronson Alcott was not a minister, like Mr. March in the book, but he was a philosopher, writer, and educator, who was dedicated to improving mankind. He was an important figure in a literary and spiritual movement called Transcendentalism. Members of this movement believed that if people's minds were properly molded, they could develop a direct, intuitive connection to God. Ralph Waldo Emerson and Henry David Thoreau, both of whom lived in nearby Concord, Massachusetts, were also leading figures in this movement and were close friends of Bronson Alcott's. When Louisa May Alcott was eight, her family moved to Concord, so that her father could be closer to his friends. This little New England town, where Alcott spent the formative years of her childhood, appears to be the setting for *Little Women*, although the name of the town is never mentioned in the book.

Like many of their associates, Alcott's parents were both highly intelligent and their beliefs were quite progressive. Because Transcendentalists felt that the key to spiritual enlightenment was proper development of the mind, they believed that everyone, including Africans and women, should be educated. Abigail, or "Abba" as she was called, was a dedicated abolitionist, who protested slavery in the years leading up to the Civil War. She was also a suffragette, someone who fought for women's right to vote. During the Victorian era, women in the United States did not have the right to vote, nor many of the other rights that men had. Most people at that time did not think women should be able vote. They thought women should not get involved in politics, but should simply support what their husbands and fathers believed.

Like her mother, and like Jo in the book, Alcott had strong beliefs and opinions of her own. She never felt as though she was suited to fill the role of the proper Victorian woman. As a child, she was painfully aware of the fact that her father did not approve of her wild, irrepressible spirit. She was forever trying to live up to his ideals, to no avail. Despite her rebelliousness and independence, Alcott was deeply influenced by her father. She came to believe, as he did, that her difficulty in accepting her role as a dutiful, reserved woman indicated a major flaw in her character. Outspokenness and resistance to rules were her demons, which she passed on to Jo. And like Jo, Alcott worked through these demons by writing.

Alcott's early literary efforts, much like Jo's in the novel, were devoted to writing plays that she and her sisters performed. In 1852, she became a published writer when one of her poems appeared in a magazine. That was the beginning of a long, successful literary career. Louisa had already been helping to support her family by teaching children and taking in laundry and other odd jobs. Writing gave her the chance to provide real financial security for her family. Bronson Alcott had never been a good provider, and the family was continually plagued by poverty and dependent on wealthy relatives for support—yet another feature of the March family story that coincides with the Alcott's.

Alcott wrote numerous short stories and several novels, gaining some recognition for her talent. Then her publisher asked her to write a "girls' story." Her father had been encouraging her to write a morality story, so Alcott combined the two goals and produced *Little Women*. An indication of her father's influence on her is evident in Alcott's use of one of his favorite books, Pilgrim's Progress, to shape the plot of her novel. Pilgrim's Progress is an allegory—a story in which the characters and places symbolize ideas. The main character, Christian, represents all Christians. He embarks on a difficult journey to reach the Celestial City (Heaven) and must overcome many obstacles along the way, which represent the temptations and sins that humans struggle with. The first mention of Pilgrim's Progress appears in chapter one of *Little Women*, as the March girls reminisce about a game they used to play based on the story. They decide to use the game to aid them in their efforts to improve themselves and become worthy "little women." References to the story continue to surface throughout the book, perhaps as reminders that the March girls, like Christian, are also on a spiritual journey.

Alcott completed the first half of *Little Women* (Part 1) in about two and a half months. The novel, published September 30, 1868, was an instant success. Much to Alcott's surprise, more than 2,000 copies sold immediately. In April of 1869, the second volume (Part 2) was released and more than 13,000 copies flew off the shelves. Since the completion of Part 2, the two parts of the novel have always been published together as one book.

Little Women came out just three years after the Civil War (1861-1865) ended. The war began as a result of deep divisions between people in the North and people in the South. Southerners whose livelihood and traditions depended on slavery, argued that each state should be able to determine whether slavery was legal within its borders. Northerners who were morally opposed to slavery believed that the federal government should be able to pass laws banning it throughout the country. After many decades of trying to compromise over the issue, the two sides reached a breaking point, and the southern states seceded, or withdrew from the Union. To many in the North, the war was about keeping all the states together and preserving the Union. To many white people in the South, it was about protecting their traditional culture and way of life.

The war lasted four long, painful years. In all, more than 600,000 men died and few families escaped without the loss of a loved one. In some cases, brother fought against brother, cousin against cousin. The scars of the war lasted for a very long time. As an abolitionist who was deeply opposed to slavery, Alcott's sympathies clearly lay with the Union (or North). In *Little Women*, Mr. March joins the Union army, and Jo talks about "facing a rebel or two down South." Alcott's references to the conflict remain vague, however, and her sympathetic portrayal of soldiers would have appealed to readers who were still suffering the wounds of war.

Although much of the plot and the characters in *Little Women* are based on Alcott's own experiences, there are some significant differences between her story and Jo's. Unlike in the book, it was Louisa May Alcott, not her father, who signed up to do her duty when the Civil War broke out. She went to Washington, D.C., where she served as a nurse, tending to wounded soldiers. While there, she came down with typhoid, a very dangerous disease. At that time, the common treatment for typhoid was a poison called mercury, which left many survivors with permanent pain and health problems. Alcott was a victim of mercury poisoning and lived with chronic pain for the rest of her life. The moving descriptions of Beth's pain in the novel are likely based on her own suffering.

Another major difference between Jo and Alcott is that Alcott never did accept the role of a little woman. Her writing gave her the financial freedom that few women of her era enjoyed. As a result, she was able to live a fairly independent lifestyle. She never married or had a family of her own; she called her books her little children. As much as her father disapproved of her willfulness and fierce independence, it was these same qualities that enabled her to support him for much of her adult life. She wrote *Little Women* in part to please him and did not think the book would receive any recognition. Nevertheless, it has captured the imagination of generations of readers and provides a fairly accurate idea of what life was like, especially for women, in the late 1800s in New England.

Victoria Fortune
Boxford, Massachusetts

CHAPTER 1

Playing Pilgrims

"Christmas won't be Christmas without any presents," grumbled Jo, lying on the rug.

"It's so dreadful to be poor!" sighed Meg, looking down at her old dress.

"I don't think it's fair for some girls to have plenty of pretty things, and other girls nothing at all," added little Amy, with an injured sniff.

"We've got Father and Mother, and each other," said Beth **contentedly** from her corner.

The four young faces brightened at the cheerful words, but darkened again as Jo said sadly, "We haven't got Father and shall not have him for a long time." Each girl silently added "perhaps never," thinking of Father far away, where the fighting was.

Where has Father gone? Why are the girls worried that they will not see him again?

Nobody spoke for a minute; then Meg said, "Mother thinks we ought not to spend money for presents, when our men are suffering so in the army. We can't do much, but we can make our little sacrifices, and ought to do it gladly. But I am afraid I don't," said Meg regretfully, as she thought of all the pretty things she wanted.

"But I don't think the dollar we've each got to spend would do the army much good. I agree not to expect anything from Mother or you, but I do want to buy *Undine and Sintram*[1] for myself. I've wanted it so long," said Jo, who was a bookworm.

"I planned to spend mine in new music," said Beth, with a little sigh, which no one heard.

---

[1] *Undine and Sintram.* Popular romance novel by German author Frederick de la Motte Fouque (1777–1843)

Vocabulary in Place
contentedly, *adv.* With a calm, quiet feeling of comfort or satisfaction

"I was going to buy a nice box of drawing pencils; I really need them," said Amy decidedly.

"Mother won't wish us to give up everything. Let's each buy what we want and have a little fun; I'm sure we work hard enough to earn it," cried Jo.

"I know I do—teaching those tiresome children nearly all day," began Meg, in the complaining tone again.

"You don't have half such a hard time as I do," said Jo. "How would you like to be shut up for hours with a fussy old lady, who is never satisfied and worries you till you're ready to fly out the window?"

"It's naughty to fret, but I do think washing dishes and keeping things tidy is the worst work in the world. My hands get so stiff, I can't practice well at all." Beth looked at her rough hands with a sigh that any one could hear that time.

"I don't believe any of you suffer as I do," cried Amy, "for you don't have to go to school with girls who laugh at your dresses, and *label* your father if he isn't rich, and insult you when your nose isn't nice."

Why does Jo laugh?

"If you mean **libel,** then say so, and don't talk about labels, as if Papa was a pickle bottle," advised Jo, laughing.

"You needn't be *statirical*[2] about it. It's proper to use good words, and improve your *vocabilary*," returned Amy, with dignity.

"Don't peck at one another, children. Don't you wish we had the money Papa lost when we were little, Jo? Dear me! How happy we'd be!" said Meg, who could remember better times.

"You said, the other day, you thought we were a good deal happier than the King children, for they were fighting and fretting all the time, in spite of their money."

"So I did, Beth. Well, I think we are. For though we do have to work, we are a pretty jolly set, as Jo would say."

---

[2] **statirical.** Amy meant to say *satirical*, or *sarcastic*, because she thought Jo was making fun of her. (See also Vocabulary in Place, page 77.)

Vocabulary in Place
libel, *v.* To make a false written or spoken statement that damages someone's reputation

"Jo does use such slang words!" observed Amy, with a **reproving** look at the long figure stretched on the rug.

Jo immediately sat up and began to whistle.

"Don't, Jo. It's so boyish!"

"That's why I do it."

"I detest rude, unladylike girls!"

"I hate **affected,** niminy-piminy chits!"³

"Birds in their little nests agree," sang Beth, the peacemaker, with such a funny face that both sharp voices softened to a laugh.

"Really, girls, you are both to be blamed," said Meg, beginning to lecture in her elder-sisterly fashion. Margaret, the oldest of the four sisters, was sixteen, and very pretty, being plump and fair, with large eyes, plenty of soft brown hair, a sweet mouth, and white hands, of which she was rather **vain**.

"You are old enough to leave off boyish tricks, Josephine. It didn't matter so much when you were a little girl, but now you are so tall, and turn up your hair; you should remember that you are a young lady."

"I'm not! And if turning up my hair makes me one, I'll wear it in two tails till I'm twenty," cried Jo, pulling off her net, and shaking down a chestnut mane.

Fifteen-year-old Jo was very tall, thin, and brown, and reminded one of a colt, for her long limbs were very much in her way. She had a decided⁴ mouth, a comical nose, and sharp, gray eyes, which appeared to see everything. Her long, thick hair was her one beauty, but it was usually bundled into a net, to be out of her way. She had big hands and feet, a flyaway look to her clothes, and the uncomfortable appearance of a girl who was rapidly shooting up into a woman and didn't like it.

Who is squabbling here, and what are they arguing about?

---

³ **niminy-piminy chit.** Bad-mannered child
⁴ **decided.** Well-defined

Vocabulary in Place

reproving, *adj.* Disapproving

affected, *adj.* Speaking or acting in an artificial way in order to make an impression

vain, *adj.* Excessively proud of one's appearance or accomplishments

Why is Jo knitting a blue army sock? What would she rather be doing?

"I hate to think I've got to grow up, and be Miss March, and wear long gowns, and look prim! It's bad enough to be a girl, anyway, when I like boy's games and work and manners! And it's worse than ever now, for I'm dying to go and fight with Papa. And I can only stay home and knit, like an old woman!" And Jo shook the blue army sock she was knitting till the needles rattled like castanets,[5] and her ball bounded across the room.

"Poor Jo! It's too bad, but it can't be helped. So you must try to be contented with making your name boyish, and playing brother to us girls," said Beth, stroking the rough head with a hand that all the dish washing and dusting in the world could not make ungentle in its touch.

Elizabeth, or Beth, as everyone called her, was a rosy, smooth-haired, bright-eyed girl of thirteen. She had a shy manner, a timid voice, and a peaceful expression which was seldom disturbed. Her father called her "Little Miss **Tranquility**," and the name suited her excellently, for she seemed to live in a happy world of her own, only venturing out to meet the few whom she trusted and loved.

"As for you, Amy," continued Meg, "you are altogether too particular and prim. You'll grow up an affected little goose, if you don't take care. I like your nice manners and **refined** ways of speaking, but your absurd words are as bad as Jo's slang."

Amy, though the youngest, was a most important person, in her own opinion at least. A regular snow maiden, with blue eyes, and yellow hair curling on her shoulders, pale and slender, she always carried herself like a young lady mindful of her manners.

"If Jo is a tomboy and Amy a goose, what am I, please?" asked Beth, ready to share the lecture.

---

[5] **castanets.** A small hand-held instrument that makes a clapping sound

> **Vocabulary in Place**
>
> **tranquility,** *n.* A state of being calm, peaceful, and unruffled; not easily disturbed
>
> **refined,** *adj.* Smooth and polished; improved through hard work and effort

"You're a dear, and nothing else," answered Meg warmly, and no one contradicted her, for the "Mouse" was the pet of the family.

The four sisters sat knitting away in the twilight, while the December snow fell quietly without, and the fire crackled cheerfully within. It was a comfortable room, though the carpet was faded and the furniture very plain, for a good picture or two hung on the walls, books filled the **recesses,** chrysanthemums[6] and Christmas roses bloomed in the windows, and a pleasant atmosphere of home peace **pervaded** it.

The clock struck six and everyone brightened, for Mother was coming home. Having swept up the hearth, Beth put a pair of slippers down to warm.

What do the girls do when the clock strikes six?

"They are quite worn out. Marmee must have a new pair."

"I thought I'd get her some with my dollar," said Beth.

"No, I shall!" cried Amy.

"I'm the oldest," began Meg, but Jo cut in with a decided tone. "I'm the man of the family now that Papa is away, and I shall provide the slippers, for he told me to take special care of Mother while he was gone."

"I'll tell you what we'll do," said Beth. "Let's each get her something for Christmas, and not get anything for ourselves."

"That's like you, dear! What will we get?" exclaimed Jo.

Everyone thought for a minute, then Meg announced, as if the idea was suggested by the sight of her own pretty hands, "I shall give her a nice pair of gloves."

"Army shoes, best to be had," cried Jo.

"Some handkerchiefs, all hemmed," said Beth.

"I'll get a little bottle of cologne. She likes it, and it won't cost much, so I'll have some left to buy my pencils," added Amy.

Why is Amy planning to get the little bottle?

---

[6] **chrysanthemum.** A type of flower with large flower heads

Vocabulary in Place
recess, *n.* An indentation or niche (in this case, along a wall or between furniture)
pervade, *v.* To spread into every corner

"We must go shopping tomorrow afternoon, Meg," said Jo, marching up and down with her hands behind her back and her nose in the air. "There is so much to do about the play for Christmas night."

"I don't mean to act any more after this time. I'm getting too old for such things," observed Meg, who was as much a child as ever about "dressing-up" frolics.

"You won't stop, I know, as long as you can trail round in a white gown with your hair down, and wear gold-paper jewelry. You are the best actress we've got, and there'll be an end of everything if you quit," said Jo. "We ought to rehearse tonight. Come here, Amy, and do the fainting scene, for you are as stiff as a poker[7] in that."

"I can't help it. I never saw anyone faint, and I don't choose to make myself all black and blue, tumbling flat as you do. If I can go down easily, I'll drop. If I can't, I shall fall into a chair and be graceful. I don't care if Hugo does come at me with a pistol," returned Amy, who was not gifted with dramatic power, but was chosen because she was small enough to be carried out shrieking by the villain of the piece.

"Do it this way. Clasp your hands so, and stagger across the room, crying frantically, 'Roderigo! Save me! Save me!'" and away went Jo, with a melodramatic scream, which was truly thrilling.

Amy followed, but she poked her hands out stiffly before her, and jerked herself along as if she went by machinery, and her "Ow!" was more suggestive of pins being run into her than of fear and anguish.

Jo gave a **despairing** groan. "It's no use! Do the best you can when the time comes, and if the audience laughs, don't blame me."

"I don't see how you can write and act such splendid things, Jo. You're a regular Shakespeare!" exclaimed Beth.

---

[7] **stiff as a poker.** A poker is an iron rod used for poking wood in a fire. The phrase "stiff as a poker" means *without expression*.

Vocabulary in Place

despairing, *adj.* Without any hope

"Not quite," replied Jo **modestly,** "but I do think *The Witch's Curse, an Operatic Tragedy*[8] is rather a nice thing."

"Hello, dearies, how have you got on today?" said a cheery voice at the door, and actors and audience turned to welcome a tall, motherly lady. She was not elegantly dressed, but a noble-looking woman, and the girls thought the gray cloak and unfashionable bonnet covered the most splendid mother in the world. "There was so much to do today that I didn't come home to dinner.[9] Has anyone called, Beth? How is your cold, Meg? Jo, you look tired to death. Come and kiss me, baby."

What is Mrs. March wearing? Do these clothes affect the way the girls look at her?

While making these motherly **inquiries,** Mrs. March got her wet things off and her warm slippers on. Sitting down in the easy chair, she drew Amy to her lap, preparing to enjoy the happiest hour of her busy day. The girls flew about, trying to make things comfortable, each in her own way. Meg arranged the tea table, as Jo brought wood and set chairs, dropping, over-turning, and clattering everything she touched. Beth trotted to and fro between parlor and kitchen, quiet and busy, while Amy gave directions to everyone, as she sat with her hands folded.

As they gathered about the table, Mrs. March said, with a particularly happy face, "I've got a treat for you after supper."

A quick, bright smile went round like a streak of sunshine. Beth clapped her hands, and Jo tossed up her napkin, crying, "A letter! A letter! Three cheers for Father!"

"Yes, a nice long letter. He is well, and sends all sorts of loving wishes for Christmas, and an especial message to you girls," said Mrs. March, patting her pocket as if she had a treasure there.

---

[8] ***The Witch's Curse, an Operatic Tragedy.*** Jo's play, which the girls are rehearsing

[9] **dinner.** The afternoon meal, called *lunch* in modern times

Vocabulary in Place

modestly, *adv.* With a moderate opinion of one's own talent and abilities

inquiry, *n.* A question about something or someone

"When will he come home, Marmee?" asked Beth, with a little quiver in her voice.

"Not for many months, dear, unless he is sick. He will stay and do his work faithfully as long as he can, and we won't ask for him back a minute sooner than he can be spared. Now come and hear the letter."

"Hurry and get done! Don't stop to smile over your plate, Amy," cried Jo, choking on her tea and dropping her bread, butter side down, on the carpet in her haste to get at the treat.

Beth ate no more but crept away to sit in her shadowy corner and think about the delight to come, till the others were ready.

What does Father do in the army? Why?

"I think it was so splendid of Father to go as chaplain when he was too old to be drafted, and not strong enough for a soldier," said Meg warmly.

"Don't I wish I could go as a drummer, a *vivan*[10]—what's its name? Or a nurse, so I could be near him and help him," exclaimed Jo, with a groan.

"It must be very disagreeable to sleep in a tent, and eat all sorts of bad-tasting things, and drink out of a tin mug," sighed Amy.

They all drew to the fire, Mother in the big chair with Beth at her feet, Meg and Amy perched on either arm of the chair, and Jo leaning on the back, where no one would see any sign of emotion if the letter should happen to be touching. Very few letters were written in those hard times that were not touching, especially those which fathers sent home. In this one little was said of the hardships endured, the dangers faced, or the homesickness conquered. It was a cheerful, hopeful letter, full of lively descriptions of camp life, marches, and military news, and only at the end did the writer's heart overflow with fatherly love and longing for the little girls at home.

What is the tone of Mr. March's letter?

"Give them all of my dear love and a kiss. Tell them I think of them by day and pray for them by night. A year seems very long to wait before I see them, but remind them that these hard days need not be wasted. I know that they will be loving children and will do their duty faithfully and improve themselves so beautifully that when I come back to them, I may be fonder and prouder than ever of my little women."

---

10 **vivan.** Short for *vivandière*, a woman who sells supplies to soldiers

Everybody sniffed when they came to that part. A great tear dropped off the end of Jo's nose and Amy hid her face on her mother's shoulder, sobbing out, "I am a selfish girl! But I'll truly try to be better, so he won't be disappointed in me."

"We all will," cried Meg. "I think too much of my looks and hate to work, but won't any more, if I can help it."

"I'll try and be what he loves to call me, 'a little woman,' and not be rough and wild," said Jo, thinking that keeping her temper at home was a much harder task than facing a rebel[11] or two down South.

Beth said nothing, but wiped away her tears and began to knit with all her might, losing no time in doing her duty. She **resolved** in her quiet little soul to be all that Father hoped her to be by the time he returned home.

Mrs. March broke the silence that followed Jo's words, by saying in her cheery voice, "Do you remember how you used to play *Pilgrim's Progress*[12] when you were little things? Nothing delighted you more than to have me tie bundles on your backs for burdens, give you hats and sticks and rolls of paper, and let you travel through the house from the cellar, which was the City of Destruction, up, up, to the housetop, where you had all the lovely things you could collect to make a Celestial City."

"What fun it was, especially going by the lions, fighting Apollyon,[13] and passing through the valley where the hobgoblins were," said Jo.

"I don't remember much about it, except that I was afraid of the cellar and always liked the cake and milk we had up at the top. If I

---

[11] **rebel.** A common name for a solider who fought for the Confederacy

[12] ***Pilgrim's Progress.*** A seventeenth-century allegorical story in which the main character, Christian—who represents all Christians—faces many obstacles on his journey from the City of Destruction to the Celestial City, or Heaven

[13] **Apollyon.** A name for the Devil in early Christian literature, including *Pilgrim's Progress*; often depicted as a terrifying, dragon-like creature

Vocabulary in Place
resolve, *v.* To make a commitment to do something

wasn't too old for such things, I'd rather like to play it over again," said Amy, who began to talk of **renouncing** childish things at the mature age of twelve.

Does Amy want to play the game?

"We never are too old for this, my dear. It is a play we are playing all the time in one way or another. Our burdens are here, our road is before us, and the search for goodness and happiness leads us through many troubles and mistakes to the peace of the Celestial City. Now, my little pilgrims, suppose you begin again, not in play, but in earnest, and see how far on you can get before Father comes home."

"Really, Mother? Where are our bundles?" asked Amy, who was very **literal**.

"Each of you told what your burden was just now, except Beth. I rather think she hasn't got any," said her mother.

"Yes, I have. Mine is dishes and dusters, and envying girls with nice pianos, and being afraid of people."

Beth's bundle was such a funny one that everybody wanted to laugh, but nobody did, for it would have hurt her feelings very much.

What is funny about Beth's "bundle"? How is it different from the girls' other bundles?

"Let us do it," said Meg thoughtfully. "It is only another name for trying to be good, and the story may help us, for it's hard work and we forget, and don't do our best."

"We ought to have a guidebook, like Christian. What shall we do about that?" asked Jo, delighted with the game, which lent a little romance to the very dull task of doing her duty.

"Look under your pillows Christmas morning, and you will find your guidebook," replied Mrs. March.

They talked over the new plan while old Hannah[14] cleared the table, then out came the four little work baskets, and the needles flew as the girls made sheets for Aunt March. It was uninteresting sewing,

---

[14] **Hannah.** Their housekeeper. (She is described in Chapter 2.)

Vocabulary in Place
renounce, *v.* To give up something, especially for good
literal, *adj.* Focused on exactly what is said, word for word

but tonight no one grumbled. They adopted Jo's plan of dividing the long seams into four parts, and calling the quarters Europe, Asia, Africa, and America, and in that way got on **capitally,** especially when they talked about the different countries as they stitched their way through them.

At nine they stopped working and sang, as usual, before they went to bed. No one but Beth could get much music out of the old piano, but she had a way of softly touching the yellow keys and making a pleasant accompaniment to the simple songs they sang. They had done this from the time they could **lisp** . . .

Crinkle, crinkle, 'ittle 'tar,

and it had become a household custom, for the mother was a born singer. The first sound in the morning was her voice as she went about the house singing, and the last sound at night was the same cheery sound, for the girls never grew too old for that familiar lullaby.

Vocabulary in Place

capitally, *adv.* Agreeably; excellently

lisp, *v.* To speak imperfectly, like a child

CHAPTER 2

A Merry Christmas

Jo was the first to wake in the gray dawn of Christmas morning. No stockings hung at the fireplace, and for a moment she felt terribly disappointed. Then she remembered her mother's promise and, slipping her hand under her pillow, drew out a little crimson-covered book. She knew it very well, for it was that beautiful old story of the best life ever lived,[1] and Jo felt that it was a true guidebook for any pilgrim going on a long journey.

Why was Jo disappointed at first?

Soon Meg and Beth and Amy woke to **rummage** and find their little books also. One was green-covered, another dove-colored, and the final blue. They each had the same picture inside, and a few words written by Marmee, which made the girls' one present very precious in their eyes. All sat looking at and talking about them, while the east grew rosy with the coming day.

"Girls," said Meg seriously, "Mother wants us to read and love and mind these books, and we must begin at once. I shall keep my book on the table here and read a little every morning as soon as I wake, for I know it will do me good and help me through the day."

Then she opened her new book and began to read. Jo put her arm round her and, leaning cheek to cheek, read also, with the quiet expression so **seldom** seen on her restless face.

---

[1] **old story . . . ever lived.** The "beautiful old story" is a reference to the Bible. The "best life ever lived" refers to that of Jesus Christ.

Vocabulary in Place
rummage, *v.* To search through a pile or layer of things
seldom, *adv.* Not often; rarely

"Come, Amy, let's do as they do. I'll help you with the hard words, and they'll explain things if we don't understand," whispered Beth, very much impressed by the pretty books and her sisters' example.

"I'm glad mine is blue," said Amy. And then the rooms were very still while the pages were softly turned, and the winter sunshine crept in to touch the bright heads and serious faces with a Christmas greeting.

"Where is Mother?" asked Meg, as she and Jo ran down to thank her for their gifts, half an hour later.

"Goodness only knows," replied Hannah, who had lived with the family since Meg was born, and was considered by them all more as a friend than a servant. "Some poor creeter came a-beggin', and your ma went straight off to see what was needed. There never was such a woman for givin' away vittles and drink, clothes and firin'."[2]

How does Mrs. March respond when someone comes begging on Christmas morning?

"She will be back soon, I think, so fry your cakes, and have everything ready," said Meg, looking over the presents, which were collected in a basket under the sofa, ready to be produced at the proper time. "Why, where is Amy's bottle of cologne?" she added, as the little flask did not appear.

"She took it out a minute ago, and went off with it to put a ribbon on it, or some such **notion**," replied Jo, dancing about the room to take the first stiffness off the new army slippers.

"How nice my handkerchiefs look, don't they?" said Beth, looking proudly at the somewhat uneven letters, which had cost her such labor.

Then a door slammed and steps sounded in the hall.

"There's Mother. Hide the basket, quick!" cried Jo.

Amy came in hastily and looked rather **abashed** when she saw her sisters all waiting for her.

---

[2] **creeter . . . firin'.** *Creeter* means creature; *vittles* refers to food; and *firin'* means firewood.

> **Vocabulary in Place**
>
> **notion,** *n.* Impulse, whim; a spur-of-the-moment idea or decision
>
> **abashed,** *past part.* Taken aback, as from embarrassment

"Where have you been, and what are you hiding behind you?" asked Meg, surprised to see that lazy Amy had been out so early.

"I went out to exchange the small bottle of cologne for a larger one," Amy explained. "You see I felt ashamed of my present, after reading and talking about being good this morning. So I ran round the corner and changed it the minute I was up, and I'm so glad, for mine is the handsomest now."

Another bang of the street door sent the basket under the sofa, and the girls to the table, eager for breakfast.

"Merry Christmas, Marmee! Thank you for our books. We read some, and mean to every day," they all cried in chorus.

"Merry Christmas, little daughters! I'm glad you began at once, and hope you will keep on. But I want to say one word before we sit down. Not far away from here lies a poor woman with a little newborn baby. Six children are huddled into one bed to keep from freezing, for they have no fire. They have nothing to eat, and the oldest boy came to tell me they were suffering hunger and cold. My girls, will you give them your breakfast as a Christmas present?"

They were all unusually hungry, having waited nearly an hour, and for a minute no one spoke. Then Jo cried out, "I'm so glad you came before we began!"

"May I go and help carry the things to the poor little children?" asked Beth eagerly.

"I shall take the cream and the muffins," added Amy, heroically giving up the article she most liked.

Meg was already covering the buckwheats,[3] and piling the bread into one big plate.

"I thought you'd do it," said Mrs. March, smiling as if satisfied. "You shall all go and help me, and when we come back we will have bread and milk for breakfast, and make it up at dinnertime."

Why does Amy go out to exchange the small bottle of cologne for a larger one?

---

[3] **buckwheats,** *n.* Pancakes

They quickly got themselves ready, and the **procession** set out. Soon they arrived at the poor, bare, miserable room, with broken windows, no fire, ragged bedclothes, a sick mother, wailing baby, and a group of pale, hungry children cuddled under one old quilt, trying to keep warm. How the big eyes stared and the blue lips smiled as the girls went in.

Whose lips are blue, and why are they smiling now?

"Ach, mein Gott![4] It is good angels come to us!" said the poor woman, crying for joy.

In a few minutes it really did seem as if kind spirits had been at work there. Hannah, who had carried wood, made a fire and stopped up the broken panes with old hats and her own cloak. Mrs. March gave the mother tea and gruel,[5] and comforted her with promises of help while she dressed the little baby tenderly. The girls meantime spread the table, set the children round the fire, and fed them like so many hungry birds, laughing, talking, and trying to understand the funny broken English.

"Das ist gut!" "Die Engel-kinder!" cried the poor things as they ate and warmed their purple hands at the comfortable blaze.

The girls had never been called angel children before, and thought it very agreeable. That was a very happy breakfast, though they didn't get any of it. And when they went away, leaving comfort behind, I think there were not in all the city four merrier people than the hungry little girls who gave away their breakfasts and contented themselves with bread and milk on Christmas morning.

"That's loving our neighbor better than ourselves, and I like it," said Meg, as they set out their presents while their mother was upstairs collecting clothes for the poor Hummels.

Not a very splendid show, but there was a great deal of love done up in the few little bundles on the table.

---

[4] **Ach, mein Gott!** A German exclamation meaning "Oh, my God!"

[5] **gruel.** Porridge

Vocabulary in Place

procession, *n.* A group of people (or vehicles) moving along in an orderly fashion

"She's coming! Strike up, Beth! Open the door, Amy! Three cheers for Marmee!" cried Jo. Beth played her gayest march, Amy threw open the door, and Meg escorted Marmee to the table with great **dignity**. Mrs. March was both surprised and touched, and smiled with her eyes full as she examined her presents and read the little notes that accompanied them. The slippers went on at once, a new handkerchief was slipped into her pocket, well scented with Amy's cologne, and the nice gloves were pronounced a perfect fit. There was a good deal of laughing and kissing and explaining, in a simple, loving fashion. Then all fell to work.

The morning charities and ceremonies took so much time that the rest of the day was devoted to preparations for the evening festivities. Necessity being the mother of invention, the girls put their **wits** to work and made whatever they needed to set the stage for Jo's play. Very clever were some of their productions—pasteboard guitars, gorgeous robes of old cotton, glittering with tin spangles, and armor covered with the same useful diamond-shaped bits left in sheets when the lids of preserve pots from a pickle factory were cut out.

The big chamber was the scene of many innocent revels.[6] No gentlemen were admitted, so Jo played male parts to her heart's content. She took **immense** satisfaction in a pair of russet[7] leather boots given her by a friend, which she wore in her masculine roles. Jo and Meg certainly deserved some credit for the hard work they did in learning three or four different parts, whisking in and out of various costumes, and managing the stage besides. It was an excellent drill for their memories and employed many hours which otherwise would have been **idle,** lonely, or spent in less profitable society.

What does the expression "necessity being the mother of invention" mean?

How is performing the play good for the girls' minds and bodies?

---

[6] **revel.** Celebration or fun
[7] **russet.** Dark reddish brown

Vocabulary in Place
dignity, *n.* The respect and honor associated with an important position
wits, *n.pl.* Intelligence and resourcefulness
immense, *adj.* Enormous; of very large size or extent
idle, *adj.* Lacking substance, value, or basis

Who is in the audience?

On Christmas night, a dozen girls piled onto the bed and sat before the curtains in a most flattering state of **expectancy**. There was a good deal of rustling and whispering behind the curtain and an occasional giggle from Amy. Presently a bell sounded, the curtains flew apart, and the *Operatic Tragedy* began.

"A gloomy wood," according to the one playbill,[8] was represented by a few shrubs in pots, green felt on the floor, and a cave in the distance, made with a clotheshorse[9] for a roof and bureaus for walls. In the cave was a black pot, with an old witch bending over it. A moment was allowed for the first thrill to subside. Then, Hugo the villain, stalked in with a clanking sword at his side, a slouching hat, black beard, mysterious cloak, and the boots.

Who is playing the part of Hugo?

—*The editors have here abridged the original text.*

[*He approached the witch and requested her aid in his plot to win the heart of the beautiful Zara and do away with her love, Roderigo. The witch agreed to help Hugo and produced two potions—one, a poison with which to kill Roderigo, the other, a love potion, to make Zara fall in love with him. After Hugo stormed off to carry out his evil scheme, the witch slyly revealed to the audience that she was plotting revenge against Hugo, and intended to stop his devilish plan.*

Act II featured Don Pedro, Zara's father, ordering Roderigo to stop pursuing his daughter, for he was penniless and had nothing to offer. When the two young lovers defied his wishes, he had them both thrown into the dungeon, where Hugo attempted to carry out his plan. The witch was to deliver the potions to the couple in prison, but she switched Hugo's cup for Roderigo's, and Hugo died a dramatic death made all the more serious by the song of the choir.

The actors performed their multiple roles with such skill and flair that all but the most critical audience would have been impressed by the final effect. Even when the tower, a masterpiece of carpentry hastily erected

---

[8] **playbill.** A poster announcing a theatrical performance
[9] **clotheshorse.** A wooden frame on which clothes are hung to dry

Vocabulary in Place
expectancy, *n.* Expectation; eager awaiting of something

between acts, came toppling down upon the hero and his love, the actors took no time in disentangling themselves and carried on as if the small disaster had been part of the plot. In the end, Roderigo and Zara were united and all the players joined in a joyful chorus, as the curtain fell upon the happy scene.]

Thunderous applause followed but was unexpectedly interrupted when the cot bed suddenly shut up and extinguished the enthusiastic audience. The actors flew to the rescue, and all were taken out unhurt, though many were speechless with laughter. The excitement had hardly subsided when Hannah appeared, offering "Mrs. March's compliments, and would the ladies walk down to supper."

This was a surprise even to the actors, and when they saw the table, they looked at one another in **rapturous** amazement. It was like Marmee to get up a little treat for them, but anything so fine as this was unheard of since the departed days of plenty. There was ice cream, actually two dishes of it, pink and white, and cake and fruit and distracting French bonbons and, in the middle of the table, four great bouquets of flowers.

When were "the departed days of plenty"? Why is this feast such a treat?

It quite took their breath away, and they stared first at the table and then at their mother, who looked as if she enjoyed it immensely.

"Is it fairies?" asked Amy.

"Santa Claus," said Beth.

"Mother did it." And Meg smiled her sweetest, in spite of her gray beard and white eyebrows.

"Aunt March had a good fit and sent the supper," cried Jo, with a sudden inspiration.

"All wrong. Old Mr. Laurence sent it," replied Mrs. March.

"The Laurence boy's grandfather! What in the world put such a thing into his head? We don't know him!" exclaimed Meg.

"Hannah told one of his servants about your breakfast party and that pleased him. He knew my father years ago, and he sent me a polite note this afternoon, saying he hoped I would allow him to

---

Vocabulary in Place

rapturous, *adj.* Ecstatic (very happy) and overcome with awe or surprise; thrilled

express his friendly feeling toward my children by sending them a few treats in honor of the day. I could not refuse, and so you have a little feast at night to make up for the bread-and-milk breakfast."

"That boy put it into his head, I know he did! He's a capital fellow, and I wish we could get acquainted. He looks as if he'd like to know us but he's bashful, and Meg is so **prim** she won't let me speak to him when we pass," said Jo, as the plates went round, and the ice began to melt out of sight, with ohs and ahs of satisfaction.

"You mean the people who live in the big house next door, don't you?" asked one of the girls. "My mother knows old Mr. Laurence, but says he's very proud and doesn't like to mix with his neighbors. He keeps his grandson shut up, when he isn't riding or walking with his tutor, and makes him study very hard. We invited him to our party, but he didn't come. Mother says he's very nice, though he never speaks to us girls."

"Our cat ran away once, and he brought her back. We talked over the fence and were getting on capitally, all about cricket, and so on, when he saw Meg coming and walked off. I mean to know him some day, for he needs fun, I'm sure he does," said Jo decidedly.

"He looks like a little gentleman, so I've no objection to your knowing him, if a proper opportunity comes," said Mrs. March. "He brought the flowers himself, and I should have asked him in, if I had been sure what was going on upstairs. He looked so **wistful** as he went away, hearing the frolic and evidently having none of his own."

"It's a mercy you didn't, Mother!" laughed Jo, looking at her boots. "But we'll have another play sometime that he can see. Perhaps he'll help act. Wouldn't that be jolly?"

"I never had such a fine bouquet before! How pretty it is!" said Meg.

"I wish I could send my bunch to Father," said Beth softly. "I'm afraid he isn't having such a merry Christmas as we are."

Vocabulary in Place

prim, *adj.* Very precise and proper; straight-laced

wistful, *adj.* Tinged with sadness or regret

Who is "the Laurence boy"? Do you think the girls will get to know him?

Why does Beth wish that she could send her flowers to her father?

Understanding the Selection

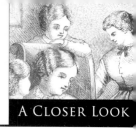

A Closer Look

Recalling (just the facts)

1. Why does Marmee think that the March family should not buy any Christmas presents for one another this year?
2. Name two things that Jo does that are considered "unladylike" behavior.
3. Who is the shy "Mouse" of the family? How can you tell?
4. Where does Marmee go first thing Christmas morning? What does she ask her daughters to do when she gets back?

Interpreting (delving deeper)

1. Is this Christmas a happy one for the March family? Why or why not?
2. How do you think teenaged girls were expected to behave in the 1860s? Is Jo comfortable with staying home and knitting, or would she rather be doing something else?
3. Which sister seems to be the most self-centered one? Which one seems to be the least selfish? How can you tell?
4. Whose idea was it to treat the March girls to such a nice supper on Christmas Day, and why did he come up with that idea?

Synthesizing (putting it all together)

1. Marmee reads the girls a letter from their father. In the letter, he urges them all to be good and "to improve themselves so . . . that he will be fonder and prouder than ever of [his] little women" when he comes back from the war. Which sister expects to have the hardest time meeting this goal? Why does she expect it to be "much harder . . . than facing a rebel or two down South?" Is she a bit of a rebel herself?
2. Is Amy really a spoiled brat, or is she just too young to know any better? Use examples from the story to support your answer.

Writing

Writing Exercise. As the curtain lifts on *Little Women,* the March girls are knitting in their living room and talking about the coming Christmas. Louisa May Alcott draws readers into the world of the March family by illustrating each character's **personality traits** and the overall atmosphere in their home. In addition to providing an initial **characterization** for each of the main characters in the book, the opening of the novel also reveals the book's **setting**—the location and historical period in which the story takes place—and gives hints as to the **plot,** or the events and conflicts surrounding the characters' lives.

On a separate sheet of paper, create a table with two columns and three rows. Follow the example below, but use your whole paper so you have room to write.

Setting	
Plot	
Characters Beth Jo Amy Meg Hannah Mrs. March	Personal traits

Fill in the table by writing responses to the following questions. Refer to these notes for future writing exercises about character and plot development.

Setting: During what historical period does *Little Women* take place? Where does the March family live?

Plot: What are the March sisters doing when Marmee comes home? What does Marmee read to them? What surprising event occurs at the end of Chapter 2?

Characterization: What is each character like? Remember: Authors reveal their characters' personalities not only by directly explaining what they are like, but also by showing what kinds of thoughts they have, the actions they perform, and what others say about them. Provide at least two examples for each character.

History Alive!

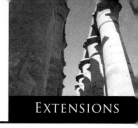

EXTENSIONS

Women in Wartime. At the outset of *Little Women,* the reader learns that Mr. March has gone off to serve in the Civil War, leaving behind his four daughters and his wife, whom the girls affectionately refer to as "Marmee." The girls' conversation about their first Christmas without their father reveals much about their individual personalities. Jo, for instance, says (page 4) that she is "dying to go and fight with Papa." Why can't she accompany him? What is she expected to do at home instead?

Women have always played important roles in wartime. During the American Revolutionary War, married women often accompanied their soldier husbands onto the battlefield. Recognized as part of the military, they attended to their children and earned pay as cooks, nurses, spies, and laundresses. Some women fought directly in battles by stepping up to fire the artillery when their husbands fell or by disguising themselves as men in order to join in frontline combat.

For those women who remained at home, the war brought additional hardships to an already labor-intensive life. In addition to caring for their extended families, growing their own food, and making many of their own domestic provisions, women often took over their husbands' businesses, took in boarders for additional money, or provided supplies and housing to the troops.

The Civil War. Women played vital roles on both the Union and Confederate sides of the Civil War. They not only provided food and provisions for military units in the field, but, like the Revolutionary War women before them, they also braved the gruesome effects of war by caring for sick and wounded soldiers on the battlefront and in makeshift medical hospitals. In fact, Louisa May Alcott, author of *Little Women,* served as a Civil War nurse, and her *Hospital Sketches,* published in 1863, is one of the few surviving accounts of this important wartime service.

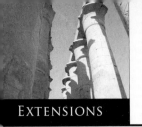

EXTENSIONS

History Alive!

Research: Women in the Civil War

Select one of the following women who performed important roles during wartime. Prepare a brief presentation for the class explaining what this woman did and at least one interesting fact about her life.

- Belle Boyd
- Rose O'Neal Greenhow
- Dr. Mary Walker
- Anna Etheridge (Anna Blair)
- Lucy Ann Cox
- Clara Barton
- Susie Baker
- Sarah Emma Edmonds ("Franklin Thompson")
- Jennie Hodgers
- Cathay Williams

World War II. Women's roles in wartime transformed dramatically during World War II. On the home-front, as American industry shifted from producing ordinary merchandise to turning out planes, ships, and other military supplies, women became the core of the work force. Many women left their housework behind and found employment drafting, riveting, welding, and working with sheet metal. As many as six million women went to work in airplane factories, shipyards, and the American railroad industry. As in the days of the Civil War, women were also relied upon to keep the economy running by operating family farms and businesses, as well as by conserving important raw materials such as copper and oil.

World War II also marked the beginning of active recruitment of women into the Armed Forces. Thousands of uniformed women served in the newly created Women's Army Corps (WAC) and the Navy's Women Accepted for Volunteer Emergency Services (WAVES). The Women Airforce Service Pilots (WASP) became the first women trained to fly American military aircraft. Women performed a diverse array of services overseas ranging from nursing the wounded (as in previous wars) to handling military communications and flying cargo planes.

History Alive!

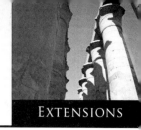

EXTENSIONS

Research and Discussion: Women During Modern Wars

1. How have the roles of women in the military expanded in the modern era? Are they restricted in any way? Are there any women officers? What is the highest rank ever achieved by a woman in the U.S. Armed Forces?
2. What happens to the children of military women who are called to duty? What if both parents are military personnel? Does the military have any regulations concerning parenting and wartime? Are pregnant women allowed to serve in active duty?

Supplemental Research and Additional Exercises

1. With the help of your teacher or librarian, research the roles of women during wartime. Start with the Revolutionary War and look for examples from the Civil War, the World Wars, the Korean War, the Vietnam War, and both Gulf wars. Work in a small group to make a compare-and-contrast chart. List examples that reveal how the role of women during wartime has changed from the eighteenth century through the present day.
2. Ask your librarian or teacher if you can listen to any or all of the following songs that were popular during and after wars in the twentieth century: "Over There," "I'll Be Home for Christmas," and "Anything You Can Do, I Can Do Better." Locate the lyrics to the songs in a music book, in album notes, on the Internet, or by listening and transcribing on your own. What do these songs have to do with women in wartime? Prepare a short presentation for the class about one of these songs.

CHAPTER 3

The Laurence Boy

"Jo! Jo! Where are you?" cried Meg at the foot of the garret[1] stairs.

"Here!" answered a husky voice from above, and, running up, Meg found her sister eating apples and crying over the *Heir of Redclyffe*,[2] on an old three-legged sofa by the sunny window. This was Jo's favorite **refuge**, and here she loved to retire with half a dozen russets[3] and a nice book. As Meg appeared, Jo shook the tears off her cheeks and waited to hear the news.

"Only see! An invitation from Mrs. Gardiner for tomorrow night!" cried Meg, waving the precious paper. She read it with girlish delight.

"'Mrs. Gardiner would be happy to see Miss March and Miss Josephine at a little dance on New Year's Eve.' Marmee is willing we should go, now what shall we wear?"

"What's the use of asking that? You know we shall wear our poplins,[4] because we haven't got anything else," answered Jo with her mouth full.

"If I only had a silk!" sighed Meg.

Why is Meg so excited?

---

[1] **garret.** An attic, or a room at the top of a house

[2] *Heir of Redclyffe.* A nineteenth-century tragic novel by Charlotte M. Yonge, which emphasizes chivalric qualities such as bravery, courtesy, and honor

[3] **russet.** A type of apple

[4] **poplin.** A ribbed fabric, often made of cotton. These are referred to elsewhere in the text as *pops*.

Vocabulary in Place
refuge, *n.* Hideout or retreat; a safe, quiet place

"Our pops are nice enough for us. Yours is as good as new, but I forgot the burn and the tear in mine. Whatever shall I do? The burn shows badly, and I can't take any out."

"You must sit still all you can and keep your back out of sight. The front is all right. I shall have a new ribbon for my hair, and Marmee will lend me her little pearl pin, and my new slippers are lovely, and my gloves will do, though they aren't as nice as I'd like."

"Mine are spoiled with lemonade, so I shall have to go without," said Jo, who never troubled herself much about dress.

"You must have gloves, or I won't go," cried Meg decidedly. "Gloves are more important than anything else. You can't dance without them. Can't you make them do?" Meg pleaded.

"I'll tell you how we can manage," Jo replied, lighting up with an idea. "We'll each wear one of your good ones and carry one of my bad ones. Don't you see?"

"Your hands are bigger than mine, and you will stretch my glove dreadfully," began Meg, whose gloves were a tender point with her.

"Then I'll go without. I don't care what people say!" cried Jo, taking up her book.

"You may have it! Only don't stain it, and do behave nicely. Don't put your hands behind you, or stare, or use slang will you?"

"Don't worry about me. I'll be as prim as I can and not get into any scrapes, if I can help it. Now go and answer your note, and let me finish this splendid story."

So Meg went away to "accept with thanks" and look over her dress while Jo finished her story and her four apples.

On New Year's Eve the two younger girls played dressing maids and the two elder were absorbed in the all-important business of "getting ready for the party." There was a great deal of running up and down, laughing and talking. At one time a strong smell of burned hair pervaded the house. Meg wanted a few curls about her face, and Jo undertook to pinch the papered locks with a pair of hot tongs.

Much to her dismay, however, Meg's pretty little ringlets came off with the papers, and the horrified hairdresser laid a row of little scorched bundles on the bureau before her victim.

What is wrong with Jo's gloves? How do she and Meg resolve the problem?

What does Jo do to Meg's hair?

"Oh, oh, oh! What have you done? I'm spoiled! I can't go! My hair, oh, my hair!" wailed Meg, looking with despair at the uneven frizzle on her forehead.

"I'm so sorry, but the tongs were too hot, and so I've made a mess," groaned poor Jo, with tears of regret. "I always spoil everything."

"It isn't spoiled. Just frizzle it, and tie your ribbon so the ends come on your forehead a bit. It will look like the latest fashion. I've seen many girls do it so," said Amy **consolingly**.

"Serves me right for trying to be fine. I wish I'd let my hair alone," cried Meg.

"So do I, it was so smooth and pretty. But it will soon grow out again," said Beth, coming to kiss and comfort her sister.

At last Meg was finished, and by the united efforts of the entire family Jo's hair was got up and her dress on. They looked very well in their simple suits, Meg's in silvery drab, with a blue velvet net for her hair, lace frills, and the pearl pin. Jo in maroon, with a stiff linen collar and a white chrysanthemum or two for her only ornament.

Each put on one nice light glove, and carried one soiled one, and all pronounced the effect "quite easy and fine." Meg's high-heeled slippers were very tight and hurt her, though she would not own it,[5] and Jo's nineteen hairpins all seemed stuck straight into her head, which was not exactly comfortable.

"Have a good time, dearies!" said Mrs. March, as the sisters went daintily down the walk. "Don't eat much supper, and come away at eleven when I send Hannah for you." As the gate clashed behind them, a voice cried from a window . . .

"Girls, girls! Have you both got nice pocket handkerchiefs?"

---

[5]**own it.** Admit or accept it

Vocabulary in Place
consolingly, *adv.* Soothingly, with encouragement and support; in a manner meant to make someone feel better

"Yes, yes," cried Jo, adding with a laugh as they went on, "I do believe Marmee would ask that if we were all running away from an earthquake."

"It is quite proper, for a real lady is always known by neat boots, gloves, and handkerchiefs," replied Meg.

As they arrived at Mrs. Gardiner's, Meg said. "Is my sash right? And does my hair look very bad? Now don't forget to keep the bad breadth of your dress out of sight, Jo."

"I know I shall forget. If you see me doing anything wrong, just remind me by a wink, will you?" returned Jo, giving her collar a twitch and her head a hasty brush.

"No, winking isn't ladylike. I'll lift my eyebrows if anything is wrong, and nod if you are all right. Now hold your shoulders straight, and take short steps, and don't shake hands if you are introduced to anyone. It isn't the thing."

"How do you learn all the proper ways? I never can. Isn't that music gay?"

In they went, feeling a **trifle** timid, for they seldom went to parties. Mrs. Gardiner, a stately old lady, greeted them kindly and handed them over to her daughter Sallie. Meg knew Sallie and was at her ease very soon, but Jo, who didn't care much for girls or girlish gossip, stood about, with her back carefully against the wall, and felt as much out of place as a colt in a flower garden.

Half a dozen lads were talking about skates in another part of the room, and Jo longed to go and join them, for skating was one of the joys of her life. She telegraphed[6] her wish to Meg, but the eyebrows went up so alarmingly that she dared not stir. Meg was asked to dance at once, and the tight slippers tripped about so briskly that none would have guessed the pain their wearer suffered smilingly. Jo saw a big red-headed youth approaching her corner, and fearing he meant

Why does Marmee care so much about their handkerchiefs?

---

[6] **telegraphed.** Made known by nonverbal means

Vocabulary in Place
trifle, *n.* A small amount. (The phrase *a trifle* is idiomatic and actually functions as an adverb.)

Who else is behind the curtain when Jo slips into the corner?

to ask her to dance, she slipped into a curtained recess, intending to watch and enjoy herself in peace. Unfortunately, another **bashful** person had chosen the same refuge, for, as the curtain fell behind her, she found herself face to face with the "Laurence boy."

"Dear me, I didn't know anyone was here!" stammered Jo, preparing to back out as speedily as she had bounced in.

But the boy laughed and said pleasantly, though he looked a little startled, "Don't mind me, stay if you like."

"Shan't I disturb you?"

"Not a bit. I only came here because I don't know many people and felt rather strange at first, you know."

"So did I. Don't go away, please, unless you'd rather."

The boy sat down again and looked at his shoes, till Jo said, trying to be polite, "I think I've had the pleasure of seeing you before. You live near us, don't you?"

"Next door." And he laughed outright, for Jo's prim manner was rather funny when he remembered how they had chatted about cricket when he brought the cat home.

Do Jo and the Laurence boy enjoy one another's company? How do you know?

That put Jo at her ease and she laughed, too, as she said, in her heartiest way, "We did have such a good time over your nice Christmas present."

"Grandpa sent it."

"But you put it into his head, didn't you, now?"

"How is your cat, Miss March?" asked the boy, trying to look **sober** while his black eyes shone with fun.

"Nicely, thank you, Mr. Laurence. But I am not Miss March, I'm only Jo," returned the young lady.

"I'm not Mr. Laurence, I'm only Laurie."

"Laurie Laurence, what an odd name."

Vocabulary in Place
bashful, *adj.* Shy
sober, *adj.* Serious

"My first name is Theodore, but I don't like it, for the fellows called me Dora, so I made them say Laurie instead."

"I hate my name, too—so **sentimental!** I wish every one would say Jo instead of Josephine. How did you make the boys stop calling you Dora?"

"I thrashed 'em."

"I can't thrash Aunt March, so I suppose I shall have to bear it." And Jo **resigned** herself with a sigh.

"Don't you like to dance, Miss Jo?" asked Laurie.

"I like it well enough if there is plenty of room, and everyone is lively. In a place like this I'm sure to upset something or tread on people's toes. Don't you dance?"

"Sometimes. I've been abroad[7] a good many years, and haven't been into company enough yet to know how you do things here."

"Abroad!" cried Jo. "Oh, tell me about it! I love dearly to hear people describe their travels."

Laurie didn't seem to know where to begin, but Jo's eager questions soon set him going. He told her how he had been at school in Vevay,[8] and spent last winter in Paris.

"Can you talk French?"

"Oui, mademoiselle. Quel nom a cette jeune demoiselle en les pantoufles jolis?"

"How nicely you do it! Let me see . . . you said, 'Who is the young lady in the pretty slippers,' didn't you?"

"Oui, mademoiselle."

"It's my sister Margaret, and you knew it was! Do you think she is pretty?"

"Yes, she looks so fresh and quiet, and dances like a lady."

Where did Laurie learn to speak French so well?

---

[7] **abroad.** In another country
[8] **Vevay.** A town in Switzerland

Vocabulary in Place
sentimental, *adj.* Characterized or influenced by emotion as opposed to reason; overly emotional
resign, *v.* To accept as inevitable; to submit

Why is Jo so happy when Laurie compliments Meg?

Jo glowed with pleasure at this boyish praise of her sister, and stored it up to repeat to Meg. Both watched the dancers and criticized and chatted till they felt like old acquaintances. Jo liked the Laurence boy better than ever and took several good looks at him, so that she might describe him to the girls, for boys were almost unknown creatures to them.

"Curly black hair, brown skin, big black eyes, handsome nose, fine teeth, small hands and feet, taller than I am, very polite, for a boy, and altogether jolly. Wonder how old he is?"

It was on the tip of Jo's tongue to ask, but she checked herself in time and, with unusual **tact**, she tried to find out in a round-about way.

"I suppose you are going to college soon? I see you pegging away at your books, no, I mean studying hard." And Jo blushed at the dreadful "pegging" which had escaped her.

Laurie smiled but didn't seem shocked, and answered with a shrug. "Not for a year or two, when I'm seventeen."

"Aren't you but fifteen?" asked Jo, looking at the tall lad, whom she had imagined seventeen already.

"Sixteen, next month."

"How I wish I was going to college! You don't look as if you liked it."

"I hate it!"

"What do you like?"

"To live in Italy, and to enjoy myself in my own way."

Jo wanted very much to ask what his own way was, but his black brows looked rather threatening as he knit them, so she changed the subject by saying, "That's a splendid polka![9] Why don't you go and try it?"

---

[9] **polka.** A lively dance performed by couples. It originated in Bohemia, a former kingdom that was located in the present-day Czech Republic

---

Vocabulary in Place

tact, *n.* Polite sense of restraint; ability to say and do the right thing at the right time

"If you will come too," he answered, with a **gallant** little bow.

"I can't, for I told Meg I wouldn't, because . . . " There Jo stopped, and looked undecided whether to tell or to laugh.

"Because, what?"

"You won't tell?"

"Never!"

"Well, I have a bad trick of standing before the fire, and so I burn my frocks, and I scorched this one. Meg told me to keep still so no one would see it. You may laugh, if you want to. It is funny, I know."

But Laurie didn't laugh. He only looked down a minute, and then said very gently, "Never mind that. I'll tell you how we can manage. There's a long hall out there, and we can dance grandly, and no one will see us. Please come."

Jo thanked him and gladly went, wishing she had two neat gloves when she saw the nice, pearl-colored ones her partner wore. The hall was empty, and they had a grand polka, for Laurie danced well, and taught her the German step, which delighted Jo, being full of swing and spring. When the music stopped, they sat down on the stairs to get their breath, and Laurie was in the midst of an account of a students' festival at Heidelberg[10] when Meg appeared in search of her sister. She beckoned, and Jo reluctantly followed her into a side room, where she found her on a sofa, holding her foot, and looking pale. "That stupid high heel turned and I've sprained my ankle. It aches so, I can hardly stand. I don't know how I'm ever going to get home," she said, rocking to and fro in pain.

"I knew you'd hurt your feet with those silly shoes. I'm sorry. But I don't see what you can do, except get a carriage, or stay here all night," answered Jo, softly rubbing the poor ankle as she spoke.

How does Meg sprain her ankle? How will she get home?

---

[10] **Heidelberg.** A city of southwest Germany

Vocabulary in Place
gallant, *adj.* Courteous, very polite; flirtatious

"I can't have a carriage without its costing ever so much. I dare say I can't get one at all, for most people come in their own, and it's a long way to the stable, and no one to send."

"I'll go."

"No, indeed! It's past nine, and dark as coal. I can't stop here, for the house is full. Sallie has some girls staying with her. I'll rest till Hannah comes, and then do the best I can."

"I'll ask Laurie. He will go," said Jo, looking relieved as the idea occurred to her.

"Mercy, no! Don't ask or tell anyone. Get me my rubbers,[11] and put these slippers with our things. I can't dance anymore, but as soon as supper is over, watch for Hannah and tell me the minute she comes."

"They are going out to supper now. I'll stay with you. I'd rather."

"No, dear, run along, and bring me some coffee. I'm so tired I can't stir."

So Meg **reclined,** with rubbers well hidden, and Jo went blundering away to the dining room, which she found after going into a china closet, and opening the door of a room where old Mr. Gardiner was taking a little private refreshment. Making a dart at the table, she secured the coffee, which she immediately spilled, thereby making the front of her dress as bad as the back.

"Oh, dear, what a blunderbuss[12] I am!" exclaimed Jo, finishing Meg's glove by scrubbing her gown with it.

"Can I help you?" said a friendly voice. And there was Laurie, with a full cup in one hand and a plate of ice in the other.

"I was trying to get something for Meg, who is very tired, and someone shook me, and here I am in a nice state," answered Jo, glancing dismally from the stained skirt to the coffee-colored glove.

"Too bad! I was looking for someone to give this to. May I take it to your sister?"

"Oh, thank you! I'll show you where she is. I don't offer to take it myself, for I should only spill it if I did."

Laurie drew up a little table and waited on both girls so **obligingly** that even particular Meg pronounced him a "nice boy."

---

[11] **rubbers.** Rain boots

[12] **blunderbuss.** A short gun with a bell-shaped muzzle that sprayed shot in all directions when fired. The term is also used as a metaphor for someone or something that is clumsy or reckless.

Vocabulary in Place
recline, *v.* To lie back, rest
obligingly, *adv.* Agreeably; without complaining

They had a merry time and were in the midst of a quiet game when Hannah appeared. Meg forgot her foot and rose so quickly that she was forced to catch hold of Jo, with an exclamation of pain.

"Hush! Don't say anything," she whispered, adding aloud, "It's nothing. I turned my foot a little, that's all," and limped upstairs to put her things on.

Why is Meg trying to cover up the fact that she is injured?

Laurie, who saw the state Meg was in, offered his grandfather's carriage, which had just come for him.

"It's so early! You can't mean to go yet?" began Jo, looking relieved but hesitating to accept the offer.

"I always go early, I do, truly! Please let me take you home. It's on my way, you know, and they say it may rain."

That settled it. Telling him of Meg's mishap, Jo gratefully accepted and rushed up to bring down the rest of the party. Hannah hated rain as much as a cat does so she made no trouble, and they rolled away in the luxurious carriage, feeling very festive and elegant. When they were at home, they said good night with many thanks and crept in, hoping to disturb no one, but the instant their door creaked, two little nightcaps bobbed up, and two sleepy but eager voices cried . . .

"Tell about the party! Tell about the party!"

Who is still awake when Jo and Meg get home?

Meg talked happily of what a good time she had and how Sallie's friend, Annie Moffat, had asked her to come and spend a week with her when Sallie goes in the spring, and Jo told all about Laurie. Jo had saved some bonbons for the little girls, and after hearing the most thrilling events of the evening, they soon headed off to bed.

"I declare, it really seems like being a fine young lady, to come home from the party in a carriage and sit in my dressing gown with a maid to wait on me," said Meg, as Jo bound up her foot and brushed her hair.

"I don't believe fine young ladies enjoy themselves a bit more than we do, in spite of our burned hair, old gowns, one glove apiece and tight slippers." And I think Jo was quite right.

Words to Keep

The following sentences contain important words from the Vocabulary in Place boxes in Chapters 1–3 of *Little Women*. In your notebook, or on a separate sheet of paper, write the part of speech of each boldface word, a synonym (or a short definition in your own words), and a new sentence of your own.

1. The dog settled down **contentedly** in his favorite corner of the couch.
2. His mother corrected him with a **reproving** look when he put his elbows on the table.
3. The bubbling fountain at the center of the courtyard created a sense of **tranquility**.
4. A haze of wood smoke **pervaded** the valley.
5. "It's hopeless," he said with a **despairing** sigh. "We'll never find water in this desert."
6. Sue smiled **modestly** and praised her teammates' after the game, even though everyone knew that she had scored all the goals.
7. Tom answered her **inquiries** in a letter.
8. She **resolved** to try harder in the future.
9. Matt brought in the new year by **renouncing** all of his bad habits.
10. She had to **rummage** through her pockets for change to give the bus driver.
11. We **seldom** go that way, so it is no wonder that we got lost.
12. Where did Kelley get the **notion** that she could ace the test without studying?
13. If you're ever lost in the woods, keep your **wits** and try to think your way out.
14. They sat on the edge of their seats, peering around the corner with great **expectancy**.
15. In the summertime, her favorite **refuge** was the treehouse in the backyard.
16. "You'll do better next time," the coach said to him **consolingly** after he struck out for the second time in a row at bat.
17. I felt a **trifle** sick this morning, but I am much better now.
18. She was so **bashful** that she usually stayed in the back of the room, hoping not to be noticed.

Chapter 4

Burdens

"I wish it was Christmas or New Year's all the time," sighed Meg the morning after the party.

"Wouldn't it be fun?" answered Jo, yawning **dismally**.

"It does seem so nice to go to parties, and drive home, and read and rest, and not work. I always envy girls who do such things; I'm so fond of luxury," said Meg, trying to decide which of two shabby gowns was the least shabby.

"Well, we can't have it, so don't let us grumble but shoulder our bundles and trudge along as cheerfully as Marmee does."

But Meg didn't brighten, for her burden, consisting of four spoiled King children, seemed heavier than ever.

"I shall have to toil and moil[1] all my days, with only little bits of fun now and then, and get old and ugly and sour, because I'm poor and can't enjoy my life as other girls do. It's a shame!"

Meg went down, wearing an injured look, and wasn't at all agreeable at breakfast time. Everyone seemed rather out of sorts. Beth had a headache and lay on the sofa, comforting herself with her cats. Amy was fretting because her lessons were not learned. Mrs. March was very busy trying to finish a letter, which must go at once, and Hannah had the grumps, for being up late didn't suit her.

"There never was such a cross family!" cried Jo, losing her temper when she had upset an inkstand, broken both boot lacings, and sat down upon her hat.

"You're the crossest person in it!" returned Amy.

> *What is the overall mood in the house? Why?*

---

[1] **moil.** A synonym for *toil,* to work continuously

Vocabulary in Place
dismally, *adv.* Hopelessly; with despair

"Girls, girls, do be quiet one minute! I must get this off by the early mail, and you drive me distracted with your worry," cried Mrs. March, crossing out the third spoiled sentence in her letter.

There was a momentary lull, broken by Hannah, who stalked in, laid two hot turnovers on the table, and stalked out again. The girls called these turnovers "muffs,"[2] for they had no others and found the hot pies very comforting to their hands on cold mornings. Hannah never forgot to make them, no matter how busy or grumpy she might be, for the walk was long and bleak. The poor things got no other lunch and were seldom home before two.

"Cuddle your cats and get over your headache, Bethy. Goodbye, Marmee. We are rascals this morning, but we'll come home regular angels. Now then, Meg!" And Jo tramped away, feeling that the pilgrims were not setting out as they ought to do.

They always looked back before turning the corner, for their mother was always at the window to nod and smile, and wave to them. Whatever their mood might be, the last glimpse of that motherly face was sure to affect them like sunshine.

"If Marmee shook her fist instead of kissing her hand to us, it would serve us right," cried Jo, taking a **remorseful** satisfaction in the snowy walk and bitter wind.

"Don't use such dreadful expressions," Meg **chided**. "Call yourself any names you like, but I am neither a rascal nor a wretch and I don't choose to be called so."

"You're cross today because you can't sit in the lap of luxury all the time. Poor dear, just wait till I make my fortune, and you shall have carriages and ice cream and high-heeled slippers, and posies, and parties."

---

[2] **muff.** A small cylindrical fur or cloth cover, open at both ends, in which the hands are placed for warmth

Vocabulary in Place
remorseful, *adj.* Full of regret for one's actions
chide, *v.* To scold

"How ridiculous you are, Jo!" But Meg laughed and felt better in spite of herself.

"Lucky for you I am. Thank goodness, I can always find something funny to keep me up. Don't croak any more, but come home jolly, there's a dear."

Jo gave her sister an encouraging pat on the shoulder as they parted for the day. Each went a different way, trying to be cheerful in spite of wintry weather, hard work, and the unsatisfied desires of youth.

When Mr. March lost his property in trying to help an unfortunate friend, the two oldest girls begged to be allowed to do something toward their own support, at least. Margaret found a place as nursery governess and felt rich with her small salary. As she said, she was "fond of luxury," and her chief trouble was poverty. She found it harder to bear than the others because she could remember a time when want of any kind was unknown. She tried not to be envious of the Kings, for there she daily saw all she wanted. Poor Meg seldom complained, but a sense of injustice made her feel bitter toward everyone sometimes. She had not yet learned to know how rich she was in the blessings that alone can make life happy.

Jo happened to suit Aunt March, who was lame and needed an active person to wait upon her. The childless old lady had offered to adopt one of the girls when the troubles came, but the **unworldly** Marches only said . . .

"We can't give up our girls. Rich or poor, we will keep together and be happy in one another."

The old lady was much offended and wouldn't speak to them for a time. But happening to meet Jo at a friend's, the girl's comical face and blunt manners struck the old lady's fancy, and she proposed to take her for a companion. This did not suit Jo at all, but she accepted the place since nothing better appeared. To everyone's surprise, she got on remarkably well with her **irascible** relative. There was

Why do Meg and Jo have to go to work?

In what way is Meg already rich?

Vocabulary in Place

unworldly, *adj.* More concerned with other things besides money or material possessions

irascible, *adj.* Crabby; difficult to get along with

an occasional **tempest,** and once Jo marched home, declaring she couldn't bear it longer, but Aunt March always cleared things up quickly, and sent for Jo to come back again with such urgency that she could not refuse, for in her heart she rather liked the peppery old lady.

I suspect that the real attraction for Jo was a large library of fine books, which was left to dust and spiders since Uncle March died. The dim, dusty room contained a wilderness of books in which she could wander where she liked.

The moment Aunt March took her nap, or was busy with company, Jo hurried to this quiet place, and curling herself up in the easy chair, devoured poetry, romance, history, and travels like a regular bookworm. But, like all happiness, it did not last long. As sure as she had just reached the heart of the story a shrill voice called, "Josy-phine! Josy-phine!" and she had to leave her paradise to wind yarn, wash the poodle, or read *Belsham's Essays*[3] by the hour.

Jo found her greatest **affliction** in the fact that she couldn't read, run, and ride as much as she liked. A quick temper, sharp tongue, and restless spirit were always getting her into scrapes. But the training she received at Aunt March's was just what she needed, and the thought that she was doing something to support herself made her happy in spite of the perpetual "Josy-phine!"

What is Jo's "greatest affliction"?

Beth was too bashful to go to school and did her lessons at home with her father. Even when he went away, and her mother was called to devote her skill and energy to Soldier's Aid Societies, Beth went faithfully on by herself and did the best she could. She was a housewifely little creature, and helped Hannah keep the home neat and comfortable for the workers, never thinking of any reward but

Why doesn't Beth attend school? What does she do during the day?

---

[3] *Belsham's Essays*. The writings of William Belsham (1752–1827), an English historian and political essayist

Vocabulary in Place
tempest, *n.* A violent storm; also, turmoil, uproar, commotion
affliction, *n.* A cause of pain, stress, or suffering

to be loved. Long, quiet days she spent, not lonely nor idle, for her little world was filled with imaginary friends. There were six dolls to be awoken and dressed every morning, for Beth was a child still and loved her dolls as well as ever. All were outcasts her older sisters had outgrown and Amy would have nothing to do with, for they were old or ugly. Beth cherished them all the more tenderly for that very reason, and set up a hospital for infirm dolls. All were fed and clothed, nursed and caressed with an affection that never failed.

Beth had her troubles as well as the others. She often "wept a little weep" as Jo said, because she couldn't take music lessons and have a fine piano. She loved music so dearly, and practiced away so patiently at the jingling old instrument. Nobody saw Beth wipe the tears off the yellow keys that wouldn't keep in tune, when she was all alone. She sang like a little lark about her work, and day after day said hopefully to herself, "I know I'll get my music some time, if I'm good."

Why does Beth sometimes cry over the piano?

There are many Beths in the world, shy and quiet, sitting in corners till needed, and living for others so cheerfully that no one sees the sacrifices till the sweet, sunshiny presence vanishes, leaving silence and shadow behind.

If anybody had asked Amy what the greatest trial of her life was, she would have answered at once, "My nose." When she was a baby, Jo had accidentally dropped her into the coal bin, and Amy insisted that the fall had ruined her nose forever. It was not big, nor red; it was only rather flat, and all the pinching in the world could not give it an **aristocratic** point. No one minded it but herself, and it was doing its best to grow, but Amy felt deeply the want of an aristocratic nose.

Why do Amy's sisters call her "Little Raphael"?

"Little Raphael,"[4] as her sisters called her, had a talent for drawing, and was never so happy as when copying flowers, designing fairies, or illustrating stories. Her teachers complained that instead

---

[4] **Raphael.** Raphael Sanzio (1483–1520), one of the greatest painters of the Italian Renaissance

Vocabulary in Place

aristocratic, *adj.* Characteristic of the ruling class or nobility

of doing her sums she covered her slate with animals. She was a great favorite with her schoolmates. Her little airs and graces and accomplishments were much admired. Besides her drawing, she could play twelve tunes, crochet, and read French without mispronouncing more than two-thirds of the words. Her long words were considered "perfectly elegant" by the girls.

Amy was on her way to becoming spoiled, for everyone petted[5] her. One thing, however, rather **quenched** her vanities. She had to wear her cousin's clothes, and Florence's mama hadn't a particle of taste. Everything was good, well made, and little worn, but Amy's artistic eyes were much afflicted, especially this winter, when her school dress was a dull purple with yellow dots and no trimming.

Meg was Amy's **confidant,** and by some strange attraction of opposites Jo was gentle Beth's. The two older girls meant a great deal to one another, but each took one of the younger sisters into her keeping and watched over her in her own way.

> Which sisters confide in one another?

"Has anybody got anything to tell?" said Meg, as they sat sewing together that evening. "It's been such a dismal day. I'm really dying for some amusement."

"I had a **queer** time with Aunt today, and, as I got the best of it, I'll tell you about it," began Jo, who dearly loved to tell stories.

"I was reading aloud those dreadful essays by Belsham, and reciting away as I always do. Aunt usually drops off, and then I take out some nice book, and read like mad until she wakes up. So, the minute her cap began to bob like a top-heavy dahlia flower, I whipped the *Vicar of Wakefield*[6] out of my pocket, and read away, with

---

[5] **petted.** Indulged; showed excessive fondness toward

[6] *Vicar of Wakefield.* A novel by British author Oliver Goldsmith (1728–1774)

Vocabulary in Place
quench, *v.* To put a limit on
confidant, *n.* A trusted friend with whom one shares secrets
queer, *adj.* Strange; odd

one eye on him and one eye on Aunt. I'd just got to where they all tumbled into the water when I forgot and laughed out loud. Aunt woke up and, being more good-natured after her nap, told me to read it a bit and show what **frivolous** work I preferred to the worthy and instructive Belsham. I did my very best, and she liked it."

"Did she own she liked it?" asked Meg.

"Oh, bless you, no! But she let old Belsham rest. And when I ran back after my gloves this afternoon, there she was, so absorbed in the novel that she didn't hear me laugh as I danced a jig in the hall. What a pleasant life she might have if only she chose! I don't envy her much, in spite of her money. After all, rich people have about as many worries as poor ones, I think," added Jo.

Why doesn't Jo envy her Aunt?

"That reminds me," said Meg, "that I've got something to tell, though it isn't funny, like Jo's story. At the Kings' today I found everybody in a flurry. One of the children said that her oldest brother had done something dreadful, and Papa had sent him away. I heard Mrs. King crying and Mr. King talking very loud, and the girls' eyes were red and swollen from crying. I didn't ask any questions, of course, but I felt so sorry for them and was rather glad I hadn't any wild brothers to do wicked things and disgrace the family."

"I think being disgraced in school is a great deal tryinger[7] than anything bad boys can do," said Amy, shaking her head. "Susie Perkins came to school today with a lovely red carnelian[8] ring. I wanted it dreadfully, and wished I was her with all my might. Then, she drew a wicked picture of Mr. Davis and we were laughing over it when all of a sudden he ordered Susie to bring up her slate. She was *parrylized* with fright, but she went, and oh, what do you think he did? He took her by the ear—the ear! Just fancy how horrid!—and led her to the recitation platform, and made her stand

---

7 **tryinger.** Amy's means to say "more trying," or "more difficult"
8 **carnelian.** A type of gemstone that is pale to deep red or reddish-brown

Vocabulary in Place
frivolous, *adj.* Trivial; of little meaning or importance

there half an hour, holding the slate so everyone could see. I didn't envy her then, for I felt that millions of carnelian rings wouldn't have made me happy after that. I never, never should have got over such an agonizing **mortification**." And Amy went on with her work, with an air of pride in her own virtue and the use of two long words in a breath.

Why was Amy proud of herself?

"I saw something I liked this morning, and I meant to tell it at dinner, but I forgot," said Beth, putting Jo's topsy-turvy basket in order as she talked. "When I went to get some oysters for Hannah, I saw Mr. Laurence in the fish shop, busy with Mr. Cutter the fishman. A poor woman came in with a pail and a mop, and asked Mr. Cutter if he would let her do some scrubbing for a bit of fish, because she hadn't any dinner for her children. Mr. Cutter was in a hurry and said 'No,' rather crossly. She was going away, looking hungry and sorry, when Mr. Laurence hooked up a big fish with the crooked end of his cane and held it out to her. She was so glad and surprised she took it right into her arms, and thanked him over and over. He told her to 'go along and cook it,' and she hurried off, so happy! Wasn't it good of him? Oh, she did look so funny, hugging the big, slippery fish."

What sort of man is Mr. Laurence?

When they had laughed at Beth's story, they asked their mother for one, and after a moment's thought, she said soberly, "As I sat cutting out blue flannel jackets today, I felt very anxious about Father, and thought how lonely and helpless we should be, if anything happened to him. Then an old man came in with an order for some clothes. He sat down near me, and I began to talk to him, for he looked poor and tired and anxious.

"'Have you sons in the army?' I asked.

"'Yes, ma'am. I had four, but two were killed, one is a prisoner, and I'm going to the other, who is very sick in a Washington hospital,' he answered quietly.

Vocabulary in Place
mortification, *n.* A feeling of shame, humiliation

Why is Marmee ashamed of herself when she hears the old man's story? What is the moral, or lesson, of Marmee's story?

"'You have done a great deal for your country, sir,' I said, feeling respect now, instead of pity.

"'Not a mite more than I ought, ma'am. I'd go myself, if I was any use. As I ain't, I give my boys, and give 'em free.'

"He spoke so cheerfully and seemed so glad to give his all that I was ashamed of myself. I'd given one man and thought it too much, while he gave four without grudging them. I had all my girls to comfort me at home, and his last son was waiting, miles away, to say good-bye to him, perhaps! I felt so rich, so happy thinking of my blessings, that I made him a nice bundle, gave him some money, and thanked him heartily for the lesson he had taught me."

"Tell another story, Mother, one with a moral to it, like this," said Jo, after a minute's silence.

Mrs. March smiled and began at once, for she had told stories to this little audience for many years, and knew how to please them.

"Once upon a time, there were four girls, who had enough to eat and drink and wear, a good many comforts and pleasures, kind friends and parents who loved them dearly, and yet they were not contented."

(Here the listeners stole sly looks at one another and began to sew steadily.)

"These girls wanted to be good and made many excellent resolutions, but they did not keep them very well. They were constantly saying, 'If only we had this,' or 'If we could only do that,' quite forgetting how much they already had, and how many things they actually could do. So they asked an old woman what spell they could use to make them happy, and she said, 'When you feel **discontented**, think over your blessings, and be grateful.'

Why does Marmee tell them this story?

"They decided to try her advice, and soon were surprised to see how well off they were. One discovered that money couldn't keep shame and sorrow out of rich peoples' houses. Another found that, though she was poor, she was a great deal happier, with her youth, health, and good spirits, than a certain fretful, feeble old lady who

---

Vocabulary in Place

discontented, *adj.* Unhappy or dissatisfied

couldn't enjoy her comforts. A third discovered that, disagreeable as it was to help get dinner, it was harder still to go begging for it and the fourth, that even carnelian rings were not so valuable as good behavior. So they agreed to stop complaining, to enjoy the blessings already possessed, and try to deserve them, lest they should be taken away entirely. And I believe they were never disappointed or sorry that they took the old woman's advice."

"Now, Marmee, that is very **cunning** of you to turn our own stories against us, and give us a sermon!" cried Meg.

"I like that kind of sermon. It's the sort Father used to tell us," said Beth thoughtfully.

"We needed that lesson, and we won't forget it," said Jo, taking it to heart as much as any of them.

Vocabulary in Place

cunning, *adj.* Clever

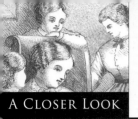

A Closer Look

Understanding the Selection

Recalling (just the facts)

1. Who refuses to go to the formal dance unless her sister wears gloves?
2. When Meg sprains her ankle, how does Laurie come to the rescue?
3. Why is the March family poor? How did Mr. March lose his property?
4. How do Meg and Jo try to help out with the family's financial situation? How does Aunt March offer to help? Are her offers accepted?

Interpreting (delving deeper)

1. What is Jo's attitude about the dance? How can you tell?
2. Do Jo and Laurie get along well? Use examples from the text to support your answer.
3. Why is everyone in such a bad mood after the party?
4. How do Jo and Aunt March get along? What do they have in common? Why does Jo feel sorry for Aunt March?

Synthesizing (putting it all together)

1. How does Marmee compare her sacrifice to the sacrifices of the old man she meets? Why does Marmee tell the girls this story? Are their "burdens" small by comparison?
2. Describe at least one important characteristic that was revealed about each sister in Chapter 4.

Writing

EXTENSIONS

Conflict and Characterization. As you learned in Chapter 1, Jo and her sisters enjoy "playing pilgrims," marching up to the attic room with bundles on their backs. Now that Mr. March has gone off to war, Marmee reminds them that they will have to play this game for real; the sisters each have their own burdens, or "bundles," which they must take up (like pilgrims in the game) on their journey toward becoming "little women."

On a separate sheet of paper, briefly describe, in your own words or using a quotation from the text, each sister's bundle.

Jo's bundle:

Meg's bundle:

Beth's bundle:

Amy's bundle:

Revealing the burdens that each sister must deal with is one way in which Louisa May Alcott differentiates the people in her narrative. As mentioned in the previous Writing extension on page 22, **characterization** refers to the writing techniques an author uses to describe a certain character's personality. Remember that character traits are not always static, or unchanging, for characters often must adapt to the circumstances in their lives.

As you read *Little Women*, you will notice that the main characters change in response to important events. These circumstances, or **conflicts**, may be either external or internal. For instance, all the girls must cope with living during wartime, missing their father, having fewer financial resources than they used to have, and sharing a home with several sisters. In addition to these external events over which the characters have little control, they all struggle with internal conflicts—the ways in which they manage their individual temperaments.

EXTENSIONS

Writing

Choose one of the March sisters as the subject of a character sketch, or short essay, about your chosen character's personality and the internal and external conflicts that she faces. The first part of your sketch should provide summary information about the character's personal traits, including her behavior toward others and her likes and dislikes. For the second part, identify and analyze the external and internal forces that are acting upon this character. Note that many of the external conflicts will be the same for all the sisters, though internal conflicts should differ. In analyzing the internal conflicts, identify both the cause of the conflict and the way in which you think this sister will deal with it based on what you know about her personality.

Write a rough draft of your character sketch and then revise it by referring to the Revision and Proofreading checklists on pages 253–256.

Understanding Literature

EXTENSIONS

The Novel. Working in small groups or as a class, discuss and write brief responses to the following questions or topics. When you have finished, read the passage in the box and revise your answers before completing the final exercise.

1. What is a novel? List at least two things that you think a literary work should have in order for it to be called a novel. List three novels that you have read or would like to read.
2. Who are the main characters in *Little Women*? Identify important events, circumstances, and minor characters—inside and outside the home—that influence the main characters.
3. Which of the four March sisters do you find to be most interesting? Describe her personality. How do you think that she will change over the course of the story and what impact might she have on other characters? How can you plan to trace the development of her character over the course of the book?

> A **novel** is simply an extended written work of fiction, usually in the form of a story. The writer of a novel, or a **novelist**, reveals how a character (usually, but not necessarily human) is influenced by the environment and by major events. Novels are works of **fiction**, which means that the actions and words of the main characters, and perhaps the physical setting itself, are imaginary. However, the events to which the characters react may be based on fact. For example, in *Little Women*, the Civil War marks a real period in American history, but the March sisters are fictional. Characters in a novel can also be "real" people, such as presidents, celebrities, or other historical figures. In any case, the novelist uses his or her imagination to fictionalize the story—creating dialogue, details of setting, and events—in order to make the story interesting and to help emphasize themes.

EXTENSIONS

Understanding Literature

Louisa May Alcott's *Little Women* is a novel about growing up, specifically in the northeastern United States during the 1860s. The March sisters are the main characters and they are directly affected by secondary characters such as Mrs. March, Laurie, and Hannah, as well as by outside events like the Civil War, fashion and manners, the economy, and other factors.

Of the four sisters, many readers agree that Jo is truly the central character because, over the course of the novel, she receives more attention than her sisters. Jo has the most complex personality and is a constant source of courage, creativity, and curiosity for other characters. A character's personality—how she acts in response to society and events—helps readers to understand the setting and to remain interested in the plot of the story. In order to identify a character's key personality traits, readers should analyze the ways in which that character reacts to her surroundings and to the actions of the other characters.

Complete the following exercises on a separate sheet of paper, working either individually or in small groups.

A. Louisa May Alcott's *Little Women* can be classified as a particular type of novel known as a **Bildungsroman.** Where would you look to learn this word's origin, meaning, pronunciation, and how it pertains to *Little Women*? Make a list of resources from the Internet, the school library, or around the classroom that you can use to find out more about the Bildungsroman.

B. Write a definition of Bildungsroman and then answer each of the following questions: From what language does this word come? What was the first Bildungsroman? Are there different types of Bildungsromans?

C. List at least three examples of Bildungsromans that you have read or that have familiar titles.

D. Write a paragraph explaining why *Little Women* qualifies as a Bildungsroman.

CHAPTER 5

Being Neighborly

"What in the world are you going to do now, Jo?" asked Meg one snowy afternoon, as her sister came tramping through the hall in rubber boots, with a broom in one hand and a shovel in the other.

"Going out for exercise," answered Jo with a mischievous twinkle in her eyes.

"Two long walks this morning weren't enough? I advise you to stay warm and dry by the fire, as I do," said Meg with a shiver.

"Never take advice! Can't keep still all day. I like adventures, and I'm going to find some," Jo answered briskly.

Meg went back to toast her feet and read, as Jo began to dig paths with great energy. She soon swept a path all round the garden for Beth to walk in when the sun came out and her little dolls needed air.

The garden separated the Marches' house from that of Mr. Laurence. Both stood in a suburb of the city, which was still countrylike, with groves and lawns, large gardens, and quiet streets. On one side of a low hedge was an old, brown house, looking rather bare and shabby. On the other side was a stately stone mansion with every sort of comfort and luxury. Yet it seemed a lonely, lifeless sort of house, for no children frolicked on the lawn, no motherly face ever smiled at the windows, and few people went in and out, except the old gentleman and his grandson.

Which house belongs to the Marches?

To Jo's lively imagination, this fine house seemed a kind of **enchanted** palace, full of splendors and delights, which no one enjoyed. She had long wanted to behold its hidden glories and to know the Laurence boy, who looked as if he would like to be known, if he only knew how to begin. Since the party, she had planned many

---

Vocabulary in Place

enchant, *v.* To cast a spell over; to attract or delight

ways of making friends with him, but he had not been seen lately. Peering up, she spied a brown face at an upper window, looking wistfully down into their garden.

"That boy is suffering for society and fun," she said to herself. "His grandpa does not know what's good for him and keeps him shut up all alone. He needs somebody young and lively to play with, and I've a great mind to go over and tell the old gentleman so!"

Where is Jo headed? Has she been invited?

The idea amused Jo, who liked to do daring things. She resolved to try what could be done. When she saw Mr. Laurence drive off, she dug her way down to the hedge, where she paused and took a survey. All quiet, curtains down, servants out of sight. Nothing visible but a curly black head at the upper window.

"Poor boy!" thought Jo, and she tossed up a snowball to make him look out. The head turned at once, as the big eyes brightened and the mouth began to smile. Jo **flourished** her broom and called out . . .

"How do you do? Are you sick?"

Laurie opened the window, and croaked out as hoarsely as a raven . . .

"Better, thank you. I've had a bad cold, and been shut up a week."

"I'm sorry. What do you amuse yourself with?"

"Nothing. It's dull as tombs up here."

"Don't you read?"

"Not much. They won't let me."

"Have someone come and see you then."

"There isn't anyone I'd like to see. Boys make such a row,[1] and my head is weak."

"Isn't there some nice quiet girl who'd read to you and amuse you?"

"Don't know any."

"You know us," Jo laughed.

"So I do! Will you come, please?" cried Laurie.

---

[1] **row.** Quarrel or uproar

Vocabulary in Place
flourish, *v.* To wave about

With that, Jo shouldered her broom and marched into the house, wondering what they would all say to her. Laurie was in a flutter of excitement at the idea of having company, and flew about to get ready, for as Mrs. March said, he was "a little gentleman" and did honor to the coming guest by brushing his hair and trying to tidy up the room, which in spite of half a dozen servants, was anything but neat. Presently there came a loud ring at the door, then a decided voice, asking for "Mr. Laurie," and a surprised-looking servant came running up to announce a young lady.

"Show her up, it's Miss Jo," said Laurie, going to the door of his little parlor to meet Jo. She appeared, looking rosy and quite at her ease, with a covered dish in one hand and Beth's three kittens in the other.

"Here I am, bag and baggage," she said briskly. "Meg wanted me to bring some of her blancmange,[2] and Beth thought her cats would be comforting. I knew you'd laugh at them, but I couldn't refuse, she was so anxious to do something."

It so happened that in laughing over Beth's funny loan, Laurie forgot his bashfulness and grew **sociable** at once.

"What a cozy room this is!" said Jo, glancing around.

"It might be if it was kept nice, but the maids are lazy."

"I'll right it up in two minutes."

As she laughed and talked, Jo whisked things into place and gave quite a different air to the room. When she finished they sat down on the sofa and Laurie sighed with satisfaction. "How kind you are!" he said gratefully. "Yes, that's what it wanted. Now let me do something to amuse my company."

"No, I came to amuse you. Shall I read aloud?" and Jo looked toward some inviting books near by.

What does Jo do to Laurie's room?

---

[2] **blancmange.** A sweetened milk pudding

Vocabulary in Place
sociable, *adj.* Friendly; eager to make friends

63

"Thank you! I've read all those, and if you don't mind, I'd rather talk," answered Laurie.

"Not a bit. I'll talk all day if you'll only set me going. Beth says I never know when to stop."

"Is Beth the rosy one, who stays at home a good deal and sometimes goes out with a little basket?" asked Laurie with interest.

"Yes, that's Beth. She's my girl, and a regular good one she is, too."

"The pretty one is Meg, and the curly-haired one is Amy, I believe?"

"How did you find that out?"

Laurie blushed, but answered frankly, "Why, you see I often hear you calling to one another, and I can't help looking over at your house. You always seem to be having such good times. I beg your pardon for being so rude, but sometimes you forget to put down the curtain at the window, and it's like looking at a picture to see the fire, and you all around the table with your mother. Her face looks so sweet, I can't help watching it. I haven't got any mother, you know."

And Laurie poked the fire to hide a little twitching of the lips that he could not control. The solitary, hungry look in his eyes went straight to Jo's warm heart, and feeling how rich she was in home and happiness, she gladly tried to share it with him.

Her voice was unusually gentle as she said, "I give you leave to look as much as you like. I just wish, though, instead of peeping, you'd come over and see us. Beth would sing to you if I begged her to, and Amy would dance. Meg and I would make you laugh over our funny stage properties, and we'd have jolly times. Wouldn't your grandpa let you?"

"I think he would, if your mother asked him. He's very kind, though he does not look so. He lets me do what I like, pretty much, only he's afraid I might be a bother to strangers," began Laurie, brightening more and more.

"We are not strangers, we're neighbors, and you needn't think you'd be a bother. We want to know you. I've been trying to do this ever so long. We've got acquainted with all our neighbors but you."

"You see, Grandpa lives among his books, and doesn't mind much what happens outside. Mr. Brooke, my tutor, doesn't stay here,

How does Laurie know which sister is which? Why does he blush when he explains this to Jo?

Why does Laurie have a "hungry" look in his eyes?

Where does Grandpa live? What does Laurie mean by this?

you know, and I have no one to go about with me, so I just stop at home and get on as I can."

"That's bad. You ought to make an effort and go visiting everywhere you are asked. Then you'll have plenty of friends, and if you keep going, you won't be bashful for long."

Laurie turned red again, but wasn't offended, for it was impossible not to take Jo's **blunt** speeches as kindly as they were meant.

"Do you like your school?" asked the boy, changing the subject, after a little pause.

"Don't go to school, I'm a businessman—girl, I mean. I go to wait on my great-aunt, and a dear, cross old soul she is, too," answered Jo. She gave him a lively description of the fidgety old lady, her fat poodle, and the parrot that talked Spanish.

The boy lay back and laughed till the tears ran down his cheeks.

"Oh! That does me no end of good. Tell on, please," he said, his face red and shining with merriment.

Much **elated** with her success, Jo did "tell on," all about their plays and plans, their hopes and fears for Father, and the most interesting events of her little world. Then they got to talking about books, and to Jo's delight, she found that Laurie loved them as well as she did.

"If you like them so much, come down and see ours. Grandfather is out, so you needn't be afraid," said Laurie, getting up.

"I'm not afraid of anything," returned Jo, with a toss of the head.

"I don't believe you are!" exclaimed the boy, looking at her with much admiration. Privately he thought she would have good reason to be a trifle afraid of the old gentleman, if she met him in some of his moods.

Laurie led Jo to the library, where she clapped her hands and pranced, as she always did when especially delighted. It was lined

Vocabulary in Place
blunt, *adj.* Abrupt and often embarassingly frank
elated, *adj.* Thrilled; very happy and excited

with books, and there were pictures, statues, and cabinets full of coins and curiosities, and best of all, a great open fireplace with tiles all round it.

"What richness!" sighed Jo, sinking into a velvet chair and gazing about her with an air of satisfaction. "Theodore Laurence, you ought to be the happiest boy in the world," she added impressively.

"A fellow can't live on books," said Laurie, shaking his head. Before he could say more, a bell rang, and Jo flew up, exclaiming with alarm, "Mercy me! It's your grandpa!"

"Well, what if it is? You are not afraid of anything, you know," returned the boy, looking wicked.

Why does Jo think she might be "a little bit" afraid of Laurie's grandfather?

"I think I am a little bit afraid of him, but I don't know why I should be. Marmee said I might come, and I don't think you're any the worse for it," said Jo, **composing** herself, though she kept her eyes on the door.

"I'm a great deal better for it. It was so pleasant, I couldn't bear to stop," said Laurie gratefully.

"The doctor to see you, sir," said the maid, beckoning.

"Would you mind if I left you for a minute? I suppose I must see him," said Laurie.

"Don't mind me. I'm happy as a cricket here," answered Jo.

Laurie went away, and his guest amused herself in her own way. She was standing before a fine portrait of the old gentleman when the door opened again, and without turning, she said decidedly, "I'm sure now that I shouldn't be afraid of him, for he's got kind eyes, though his mouth is grim, and he looks as if he has a tremendous **will** of his own. He isn't as handsome as my grandfather, but I like him."

"Thank you, ma'am," said a gruff voice behind her, and there, to her great **dismay**, stood old Mr. Laurence.

Vocabulary in Place

compose, *v.* To make oneself calm

will, *n.* The part of the mind by which one deliberately chooses a course of action; determination

dismay, *n.* A feeling of disappointment or alarm

Poor Jo blushed till she couldn't blush any redder, as she thought what she had said. For a minute a wild desire to run away possessed her, but a second look showed her that the eyes under the bushy eyebrows were kinder even than the painted ones. There was a sly twinkle in them, which lessened her fear a good deal. After a dreadful pause the old gentleman said, "So you're not afraid of me, hey?"

"Not much, sir."

"And you don't think me as handsome as your grandfather?"

"Not quite, sir."

"And I've got a tremendous will, have I?"

"I only said I thought so."

"But you like me in spite of it?"

"Yes, I do, sir."

That answer pleased the old gentleman. He gave a short laugh and shook hands with her, examining her face **gravely**. With a nod, he said, "You've got your grandfather's spirit, if you haven't his face. He was a fine man, my dear, but what is better, he was a brave and an honest one. I was proud to be his friend."

"Thank you, sir," And Jo was quite comfortable after that, for it suited her exactly.

"What have you been doing to this boy of mine, hey?" was the next question, sharply put.

"Only trying to be neighborly, sir." And Jo told how her visit came about.

"You think he needs cheering up a bit, do you?"

"Yes, sir, he seems a little lonely, and we girls would be glad to help if we could, for we don't forget the splendid Christmas present you sent us," said Jo eagerly.

"Tut, tut, tut! That was the boy's affair. How is the poor woman?"

"Doing nicely, sir." And Jo told all about the Hummels.

"Just her father's way of doing good. I shall come and see your mother some fine day. Tell her so. There's the tea bell. Come down

What is it about Jo that Laurie's grandfather likes so much? Does she remind him of someone else?

Vocabulary in Place
gravely, *adv.* Very seriously

67

and go on being neighborly." And Mr. Laurence offered her his arm with old-fashioned courtesy.

"What would Meg say to this?" thought Jo, as she was marched away. Her eyes danced with fun as she imagined herself telling the story at home.

"Hey! Why, what the dickens³ . . . ?" said the old gentleman, as Laurie came running downstairs. He stopped short, surprised at the sight of Jo arm in arm with his grandfather.

Jo gave him a **triumphant** little glance.

"Come to your tea, sir, and behave like a gentleman."

The old gentleman did not say much as he drank his four cups of tea. He quietly watched the young people chatting away like old friends, and noticed the change in his grandson. There was color, light, and life in the boy's face now and genuine merriment in his laugh.

What effect has Jo's visit had on Laurie?

"She's right, the lad is lonely. I'll see what these little girls can do for him," thought Mr. Laurence, as he looked and listened. He liked Jo. Her odd, blunt ways suited him, and she seemed to understand the boy almost as well as if she had been one herself.

As she rose to go, Laurie said he had something more to show her and took her away to the conservatory.⁴ It seemed quite fairylike to Jo, as she went up and down the walks, enjoying the blooming walls on either side, the soft light, the damp sweet air, and the wonderful vines and trees that hung about her. Her new friend cut the finest flowers till his hands were full. Then he tied them up, saying happily, "Please give these to your mother, and tell her I like the medicine she sent me very much."

---

³ **dickens.** A name for the devil. *What the dickens* is an expression of surprise.

⁴ **conservatory.** A greenhouse for displaying plants

Vocabulary in Place
triumphant, *adj.* Proud and victorious

They found Mr. Laurence standing before the fire in the great drawing room, by a grand piano, which stood open.

"Do you play?" she asked, turning to Laurie with a respectful expression.

"Sometimes," he answered modestly.

"Please do now. I want to hear it, so I can tell Beth."

As Jo listened, her regard for the "Laurence" boy increased very much, for he played remarkably well and didn't put on any airs.[5] She praised him till he was quite abashed, and his grandfather came to his rescue.

"That will do, that will do, young lady. His music isn't bad, but I hope he will do more important things. My respects to your mother. I hope you'll come again. Goodnight, Doctor Jo."

Why does Mr. Laurence call her "Doctor Jo"?

He shook hands kindly, but **glowered** as if something did not please him. When they got into the hall, Jo asked if she had said something **amiss.** Laurie shook his head.

"No, it was me. He doesn't like to hear me play."

"Why not?"

"I'll tell you some day. You will come again, I hope?"

"If you promise to come and see us after you are well."

"I will."

"Good night, Laurie!"

"Good night, Jo, good night!"

When Jo was through telling the afternoon's adventures, the whole family wanted to go visiting, for each found something very attractive in the big house on the other side of the hedge. Mrs. March wanted to talk of her father with the old man who had not forgotten him, Meg longed to walk in the conservatory, Beth sighed for the grand piano, and Amy was eager to see the fine pictures and statues.

---

[5]**put on . . . airs.** Act stuck up, as if superior to others

Vocabulary in Place
glower, *v.* To look angrily
amiss, *adj.* Out of place

69

Jo asked her mother why Mr. Laurence didn't like to have Laurie play piano.

"I think it was because his son, Laurie's father, married an Italian musician, which displeased the old man. The lady was lovely and accomplished, but he did not like her, and never saw his son after he married. They both died when Laurie was a little child, and then his grandfather took him home. Laurie comes naturally by his love of music, for he is like his mother, and I dare say he fears that Laurie may want to be a musician. At any rate, the boy's skill reminds him of the woman he did not like, and so he 'glowered' as Jo said."

"Dear me, how romantic!" exclaimed Meg.

"How silly!" said Jo. "Let him be a musician if he wants to, and don't send him to college, when he hates to go. What do you say, Beth?"

"I was thinking about our *Pilgrim's Progress*," answered Beth, who had not heard a word. "Maybe the house over there, full of splendid things, is going to be our Palace Beautiful."⁶

"We have got to get by the lions first," said Jo, as if she rather liked the idea. ■

> *Why does Laurie live with his grandfather instead of his parents?*

> *Why does Beth think that the house next door is like the Palace Beautiful?*

---

⁶ **Palace Beautiful.** In *Pilgrim's Progress,* a palace established in order to provide "relief and security of pilgrims"

CHAPTER 6

Beth Finds the Palace Beautiful

The big house did prove a Palace Beautiful, though it took some time for all to get in, and Beth found it very hard to pass the lions. Old Mr. Laurence was the biggest one, but after he had called several times and said something funny or kind to each one of the girls, nobody felt much afraid of him, except timid Beth.

What are the "lions" that the girls must pass to get into the Laurence house?

The other lion was the fact that they were poor and Laurie rich. This made them shy of accepting favors, which they could not return. But, after a while, they found that he considered them the **benefactors**. He could not do enough to show how grateful he was for the comfort he took in that humble home of theirs. So they soon forgot their pride and interchanged kindnesses without stopping to think which was the greater.

Everyone liked Laurie, and he privately informed his tutor, Mr. Brooke, that "the Marches were regularly splendid girls." With delightful enthusiasm, they took the solitary boy into their midst and made much of him.

What good times they had, to be sure. Such plays and sleigh rides and skating frolics, such pleasant evenings in the old parlor, and now and then such gay little parties at the great house. Meg walked in the conservatory whenever she liked to delight in the bouquets; Jo read **voraciously** and amused the old gentleman with her criticisms;[1] Amy copied beautiful pictures to her heart's content; and Laurie played "lord of the manor" in the most delightful style.

---

[1] **criticisms.** The analyses or intepretations of literary works

Vocabulary in Place
benefactor, *n.* A person who helps another person
voraciously, *adv.* With great appetite

But Beth, though yearning for the grand piano, could not pluck up courage to go to the "Mansion of Bliss," as Meg called it. She went once with Jo, but the old gentleman, not being aware of her shyness, said "Hey!" so loud that she ran away, declaring she would never go there any more, not even for the dear piano. No persuasions or **enticements** could overcome her fear, till Mr. Laurence, hearing of the situation from Laurie, set about mending matters.

One day while visiting, he **artfully** led the conversation to music and talked away about great singers and musicians whom he had seen until Beth found it impossible to stay in her distant corner. She crept nearer and nearer, until she stopped at the back of his chair where she stood listening, her great eyes wide open and her cheeks red with excitement. Mr. Laurence talked on and presently, as if the idea had just occurred to him, he said to Mrs. March . . .

"The boy neglects his music now, and I'm glad of it, for he was getting too fond of it. Wouldn't some of your girls like to run over and practice on the piano now and then, just to keep it in tune, you know, ma'am?"

Beth took a step forward, her hands pressed tightly together to keep from clapping them. The thought of practicing on that splendid instrument quite took her breath away. Mr. Laurence went on with an odd little nod and smile . . .

"They needn't see or speak to anyone for I'm shut up in my study at the other end of the house, Laurie is out a great deal, and the servants are never near the drawing room after nine o'clock."

He rose, as if going. "Please, tell the young ladies, and if they don't care to come, why, never mind." Here a little hand slipped into his, as Beth looked up at him and said, in her **earnest** yet timid way . . .

How does Mr. Laurence get Beth to come over? Once she gets over her initial shyness, will she go there often?

Vocabulary in Place
enticement, *n.* A lure or attraction; a bribe or hint of future reward
artfully, *adv.* With skill and subtlety; not in an obvious way
earnest, *adj.* Sincere; openly honest and direct

72

"Oh sir, they do care, very very much!"

"Are you the musical girl?" he asked very kindly.

"I'm Beth. I love it dearly, and I'll come, if you are quite sure nobody will hear me and be disturbed," she added, trembling at her own boldness as she spoke.

"Not a soul, my dear. The house is empty half the day, so come and drum away as much as you like."

Beth blushed like a rose and gave the hand a grateful squeeze because she had no words to thank him. The old gentleman softly stroked the hair off her forehead, and, stooping down, he kissed her, saying, in a tone few people ever heard, "I had a little girl once, with eyes like these. God bless you, my dear! Good day, madam." And away he went, in a great hurry.

Who does Mr. Laurence remember when he sees Beth?

Next day, having seen both the old and young gentleman out of the house, Beth crept in at the side door, and made her way as noiselessly as any mouse to the drawing room where her **idol** stood. Some pretty, easy music happen to lay on the piano. After looking over her shoulder several times, Beth touched the great instrument with trembling fingers. Straightway she forgot her fear and everything else but the delight that the music gave her, like the voice of a beloved friend.

She stayed till Hannah came to take her home to dinner, but she had no appetite, and could only sit and smile upon everyone in a general state of beatitude.[2]

After that, the little brown hood slipped through the hedge nearly every day, and the great drawing room was haunted by a tuneful spirit that came and went unseen. She never knew that Mr. Laurence opened his study door to hear her play. She never saw Laurie stand guard in the hall to warn the servants away. She never

Why does Beth sneak through the hedge? What special things do Laurie and his grandfather do for her? Does she realize this?

---

[2] **beatitude.** Bliss

Vocabulary in Place
idol, *n.* An image used as an object of worship

73

suspected that the song books which she found in the rack were put there especially for her. She enjoyed herself heartily, and found, what isn't always the case, that her granted wish was all she had hoped. Perhaps it was because she was so grateful for this blessing that a greater was given her. At any rate she deserved both.

Beth decided to make a pair of slippers for Mr. Laurence, in order to express her thanks for his great generosity. After many serious discussions with Meg and Jo, the pattern was chosen, the materials bought, and the slippers begun. Beth worked away early and late. She was a **nimble** little needlewoman, and they were finished before anyone got tired of them. Then she wrote a short, simple note, and with Laurie's help, got them smuggled onto the study table one morning before the old gentleman was up.

When this excitement was over, Beth waited to see what would happen. All day passed and a part of the next and she was beginning to fear she had offended her crotchety[3] friend. On the afternoon of the second day, she went out to do an errand. As she came up the street, on her return, she saw three, yes, four heads popping in and out of the parlor windows. The moment they saw her, several hands were waved, and several joyful voices screamed . . .

"Here's a letter from the old gentleman! Come quick, and read it!"

"Oh, Beth, he's sent you . . ." began Amy, but she got no further, for Jo quenched her by slamming down the window.

Beth hurried on in a flutter of suspense. At the door her sisters seized her and led her to the parlor, all pointing and saying at once, "Look there! Look there!" Beth did look and turned pale with delight and surprise, for there stood a little cabinet piano, with a letter lying on the glossy lid, addressed to "Miss Elizabeth March."

"For me?" gasped Beth, holding onto Jo and feeling as if she should tumble down.

"Yes, all for you, my precious! Isn't it splendid of him? Don't you think he's the dearest old man in the world? Here's the key in the letter. We didn't open it, but we are dying to know what he says," cried Jo, hugging her sister and offering the note.

---

[3] **crotchety.** Stubborn

Vocabulary in Place
nimble, *adj.* Skilled in movement or action

"You read it! I can't, I feel so queer! Oh, it is too lovely!" and Beth hid her face in Jo's apron, quite upset by her present.

Jo opened the paper and began to read.

"Miss March:
Dear Madam—
I have had many pairs of slippers in my life, but I never had any that suited me so well as yours. They will always remind me of the gentle giver. I like to pay my debts, so I know you will allow 'the old gentleman' to send you something, which once belonged to the little granddaughter he lost. With hearty thanks and best wishes, I remain
Your grateful friend and humble servant,
JAMES LAURENCE."

How does Mr. Laurence thank Beth for making him a pair of slippers? To whom did her present once belong?

"There, Beth, that's an honor! Laurie told me how fond Mr. Laurence used to be of the child who died, and how he kept all her little things carefully. Just think, he's given you her piano. That comes of having big blue eyes and loving music," said Jo, trying to soothe Beth, who trembled and looked more excited than she had ever been before.

Meg opened the instrument to admire and display its beauties. Amy was much impressed by the elegance of the note and couldn't wait to tell the girls at school. Beth gave the little instrument a try, and everyone pronounced it the most remarkable piano ever heard. But, perfect as it was, I think the real charm lay in the happiest of all happy faces which leaned over it, as Beth lovingly touched the beautiful black and white keys and pressed the bright pedals.

"You'll have to go and thank him," said Jo, by way of a joke, for the idea of the child's really going never entered her head.

"Yes. I guess I'll go now, before I get frightened thinking about it." And, to the utter amazement of the assembled family, Beth walked deliberately down the garden, through the hedge, and in at the Laurences' door. They all stared after her, **rendered** quite speechless by the miracle.

Why is the family so amazed by Beth's action?

Vocabulary in Place
render, *v.* To cause to become

They would have been still more amazed if they had seen what Beth did afterward. If you will believe me, she went and knocked at the study door before she gave herself time to think. When a gruff voice called out, "come in!" she did go in, right up to Mr. Laurence.

He looked quite taken aback, as she held out her hand, saying, with only a small **quaver** in her voice, "I came to thank you, sir, for . . ." But she didn't finish, for he looked so friendly that she put both arms round his neck and kissed him.

If the roof of the house had suddenly flown off, the old gentleman wouldn't have been more astonished. But he liked it. Oh dear, yes, he liked it amazingly! He set her on his knee, and laid his wrinkled cheek against her rosy one, feeling as if he had got his own little granddaughter back again. Beth lost all fear of him at that moment and sat there talking to him as cozily as if she had known him all her life. When she went home, he walked with her to her own gate, shook hands cordially, and touched his hat in a gentlemanly manner.

When the girls saw that performance, Jo began to dance a jig, Amy nearly fell out of the window in her surprise, and Meg exclaimed, with uplifted hands, "Well, I do believe the world is coming to an end."

Why does Meg say this?

Vocabulary in Place

quaver, *n.* Shaky or trembling; unsteadiness

77

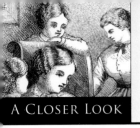

A Closer Look

Understanding the Selection

Recalling (just the facts)

1. Who lives in the old brown house that looks "rather bare and shabby"? Who lives in the mansion next door?
2. Why does Mr. Laurence encourage Beth to play the piano, even though he doesn't like to hear Laurie play?
3. Who had the hardest time getting up her courage to pass the lions next door? Of the two lions, which one did she find most intimidating?
4. What present does Beth receive? Who is it from?

Interpreting (delving deeper)

1. Why does Jo feel sorry for Laurie, even though he lives in a mansion with "every sort of comfort and luxury," including a wonderful collection of books?
2. What sort of "palace" is Beth talking about? Is it really guarded by lions?
3. Why were the March girls shy about visiting Laurie at first?
4. What does Beth do after she receives the present? Why does this surprise everyone?

Synthesizing (putting it all together)

1. Is Laurie lonely? How can you tell? How does his life change after he gets to know Jo and her sisters?
2. Why doesn't Mr. Laurence want his grandson to be a musician? Will he be disappointed if Laurie follows in his mother's footsteps? Why? Use examples from the story to support your answer.

Writing

EXTENSIONS

Journal Entry. At the end of Chapter 5, Jo describes how wonderful Laurie's house is with the conservatory full of flowers, the library stocked with numerous books, and the drawing room with its grand piano. Jo wonders whether the neighbor's fine mansion might be the "Palace Beautiful." Beth cannot wait to go and see the piano. Jo, however, reminds her that she must be willing to "get by the lions first."

In order to convey what a challenge it will be for Beth to enter the Laurence mansion, Alcott borrows imagery from *Pilgrim's Progress.* Journeying toward the "Celestial City," the novel's main character, Christian, becomes weary and wishes to rest at a pleasant inn called the "Palace Beautiful." As a trial of his faith, he must first find his way around two lions that guard the passageway to the inn. Similarly, Beth must gather up her courage to get past the obstacle of her shyness if she wants to play the coveted piano.

What sort of challenges or obstacles have you met with in your life? What sort of "lions" have you had to get by? Write a journal entry in response to one of the following topics. Your writing can be informal, but you should still write in complete sentences and use proper punctuation.

- Describe a time when you got up the nerve to try something that you weren't sure you could do at first. Tell what happened and how you felt about it. How did it work out?
- Is there something that you would really like to do or try if you had the chance? What is it? What would you have to overcome in order to try this? How might you be able to "get past the lions"? Could someone else help, or would you have to rely on yourself?

Language Alive!

EXTENSIONS

Idioms. Has anyone ever warned you never to "cry wolf"? Have you been told to "hold your horses"? Or have you ever been "in the doghouse" for making a mistake?

As in ordinary language, writers often employ expressions that cannot be taken literally. What does Alcott convey, for instance, by using the phrase "get by the lions"? She could have written something like "If Beth could get up her nerve to meet the neighbors next door, maybe she could even play the piano." But would that have made the same impression on you as the idea of getting past the lions? Although there might be a pair of stone lions guarding the steps to the elegant Laurence mansion, there are no real lions for her to get past.

Phrases such as "get by the lions" are called **idioms,** expressions that mean something different from what the words actually say. Because idioms are ways of speaking that are peculiar to a particular group of people, they are often unmatched in other languages and, therefore, cannot be directly translated. For example, when a French-speaker says "Ne tombe pas dans les pommes!" or "Do not fall into the apples!" for instance, he or she means "Do not faint!"

What are some other common idioms that we use in English? Working as a class or in small groups, read aloud the following list of idiomatic expressions and take turns explaining what they mean and how they might have become common idioms in many parts of America.

- "under the weather"
- "bend someone's ear"
- "a bad hair day"
- "not playing with a full deck"
- "chip on one's shoulder"
- "put your foot in your mouth"
- "cat's got your tongue"

Now conduct your own search for idiomatic expressions. Using old newspapers, magazines, news sites, blogs, or other Internet sources, find at least three examples of idiomatic expressions. Present your findings to the class.

CHAPTER 7

Amy's Valley of Humiliation

"That boy is a perfect Cyclops,[1] isn't he?" said Amy one day, as Laurie clattered by on horseback, with a flourish of his whip as he passed.

"How dare you say so, when he's got both his eyes? And very handsome ones they are, too," cried Jo, who resented any slighting remarks about her friend.

"I didn't say anything about his eyes, and I don't see why you need fire up when I admire his riding."

"Oh, my goodness! That little goose means a centaur,[2] and she called him a Cyclops," exclaimed Jo, with a burst of laughter.

"You needn't be so rude," **retorted** Amy. "I just wish I had a little of the money Laurie spends on that horse," she added, as if to herself, yet hoping her sisters would hear.

"Why?" asked Meg kindly.

"I need it so much. I'm dreadfully in debt, and it won't be my turn to have the rag money[3] for a month."

"In debt, Amy? What do you mean?" And Meg looked sober.

"Why, I owe at least a dozen pickled limes, and I can't pay them, you know, till I have money, for Marmee forbade my having anything charged at the shop."

Why does Jo react so quickly to Amy's comments?

---

[1] **Cyclops.** In Greek mythology, a giant with a single eye in the middle of its forehead

[2] **centaur.** In Greek mythology, one of a race of creatures with a horse's body and a human head and torso

[3] **rag money.** Extra saved money

Vocabulary in Place
retort, *v.* To reply or make a counter argument

"Tell me all about it. Are limes the fashion now? It used to be pricking bits of rubber to make balls." And Meg tried to keep her **countenance,** Amy looked so grave and important.

"Why, you see, the girls are always buying them, and unless you want to be thought mean, you must do it too. It's nothing but limes now, for everyone is sucking them in their desks in schooltime, and trading them off for pencils, bead rings, paper dolls, or something else, at recess. If one girl likes another, she gives her a lime. If she's mad with her, she eats one before her face, and doesn't offer even a suck. They treat by turns, and I've had ever so many but haven't returned them, and I ought to for they are debts of honor, you know."

"How much will pay them off and restore your credit?" asked Meg, taking out her purse.

"A quarter would more than do it, and leave a few cents over for a treat for you. Don't you like limes?"

Does Meg help Amy? What does this say about Meg's personality?

"Not much. You may take my money," said Meg. "Make it last as long as you can, for it isn't very plenty, you know."

"Oh, thank you! It must be so nice to have pocket money! I'll have a grand feast, for I haven't tasted a lime this week. I felt delicate about taking any, as I couldn't return them, and I'm actually suffering for one."

Next day Amy was rather late at school, but could not resist the temptation of displaying, with pardonable pride, a moist brown-paper parcel, before she **consigned** it to the inmost recesses of her desk. During the next few minutes the rumor that Amy March had got twenty-four delicious limes (she ate one on the way) and was going to treat circulated through her "set,"[4] and the attentions of her friends became quite overwhelming. Katy Brown invited her to

---

[4] **set.** Group of friends

Vocabulary in Place

countenance, *n.* Appearance, especially the expression of the face

consign, *v.* To set apart for a special use or purpose

her next party on the spot. Mary Kingsley insisted on lending her her watch till recess, and Jenny Snow, a **satirical** young lady, who had **basely** teased Amy upon her limeless state, promptly buried the hatchet[5] and offered to furnish answers to certain appalling sums. But Amy had not forgotten Miss Snow's cutting remarks about "some persons whose noses were not too flat to smell other people's limes, and stuck-up people who were not too proud to ask for them," and she instantly crushed "that Snow girl's" hopes, saying, "You needn't be so polite all of a sudden, for you won't get any."

A distinguished person happened to visit the school that morning, and Amy's beautifully drawn maps received praise, causing Miss March to assume the airs of a studious young peacock. But, alas, alas! Pride goes before a fall, and the revengeful Snow turned the tables with disastrous success. No sooner had the guest paid the usual stale compliments and bowed himself out, than Jenny informed Mr. Davis, the teacher, that Amy March had pickled limes in her desk.

Now Mr. Davis had declared limes a **contraband** article, and solemnly vowed to publicly ferrule[6] the first person who was found breaking the law. This man had succeeded in banishing chewing gum after a long and stormy war, had made a bonfire of forbidden novels and newspapers, had put an end to a private post office, and done all that one man could do to keep half a hundred rebellious girls in order. Boys are trying enough to human patience, goodness knows, but girls are infinitely more so, especially to nervous gentlemen with tempers and no talent for teaching. Mr. Davis knew any quantity of Greek, Latin, algebra, and "ologies" of all sorts so he was called a fine teacher. Manners, morals, feelings, and examples were not considered of any particular importance.

How does Mr. Davis discover Amy's limes?

---

[5] **buried the hatchet.** Made peace

[6] **ferrule.** Variant of *ferule;* to punish with a cane, stick, or ruler

Vocabulary in Place
satirical, *adj.* Sarcastic; intentionally insulting or humiliating others
basely, *adv.* Rudely
contraband, *adj.* Prohibited from being imported or exported

It was a most unfortunate moment for **denouncing** Amy, and Jenny knew it. Mr. Davis had evidently taken his coffee too strong that morning, and his pupils had not done him the credit which he felt he deserved. Therefore, to use the expressive, if not elegant, language of a schoolgirl, "He was as nervous as a witch and as cross as a bear." The word "limes" was like fire to powder, his face reddened, and he rapped on his desk with an energy, which made Jenny skip to her seat with unusual rapidity.

"Young ladies, attention, if you please!"

At the stern order the buzz ceased, and fifty pairs of blue, black, gray, and brown eyes were obediently fixed upon his awful countenance.

"Miss March, come to the desk."

Amy rose to comply with outward composure, but a secret fear oppressed her, for the limes weighed upon her conscience.

"Bring with you the limes you have in your desk," was the unexpected command which arrested her before she got out of her seat.

"Don't take all," whispered her neighbor, a young lady of great presence of mind.

Amy hastily shook out half a dozen and laid the rest down before Mr. Davis, feeling that any man possessing a human heart would relent when that delicious perfume met his nose. Unfortunately, Mr. Davis particularly detested the odor of the fashionable pickle, and disgust added to his wrath.

"Is that all?"

"Not quite," stammered Amy.

"Bring the rest immediately."

With a despairing glance at her set, she obeyed.

"You are sure there are no more?"

"I never lie, sir."

Vocabulary in Place

denounce, *v.* To criticize sharply or condemn

"So I see. Now take these disgusting things two by two, and throw them out of the window."

There was a simultaneous sigh, which created quite a little gust, as the last hope fled, and the treat was **ravished** from their longing lips. Scarlet with shame and anger, Amy went to and fro six dreadful times, and as each doomed couple, looking oh, so plump and juicy, fell from her reluctant hands, a shout from the street completed the anguish of the girls, for it told them that their feast was being enjoyed by the little children, who were their sworn foes. This was too much. All flashed **indignant** glances at Davis, and one passionate lime lover burst into tears.

As Amy returned from her last trip, Mr. Davis gave a "Hem!" and said, in his most impressive manner . . .

"Young ladies, you remember what I said to you a week ago. I am sorry this has happened, but I never allow my rules to be **infringed,** and I never break my word. Miss March, hold out your hand."

Amy **started,** and put both hands behind her, turning on him an imploring look which pleaded for her better than the words she could not utter.

"Your hand, Miss March!" was the only answer her mute appeal received, and too proud to cry or beg, Amy set her teeth, threw back her head defiantly, and bore without flinching several tingling blows on her little palm. They were neither many nor heavy, but that made no difference to her. For the first time in her life she had been struck, and the disgrace, in her eyes, was as deep as if he had knocked her down.

How does Amy feel about her punishment?

"You will now stand on the platform till recess," said Mr. Davis, resolved to do the thing thoroughly, since he had begun.

Vocabulary in Place

ravish, *v.* To seize and carry away by force

indignant, *adj.* Angry, especially anger brought on by something unjust or mean

infringe, *v.* To violate or break the rules

start, *v.* To move suddenly or jump when startled

That was dreadful. It would have been bad enough to go to her seat, and see the pitying faces of her friends, or the satisfied ones of her few enemies, but to face the whole school, with that shame fresh upon her, seemed impossible. For a second she felt as if she could only drop down where she stood, and break her heart with crying. A bitter sense of wrong helped her to bear it, and, taking her place, she fixed her eyes on the stove funnel[7] above what now seemed a sea of faces. She stood there so motionless and white that the girls found it hard to study with that pathetic figure before them.

During the fifteen minutes that followed, the proud and sensitive little girl suffered a shame and pain that she never forgot. To others it might seem a small affair, but to her it was a hard experience, for during the twelve years of her life she had been governed by love alone, and a blow of that sort had never touched her before. The pain of her hand and the ache of her heart were forgotten in the sting of the thought, "I shall have to tell at home, and they will be so disappointed in me!"

The fifteen minutes seemed an hour, but they came to an end at last, and the word "Recess!" had never seemed so welcome to her before.

"You can go, Miss March," said Mr. Davis, looking, as he felt, uncomfortable.

He did not soon forget the **reproachful** glance Amy gave him, as she went, without a word to anyone, straight into the coat room, snatched her things, and left the place "forever," as she passionately declared to herself. She was in a sad state when she got home, and when the older girls arrived, some time later, an indignation meeting was held at once. Mrs. March did not say much but looked disturbed, and comforted her afflicted little daughter in her tenderest manner.

What is Amy most afraid of as a result of this incident?

---

[7] **stove funnel.** The pipe through which smoke is drawn from the wood stove to the chimney

Vocabulary in Place

reproachful, *adj.* Expressing criticism, disapproval, or blame

Meg bathed the insulted hand with glycerine[8] and tears, Beth felt that even her beloved kittens would fail to soothe grief like this, Jo wrathfully proposed that Mr. Davis be arrested without delay, and Hannah shook her fist at the "villain" and pounded potatoes for dinner as if she had him under her pestle.[9]

No notice was taken of Amy's flight, except by her mates, but the sharp-eyed girls discovered that Mr. Davis was quite friendly in the afternoon, also unusually nervous. Just before school closed, Jo appeared, wearing a grim expression as she stalked up to the desk, and delivered a letter from her mother. She collected Amy's property, and departed, carefully scraping the mud from her boots on the door mat, as if she shook that dust of the place off her feet.

"Yes, you can have a vacation from school, but I want you to study a little every day with Beth," said Mrs. March that evening. "I don't approve of corporal punishment,[10] especially for girls. I dislike Mr. Davis's manner of teaching and don't think the girls you associate with are doing you any good, but I shall ask your father's advice before I send you anywhere else."

"That's good! I wish all the girls would leave, and spoil his old school. It's perfectly maddening to think of those lovely limes," sighed Amy.

"I am not sorry you lost them, for you broke the rules, and deserved some punishment for disobedience," was the severe reply, which rather disappointed the young lady, who expected nothing but sympathy.

"Do you mean you are glad I was disgraced before the whole school?" cried Amy.

"I should not have chosen that way of mending a fault," replied her mother, "but I'm not sure that it won't do you more good than

Does Mrs. March think that Amy deserved to be punished? Does she approve of Mr. Davis's methods?

---

[8] **glycerine.** Soap

[9] **pestle.** A club shaped, hand-held tool used for grinding or mashing substances

[10] **corporal punishment.** Physical punishment, such as beating or spanking

a milder method. You are getting to be rather **conceited,** my dear, and it is quite time you set about correcting it. You have a good many little gifts and virtues, but there is no need of parading them, for conceit spoils the finest genius. There is not much danger that real talent or goodness will be overlooked long, even if it is, the consciousness of possessing and using it well should satisfy one, and the great charm of all power is modesty."

"So it is!" cried Laurie, who was playing chess in a corner with Jo. "I knew a girl once who had a really remarkable talent for music, and she didn't know it, never guessed what sweet little things she composed when she was alone, and wouldn't have believed it if anyone had told her."

"I wish I'd known that nice girl. Maybe she would have helped me," said Beth, who stood beside him, listening eagerly.

"You do know her, and she helps you better than anyone else could," answered Laurie, looking at her with such mischievous meaning in his merry black eyes that Beth suddenly turned very red and hid her face in the sofa cushion, quite overcome by such an unexpected discovery.

Jo let Laurie win the game to pay for that praise of her Beth, who could not be **prevailed** upon to play for them after her compliment. So Laurie did his best, and sang delightfully, being in a particularly lively humor, for to the Marches he seldom showed the moody side of his character. When he was gone, Amy, who had been **pensive** all evening, said suddenly, as if busy over some new idea, "Is Laurie an accomplished boy?"

"Yes, he has had an excellent education, and has much talent. He will make a fine man, if not spoiled," replied her mother.

"And he isn't conceited, is he?" asked Amy.

Vocabulary in Place

conceited, *adj.* Arrogant; vain

prevail, *v.* To use persuasion. Often used with *on, upon,* or *with.*

pensive, *adj.* Deeply thoughtful

"Not in the least. That is why he is so charming and we all like him so much."

"I see. It's nice to have accomplishments and be elegant, but not to show off or get perked up," said Amy thoughtfully.

"These things are always seen and felt in a person's manner and conversations, if modestly used, but it is not necessary to display them," said Mrs. March.

"Any more than it's proper to wear all your bonnets and gowns and ribbons at once, that folks may know you've got them," added Jo, and the lecture ended in a laugh.

What does Amy mean by the phrase "perked up"?

Words to Keep

The following sentences contain important words from the Vocabulary in Place boxes in Chapters 4–7 of *Little Women*. In your notebook, or on a separate sheet of paper, write the part of speech of each boldface word, a synonym (or definition in your own words), and a new sentence of your own.

1. They stared out the window **dismally,** wondering when the rain would stop.
2. Kaz was very **remorseful** after destroying her brother's science project.
3. Gerald was finally able to cheer up his **irascible** neighbor by offering to rake her leaves.
4. Grandfather was very stern and felt any movie, regardless of its content, was **frivolous.**
5. The **cunning** fox tricked the gingerbread man into climbing onto his head.
6. We were glad to find that the new neighbors were very **sociable.**
7. When the Red Sox finally won the World Series, their fans were **elated.**
8. To my **dismay,** the essay was not in my backpack when I got to school.
9. The child **voraciously** devoured one bowl of ice cream and asked for another.
10. After his **earnest** apology, she decided to forgive him.
11. The Coast Guard discovered the **contraband** materials stowed in the ship's cargo hold.
12. Terry ignored his **reproachful** stare and continued reading the gossip column.

CHAPTER 8

Jo Meets Apollyon

"Where are you going?" asked Amy, coming into Meg and Jo's room one Saturday afternoon, and finding them getting ready to go out with an **air** of secrecy, which excited her curiosity.

"Never mind. Little girls shouldn't ask questions," returned Jo sharply.

Why does Amy feel insulted?

Amy **bridled** up at this insult, and determined to find out the secret, if she teased for an hour. She turned to Meg, who never refused her anything very long, and began to coax. Meg held her tongue, however, so Amy used her eyes. When she saw Meg slip a fan into her pocket she cried,

"I know! I know! You're going to the theater to see 'Seven Castles' with Laurie! Please let me come," she added pleadingly. "I've been sick with this cold so long, and shut up, I'm dying for some fun. Do, Meg! I'll be ever so good." Amy looked as pathetic as she could.

"Suppose we take her," began Meg.

Why doesn't Jo want Amy to come?

"If she goes I shan't," said Jo crossly, for she disliked the trouble of overseeing a fidgety child when she wanted to enjoy herself. "It will be very rude, after Laurie invited only us."

Amy began to put her boots on, saying, in her most aggravating way, "I shall go. Meg says I may . . ."

"You shan't stir a step, so you may just stay where you are," scolded Jo, crosser than ever, having just pricked her finger in her hurry.

Vocabulary in Place

air, *n.* Outward appearance; aura

bridle, *v.* To show anger; to take offense

Sitting on the floor with one boot on, Amy began to cry and Meg to reason with her, when Laurie called from below, and the two girls hurried down, leaving their sister wailing.

Just as the party was setting out, Amy called over the banisters in a threatening tone, "You'll be sorry for this, Jo March, see if you ain't."

"Fiddlesticks!" returned Jo, slamming the door.

They had a charming time, but Jo's pleasure had a drop of bitterness in it. The fairy queen's yellow curls reminded her of Amy, and between the acts she amused herself with wondering what her sister would do to make her "sorry for it."

What does Jo worry about while at the theater?

When they got home, they found Amy reading in the parlor. She assumed an injured air as they came in, never lifted her eyes from her book, or asked a single question, but let Beth inquire about the play and receive the glowing description.

On going up to her room, Jo's first look was toward the bureau, for their last quarrel had ended in Amy turning Jo's top drawer upside down on the floor. Everything was in its place, however, and Jo decided that Amy had forgiven and forgotten her wrongs.

There Jo was mistaken, for next day she made a discovery that produced a tempest. Meg, Beth, and Amy were sitting together, late in the afternoon, when Jo burst into the room, and demanded breathlessly, "Has anyone taken my book?"

Meg and Beth said "No" at once, and looked surprised. Amy poked the fire and said nothing. Jo was upon her in a minute.

"Amy, you've got it!"

"No, I haven't."

"You know where it is, then!"

"No, I don't."

"That's a fib!" cried Jo, taking her by the shoulders, and looking fierce enough to frighten a much braver child than Amy.

"Scold as much as you like, you'll never see your silly old book again," cried Amy.

"Why not?"

"I burned it up."

"What! My little book I was so fond of, and worked over, and meant to finish before Father got home? Have you really burned it?" said Jo, turning very pale, while her eyes **kindled** and her hands clutched Amy nervously.

"Yes, I did! I told you I'd make you pay for being so cross yesterday, and I have, so . . ."

Amy got no farther, for Jo's hot temper mastered her. She shook Amy till her teeth chattered in her head, crying in a passion of grief and anger . . .

"You wicked, wicked girl! I never can write it again, and I'll never forgive you as long as I live."

Meg flew to rescue Amy, and Beth to **pacify** Jo, but Jo was quite beside herself. With a parting box on her sister's ear, she rushed out of the room and up to the garret to finish her fight alone.

Is Mrs. March surprised by Jo's reaction to the loss of her book?

The storm cleared up below, for Mrs. March came home, and, having heard the story, soon brought Amy to a sense of the wrong she had done her sister. Jo's little book of fairy tales was the pride of her heart, and was regarded by her family as a literary sprout of great promise. She had just copied them with great care, and had destroyed the old manuscript, so that Amy's bonfire had consumed the loving work of several years. It seemed a small loss to others, but to Jo it was a dreadful **calamity**, and she felt that it never could be made up to her. Beth mourned as for a departed kitten, and Meg refused to defend her pet. Mrs. March looked grave and grieved, and Amy now regretted the act more than any of them.

When the tea bell rang, Jo appeared, looking so grim that it took all Amy's courage to say meekly . . .

Vocabulary in Place

kindle, *v.* To flame or become very bright; to catch on fire

pacify, *v.* To calm down

calamity, *n.* Disaster

"Please forgive me, Jo. I'm very, very sorry."

"I never shall forgive you," was Jo's stern answer, and from that moment she ignored Amy entirely.

No one spoke of the great trouble for all had learned by experience that when Jo was in that mood, words were wasted. The wisest course was to wait till some little accident softened Jo's **resentment** and healed the **breach.** It was not a happy evening, for the sweet home peace was disturbed.

As Jo received her good-night kiss, Mrs. March whispered gently, "My dear, don't let the sun go down upon your anger. Forgive each other, help each other, and begin again tomorrow."

What does Mrs. March mean by advising Jo to "not let the sun go down" on her anger?

Jo wanted to lay her head on her mother's shoulder and cry her grief and anger all away, but she felt so deeply injured that she really couldn't quite forgive yet. So she winked hard and said gruffly so that Amy could hear, "It was an **abominable** thing, and she doesn't deserve to be forgiven."

With that she marched off to bed, and there was no merry or confidential gossip that night.

The next morning, Amy was much offended that her overtures of peace had been repulsed, Jo still looked like a thunder cloud, and nothing went well all day. Aunt March had an attack of the fidgets, Meg was sensitive, Beth looked grieved and wistful when she got home, and Amy kept making aggravating remarks.

"Everybody is so hateful, I'll ask Laurie to go skating. He will put me to rights, I know," said Jo to herself, and off she went.

When Amy heard the clash of skates, she looked out and exclaimed, "She promised I should go next time, for this is the last ice we shall have. But it's no use to ask such a crosspatch to take me."

Does Amy truly understand why Jo is so upset?

Vocabulary in Place

resentment, *n.* An angry feeling, often about something that is unfair or undeserved

breach, *n.* An opening or tear; a disruption of friendly relations

abominable, *adj.* Truly awful

"Don't say that. You were very naughty, and it is hard to forgive the loss of her precious little book, but I think she might do it now," said Meg. "Go after them. Don't say anything till Jo has got good-natured with Laurie. Then do some kind thing, and I'm sure she'll be friends again with all her heart."

"I'll try," said Amy, for the advice suited her. After a flurry to get ready, she ran after the friends, who were just disappearing over the hill.

It was not far to the river, but both were ready before Amy reached them. Jo saw her coming, and turned her back. Laurie did not see, for he was carefully skating along the shore, sounding[1] the ice, for a warm spell had proceeded the cold snap.

"I'll go on to the first bend, and see if it's all right before we begin to race," Amy heard him say, as he shot away, looking like a young Russian in his fur-trimmed coat and cap.

Jo heard Amy panting after her run and blowing on her fingers as she tried to put on her skates, but Jo never turned and went slowly zigzagging down the river, taking a bitter, unhappy satisfaction in her sister's troubles. As Laurie turned the bend, he shouted back,

"Keep near the shore. It isn't safe in the middle."

Jo heard, but Amy was struggling to her feet and did not catch a word. Jo glanced over her shoulder, and a little demon said in her ear . . .

"No matter whether she heard or not, let her take care of herself."

Laurie had vanished round the bend, Jo was just at the turn, and Amy, far behind, striking out toward the smoother ice in the middle of the river. For a minute, Jo stood still with a strange feeling in her heart, then she resolved to go on. But something held and turned her round, just in time to see Amy throw up her hands and go down, with a sudden crash of rotten ice, the splash of water, and a cry that made Jo's heart stand still with fear. She tried to call Laurie, but her voice was gone. She tried to rush forward, but her feet seemed to have no strength in them, and for a second, she could only stand

Does Amy hear Laurie's warning to stay near the shore?

---

[1] **sounding.** Checking or investigating

motionless, staring with a terror-stricken face at the little blue hood above the black water.

Something rushed swiftly by her, and Laurie's voice cried out . . .

"Bring a rail. Quick, quick!"

How she did it, she never knew, but for the next few minutes she worked as if possessed, blindly obeying Laurie, who was quite **self-possessed**. Lying flat, he held Amy up by his arm and hockey stick till Jo dragged a rail from the fence, and together they got the child out, more frightened than hurt.

"Now then, we must walk her home as fast as we can. Pile our things on her," cried Laurie, wrapping his coat round Amy. Shivering, dripping, and crying, they got Amy home, and she fell asleep, rolled in blankets before a hot fire. During the bustle Jo had scarcely spoken but flown about, looking pale and wild, with her dress torn and her hands cut and bruised by ice and rails and buckles. When Amy was comfortably asleep, Mrs. March called Jo to her and began to bind up the hurt hands.

"Are you sure she is safe?" whispered Jo, looking remorsefully at the golden head, which might have been swept away from her sight forever under the **treacherous** ice.

"Quite safe, dear. She is not hurt, and won't even take cold, I think, you were so sensible in covering and getting her home quickly," replied her mother cheerfully.

"Laurie did it all. I only let her go. Mother, if she should die, it would be my fault." And Jo dropped down beside the bed in a passion of **penitent** tears, telling all that had happened.

Why does Jo blame herself?

Vocabulary in Place

self-possessed, *adj.* Cool and calm in a crisis; poised, not flustered

treacherous, *adj.* Very dangerous

penitent, *adj.* Very sorry, apologetic

"It's my dreadful temper! I try to cure it, I think I have, and then it breaks out worse than ever. Oh, Mother, what shall I do? What shall I do?" cried poor Jo, in despair.

"Watch and pray, dear, never get tired of trying, and never think it is impossible to conquer your fault," said Mrs. March, kissing Jo's wet cheeks tenderly.

"You don't know, you can't guess how bad it is! It seems as if I could do anything when I'm in a passion. I get so **savage**, I could hurt anyone and enjoy it. I'm afraid I shall do something dreadful some day, and spoil my life, and make everybody hate me."

"Don't cry so bitterly, but remember this day, and resolve with all your soul that you will never know another like it. Jo, dear, you think your temper is the worst in the world, but mine used to be just like it."

What do Jo and her mother have in common?

"Yours, Mother? Why, you are never angry!" And for the moment Jo forgot remorse in surprise.

"I've been trying to cure it for forty years, and have only succeeded in controlling it. I am angry nearly every day of my life, Jo, but I have learned not to show it, and I still hope to learn not to feel it, though it may take me another forty years to do so."

She felt comforted by the knowledge that her mother had a fault like hers. It made her own easier to bear and strengthened her resolution to cure it.

"Mother, are you angry when you fold your lips tight together and go out of the room sometimes?" asked Jo.

"Yes, I've learned to check the hasty words that rise to my lips. Then I just go away for a minute, and give myself a little shake for being so weak and wicked," answered Mrs. March with a sigh and a smile, as she smoothed and fastened up Jo's hair.

"Tell me how you do it, Marmee dear."

"Your father helps me, Jo. He never loses patience, never doubts or complains, but always hopes, and works and waits so cheerfully

---

Vocabulary in Place

savage, *adj.* Very angry; on the verge of being violent

that one is ashamed to do otherwise before him. He has helped and comforted me, and showed me that I must try to set a good example for my little girls. It was easier to try for your sakes than for my own."

"Oh, Mother, if I'm ever half as good as you, I shall be satisfied," cried Jo, much touched.

What is Mrs. March's warning to Jo?

"I hope you will be a great deal better, dear, but you must keep watch over your 'bosom enemy,' as Father calls it, or it may sadden, if not spoil your life. You have had a warning. Remember it, and try with heart and soul to master this quick temper, before it brings you greater sorrow and regret than you have known today."

"I will try, Mother, I truly will. But you must help me, remind me, and keep me from flying out . . . the way Father used to sometimes put his finger on his lips, and look at you with a very kind but sober face, and you always folded your lips tight and went away."

Jo saw that her mother's eyes filled and her lips trembled.

"Have I grieved you?" Jo whispered anxiously.

"No, dear, but speaking of Father reminded me how much I miss him, how much I owe him, and how faithfully I should watch and work to keep his little daughters safe and good for him."

"Yet you told him to go, Mother, and didn't cry when he went, and never complain now, or seem as if you needed any help," said Jo, wondering.

What does Mrs. March mean when she says that she gave her best to her country?

"I gave my best to the country I love, and kept my tears till he was gone. Why should I complain, when we both have merely done our duty and will surely be the happier for it in the end? If I don't seem to need help, it is because I have a better friend, even than Father, to comfort and sustain me. My child, the troubles and temptations of your life are beginning and may be many, but you can overcome and outlive them all if you learn to feel the strength and tenderness of your Heavenly Father as you do that of your earthly one. The more you love and trust Him, and the less you will depend on human power and wisdom. His love and care never tire or change, can never be taken from you, but may become the source of lifelong peace, happiness, and strength. Believe this heartily, and go to God with all your little cares and hopes, and sins and sorrows, as freely and confidingly as you come to your mother."

Jo's only answer was to hold her mother close, as the sincerest prayer she had ever prayed left her heart without words.

Amy stirred and sighed in her sleep, and as if eager to begin at once to mend her fault, Jo looked up with an expression on her face, which it had never worn before.

"I let the sun go down on my anger. I wouldn't forgive her, and today, if it hadn't been for Laurie, it might have been too late! How could I be so wicked?" said Jo, half aloud, as she leaned over her sister softly stroking the wet hair scattered on the pillow.

As if she heard, Amy opened her eyes, and held out her arms, with a smile that went straight to Jo's heart. Neither said a word as they hugged one another close and everything was forgiven and forgotten in one hearty kiss.

A Closer Look

Understanding the Selection

Recalling (just the facts)

1. Why is Amy in debt to her school friends? What does she owe them?
2. Why does Amy get in trouble in school? What is her punishment?
3. What does Amy do to get even with Jo for not letting her tag along to the theater? How does Jo get even with Amy?
4. What happens to Amy? Whom does Jo blame for Amy's accident?

Interpreting (delving deeper)

1. How does Amy feel about Jenny Snow? Why? How does Amy behave toward this schoolmate?
2. What is Marmee's response when she learns of Amy's experience at school? How does Jo behave when she delivers Marmee's letter to the teacher?
3. Why does Jo feel guilty about Amy's accident? Could she have prevented it?
4. How is Marmee able to comfort Jo after Amy's accident?

Synthesizing (putting it all together)

1. What lesson does Amy learn from her bad day at school?
2. What do you think Jo learns from the skating accident on the river? Why is it important not to "let the sun go down" on your anger?

Writing

EXTENSIONS

Cause and Effect. The events in Chapter 8 relay a series of causes and effects that create increasingly complicated conflicts between Jo and Amy. A **cause** details why an action or idea occurs. An **effect** describes the response that stems from the cause. In baseball, the batter's swing can cause the ball to fly over the fence. The batter's hit causes the ball to the take flight; the effect of that action is that the ball flies over the fence.

The fight between Jo and Amy involves a chain of events, each with its own related causes and effects. Think about the scenarios listed below and write, on a separate sheet of paper, Jo's or Amy's response to that action or feeling.

Cause: Jo refuses to let Amy go to the theater.
Effect: _____

Cause: Jo does not check to see if Amy hears Laurie's warning about the thin ice.
Effect: _____

Cause: Jo blames herself and seeks advice from Marmee.
Effect: _____

Writers are able to convey important themes and lessons by illustrating the causes and effects of characters' actions. In real life, the line between cause and effect is not always clear, and sometimes people with different points of view will never agree as to whom should receive blame or credit for various events. Nevertheless, readers and writers alike can benefit greatly from carefully analyzing one character's response to another character's actions and the spiral of events that often ensues. In Chapter 8, Alcott shows that Jo's anger causes her great guilt and sorrow and also compromises her sister's safety. In the end, the two sisters' actions, taken together, show that it is better to forgive than to seek revenge.

Identify three other instances from earlier chapters in which a character's action (or characters' actions) causes another character to act or feel in a certain way. (It is okay to include minor characters like Mr. Laurence or Jenny Snow.) For each example, summarize the cause and effect of characters' actions and explain what the events reveal about the character's personality. Write in complete sentences.

Language Alive!

EXTENSIONS

Creatures from Greek Mythology. In Chapter 7 of *Little Women,* Amy makes an allusion to a mythical creature from Greek mythology. An **allusion** is a reference to a well-known literary work or to a famous person, place, object, or event. Often, writers and speakers describe particular details, such as character traits, by drawing comparisons (or alluding) to things with which readers are familiar. Recall that in earilier chapters the allusion to *Pilgrim's Progress* (which would have been very familiar to much of Alcott's readership) helped to establish several themes.

There is virtually no end to the number of things to which a writer can allude. However, characters and stories from Greek mythology represent one of the most popular, time-honored sets of allusions in Western literature.

> Discuss or write short answers to each of the following questions:
> 1. Who or what is Amy describing when she alludes to the Cyclops?
> 2. Why is this allusion so confusing to Meg and Jo?
> 3. To what did Amy mean to allude?

The purpose of Amy's allusion is to compare Laurie's riding style to something that summons a clear image in her listeners' imaginations. Unfortunately, she makes her sisters think of the Cyclops instead of a centaur, but Jo realizes the error.

Characters from Greek mythology make useful allusions thanks to their distinct and often bizarre physical characteristics, which usually symbolize specific corresponding personality traits. In many cases, because of these distinct traits, the characters' names have been adapted for use as common words in the English language. One example is the mythical monster Chimera—part lion, part serpent, part goat—that terrorized the land until it was defeated by the hero Bellepheron and the winged horse Pegasus. A writer could allude to Chimera in describing a villainous character, but the name has come to mean much more than that. Over the years, Chimera's name has become common in several forms:

102

Language Alive!

EXTENSIONS

chimerical, *adj.* Created by or as if by a wildly fanciful imagination; highly improbable

chimera, *n.* An organism, organ, or part consisting of two or more tissues of different genetic composition, usually produced as a result of transplant, grafting, or genetic engineering. (The noun *chimera* has several other applications in the medical and scientific world.)

Many characters from mythology become common allusions or words in English and other languages. In a similar way, important events in myths have also come to be used as common **figures of speech,** or sayings and phrases in which the literal meaning differs from the intended meaning, as in the use of a metaphor, simile, or other figurative language.

For example, to say that someone "threw an apple of discord" means that the person did or said something that started an argument between two (or more) other people. This refers to a Greek myth in which Erin, the goddess of quarrelling, instigated an argument between Athena (goddess of wisdom), Aphrodite (goddess of love), and Hera (queen of the gods) by tossing a golden apple before them on which was inscribed "For the Most Beautiful." Eventually, this apple led to a historic war between Greece and Troy.

Conduct research in the library or on the Internet, or think about books or stories you have read in the past, in order to identify other allusions to characters or events from Greek mythology that are common in English literature.

In your notebook, begin a list of other literary or mythical allusions that Alcott uses in *Little Women*. Beside each allusion, describe the character trait or theme it is meant to signify or support. When you finish the book, you can submit your list of allusions as an extra credit assignment.

CHAPTER 9

Meg Goes to Vanity Fair

"It was so nice of Annie Moffat not to forget her promise," said Meg, one April day, as she stood packing the 'go abroady' trunk in her room, surrounded by her sisters.

"A whole fortnight[1] of fun will be regularly splendid," replied Jo, looking like a windmill as she folded skirts with her long arms.

"I wish you were all going. You have been so kind, lending me things and helping me get ready," said Meg, glancing round the room at the outfit,[2] which seemed nearly perfect in their eyes.

"What did Mother give you out of the treasure box?" asked Amy. Mrs. March kept a few **relics** of past splendor, as gifts for her girls when the proper time came.

What is in mother's "treasure box"?

"A pair of silk stockings, that pretty carved fan, and a lovely blue sash. I wanted the violet silk gown, but there isn't time to have it altered, so I must be contented with my old tarlatan."[3]

"Never mind, the tarlatan will do nicely for the big party, and you always look like an angel in white," said Amy, delighting in the little store of finery before her.

"It isn't low-necked, and it doesn't sweep enough, but it will have to do," sighed Meg, knowing how poor her accessories would look in comparison to those of her wealthy friends. "I wonder if I shall ever

---

[1] **fortnight.** Two weeks (alteration of "fourteen nights")
[2] **outfit.** A set of clothes and accessories
[3] **tarlatan.** A dress made of a sheer cotton fabric, woven for stiffness

Vocabulary in Place
relic, *n.* A treasure or leftover from the past

be happy enough to have real lace on my clothes and silk gowns?" she added impatiently.

"You said the other day that you'd be perfectly happy if you could only go to Annie Moffat's," observed Beth in her quiet way.

"So I did! Well, I am happy, and I won't fret, but it does seem as if the more one gets the more one wants, doesn't it?" said Meg, cheering up, as she glanced at all that she did have in the half-filled trunk.

The next day was fine, and Meg departed in style for a fortnight of **novelty** and pleasure. Mrs. March feared that Margaret would come back more discontented than she went, but she begged so hard, and Sallie had promised to take good care of her, so the mother yielded, and the daughter went to take her first taste of fashionable life.

Why is Mrs. March worried about letting Meg visit her friend?

The Moffats were very fashionable, and simple Meg was rather **daunted,** at first, by the splendor of the house and the elegance of its occupants. But they were kindly people, in spite of the frivolous life they led, and soon put their guest at her ease. She began to imitate the manners and conversation of those about her, and to put on little airs and graces. The more she saw of Annie Moffat's pretty things, the more she envied her and sighed to be rich.

What does Meg think of Annie Moffat's lifestyle?

She had not much time for complaining, however, for the three young girls were busily employed in "having a good time." They shopped, walked, rode, and called all day, went to theaters and operas or frolicked at home in the evening, for Annie had many friends and knew how to entertain them. Her older sisters were very fine young ladies, and one was engaged, which was extremely interesting and romantic, Meg thought. Mr. Moffat was a fat, jolly old gentleman, who knew her father, and Mrs. Moffat, a fat, jolly old lady, who took as great a fancy to Meg as her daughter had done. Everyone petted her, and "Daisy," as they called her, was in a fair way to have her head turned.

Vocabulary in Place
novelty, *n.* Something new or unusual
daunted, *adj.* Intimidated or discouraged

Why does Meg's heart feel heavy, despite the Moffats' kindness?

When the evening for the small party came, Meg's tarlatan looked older, limper, and shabbier than ever beside Sallie's crisp new one. No one said a word about it, but Sallie offered to dress her hair, and Annie to tie her sash, and Belle, the engaged sister, praised her complexion. But in their kindness Meg saw only pity for her poverty, and her heart felt very heavy. The hard, bitter feeling was getting pretty bad, when the maid brought in a box of flowers. Before she could speak, Annie had the cover off, and all were exclaiming at the lovely roses, heath,[4] and fern within.

"They are for Miss March," the man said.

"And here's a note," said the maid, holding it to Meg.

"Who are they from? Didn't know you had a lover," cried the girls, fluttering about Meg in a high state of curiosity and surprise.

"The note is from Mother, and the flowers from Laurie," said Meg simply, yet much gratified that he had not forgotten her.

"Oh, indeed!" said Annie with a funny look, as Meg slipped the note into her pocket. The few loving words had done her good, and the flowers cheered her up by their beauty.

Why doesn't Meg's dress seem "shabby" anymore?

She smiled with bright eyes as she laid her ferns against her rippling hair and fastened the roses in the dress that didn't strike her as so very shabby now.

She enjoyed herself very much that evening, for everyone was very kind. Major Lincoln asked who "the fresh little girl with the beautiful eyes" was, and Mr. Moffat insisted on dancing with her because she had such a spring in her step. Altogether she had a very nice time, till she overheard a bit of conversation, which disturbed her extremely. She was waiting for her dance partner to bring her an ice, when she heard a voice ask on the other side of the flowery wall . . .

"How old is he?"

"Sixteen or seventeen, I should say," replied another voice.

---

[4] **heath.** Another name for heather, a plant with small evergreen leaves and small urn-shaped flowers

"It would be a grand thing for one of those girls, wouldn't it? Sallie says they are very close now, and the old man quite **dotes** on them."

"Mrs. M. has made her plans, I dare say, and will play her cards well, early as it is. The girl evidently doesn't think of it yet," said Mrs. Moffat.

"She blushed quite prettily when the flowers came. Poor thing!"

"She'd be so nice if she was only got up in style. Do you think she'd be offended if we offered to lend her a dress for Thursday?" asked another voice.

"She's proud, but I don't believe she'd mind, for that **dowdy** tarlatan is all she has got. She may tear it tonight, and that will be a good excuse for offering a decent one."

Here Meg's partner appeared to find her looking much flushed and rather **agitated**. She tried to forget what she had heard, but could not, and kept repeating to herself, "Mrs. M. has made her plans" and "dowdy tarlatan," till she was ready to cry and rush home. As that was impossible, she did her best to seem gay, and she succeeded so well that no one dreamed what an effort she was making.

She was very glad when it was all over and she was quiet in her bed, where she could wonder and fume till her head ached and her cheeks were cooled by tears. Those foolish, yet well-meant words, had much disturbed the peace of her little world. Her innocent friendship with Laurie was spoiled, her faith in her mother was a little shaken by Mrs. Moffat's mention of worldly plans, and her satisfaction with her simple wardrobe was weakened by the pity of girls who thought a shabby dress one of the greatest calamities under heaven.

Who is this overheard conversation about? Why is Meg upset by what she hears?

Vocabulary in Place

dote, *v.* To be very kind and generous to

dowdy, *adj.* Lacking style or shabby

agitated, *adj.* Upset or stirred up by something

Why do Meg's friends treat her with more respect?

The next day, something in the manner of her friends struck Meg at once. They treated her with more respect, she thought, and there was a look in their eyes that plainly betrayed curiosity. She did not understand it, till Miss Belle looked up from her writing, and said,

"Daisy, dear, I've sent an invitation to your friend, Mr. Laurence, for Thursday. We should like to know him."

"It's very nice of him to send you flowers, isn't it?" said Annie, looking wise.

Meg blushed at the mention of Laurie, knowing what her friends were thinking.

"Yes, he often does, to all of us, for their house is full, and we are so fond of them," and Meg hoped they would say no more.

"It's evident Daisy isn't out yet,"[5] said Miss Clara to Belle with a nod.

"Quite innocent all round," returned Miss Belle with a shrug.

"I'm going out to get some little matters for my girls. Can I do anything for you, young ladies?" asked Mrs. Moffat, **lumbering** in like an elephant in silk and lace.

"No, thank you, ma'am," replied Sallie. "I don't want a thing."

"Nor I . . ." began Meg, but stopped because it occurred to her that she did want several things and could not have them.

"What shall you wear?" asked Sallie.

"My old white one again, if I can mend it fit to be seen, it got sadly torn last night," said Meg, trying to speak quite easily, but feeling very uncomfortable.

Why might Sallie's question be seen as foolish or naive?

"Why don't you send home for another?" said Sallie, who was not an observing young lady.

---

[5] **isn't out yet.** To be "out" means that a young woman has been officially introduced to society at a series of balls, parties, and other social events, and she is old enough to get married.

Vocabulary in Place
lumber, *v.* To be heavy on one's feet, not graceful or effortless

"I haven't got any other." It cost Meg an effort to say that, but Sallie did not see it and exclaimed in **amiable** surprise, "Only that? How funny . . ." She did not finish her speech, for Belle shook her head at her and broke in, saying kindly . . .

"Not at all. Where is the use of having a lot of dresses when she isn't out yet? There's no need of sending home, Daisy, even if you had a dozen, for I've got a sweet blue silk laid away, which I've outgrown, and you shall wear it to please me, won't you, dear?"

"You are very kind, but I don't mind my old dress if you don't," said Meg.

"Now do let me please myself by dressing you up in style. You'd be a regular little beauty with a touch here and there," said Belle in her persuasive tone.

Meg's desire to see if she would be "a little beauty" after touching up caused her to accept the kind offer and forget all her former uncomfortable feelings toward the Moffats.

On the Thursday evening, Belle and her maid went to work, and between them they turned Meg into a fine lady. They curled her hair, polished her neck and arms with some fragrant powder, and touched up her lips to make them redder. They laced her into a sky-blue dress, which was so tight she could hardly breathe and so low in the neck that modest Meg blushed at herself in the mirror. A set of silver jewelry was added, and a pair of high-heeled silk boots satisfied the last wish of her heart. Miss Belle surveyed her with the satisfaction of a little girl with a newly dressed doll.

"Come and show yourself," said Miss Belle, leading the way to the room where the others were waiting.

As Meg went rustling after, she felt as if her fun had really begun at last, for the mirror had plainly told her that she was "a little beauty." Her friends repeated the pleasing phrase enthusiastically,

Why does Meg feel as if the "fun [has] really begun."

Vocabulary in Place

amiable, *adj.* Friendly, good-natured

and for several minutes she stood, like a jackdaw in the fable, enjoying her borrowed plumes, while the rest chattered like a party of magpies.[6]

"While I dress, do you drill her, Nan, in the management of her skirt and those French heels, or she will trip herself up. Take your silver butterfly,[7] and catch up that long curl on the left side of her head, Clara, and don't any of you disturb the charming work of my hands," said Belle, as she hurried away, looking well pleased with her success.

"You don't look a bit like yourself, but you are very nice. I'm nowhere beside you, for Belle has heaps of taste, and you're quite French, I assure you. Let your flowers hang, don't be so careful of them, and be sure you don't trip," returned Sallie, trying not to care that Meg was prettier than herself.

Keeping that warning carefully in mind, Meg got safely downstairs and sailed into the drawing rooms where the Moffats and a few early guests were assembled. She very soon discovered that there is a charm about fine clothes which attracts a certain class of people and secures their respect. Several young ladies, who had taken no notice of her before, were very affectionate all of a sudden. Several young gentlemen, who had only stared at her at the other party, now not only stared, but asked to be introduced, and said all manner of foolish but agreeable things to her, and several old ladies, who sat on the sofas, and criticized the rest of the party, inquired who she was with an air of interest. She heard Mrs. Moffat reply to one of them . . .

Why do people notice Meg more this time?

"Daisy March—father a colonel in the army—one of our first families, but reverses of fortune, you know; intimate friends of the Laurences; sweet creature, I assure you; my Ned is quite wild about her."

---

[6] **jackdaw . . . magpies.** In the fable "The Vain Jackdaw," the *jackdaw* (a type of crow) finds and wears peacock plumes (feathers) and is punished for not accepting Nature's intentions. A *magpie* is a very busy, noisy type of bird; the word is sometimes used to describe a chattery woman.

[7] **silver butterfly.** Curling iron

"Dear me!" said the old lady, putting up her glass for another observation of Meg, who tried to look as if she had not heard and been rather shocked at Mrs. Moffat's fibs.

The 'queer feeling' did not pass away, but she imagined herself acting the new part of fine lady and so got on pretty well, though the tight dress gave her a side-ache, the train kept getting under her feet, and she was in constant fear lest her earrings should fly off and get lost or broken. She was flirting her fan and laughing at the feeble jokes of a young gentleman who tried to be witty, when she suddenly stopped laughing and looked confused, for just opposite, she saw Laurie. He was staring at her with undisguised surprise, and disapproval also, she thought, for though he bowed and smiled, something in his honest eyes made her blush and wish she had her old dress on.

Meg rustled across the room to shake hands with her friend.

"I'm glad you came. I was afraid you wouldn't," she said with her most grown-up air.

"Jo wanted me to come, and tell her how you looked, so I did," answered Laurie, smiling at her motherly tone.

"What shall you tell her?" asked Meg, full of curiosity to know his opinion of her, although she felt ill at ease.

"I shall say I didn't know you, for you look so grown-up and unlike yourself, I'm quite afraid of you," he said, fumbling at his glove button.

"How absurd of you! The girls dressed me up for fun, and I rather like it. Wouldn't Jo stare if she saw me?" said Meg.

"Yes, I think she would," returned Laurie gravely.

"Don't you like me so?" asked Meg, determined to make Laurie reveal his thoughts.

He glanced at her frizzled head, bare shoulders, and fantastically trimmed dress with an expression that embarrassed her.

"I don't like fuss and feathers."

That was altogether too much from a lad younger than herself, and Meg walked away, saying with an injured air, "You are the rudest boy I ever saw."

What has Mrs. Moffat fibbed about?

Does Laurie like the way Meg looks now?

What does Laurie mean by "fuss and feathers"?

111

> Why does Meg feel ashamed?

Feeling very much ruffled, she went and stood at a quiet window to cool her cheeks. As she stood there, she overheard Major Lincoln saying to his mother . . .

"They are making a fool of that little girl. I wanted you to see her, but they have spoiled her entirely. She's nothing but a doll tonight."

"Oh, dear!" sighed Meg. "I wish I'd been sensible and worn my own things, then I should not feel so uncomfortable and ashamed of myself."

She leaned her forehead on the cool pane, and stood half hidden by the curtains, till some one touched her. Turning, she saw Laurie, looking penitent, as he said, with his very best bow and his hand out . . .

"Please forgive my rudeness, and come and dance with me."

"I'm afraid it will be too disagreeable to you," said Meg, trying to look offended and failing entirely.

"Not a bit of it. Come, I'll be good. I don't like your gown, but I do think you are just splendid." And he waved his hands, as if words failed to express his admiration.

Meg smiled and whispered as they stood waiting to join the dance, "Take care my skirt doesn't trip you up. I was a silly goose to wear it."

"Pin it round your neck, and then it will be useful," said Laurie, looking down at the little blue boots, which he evidently approved of.

Having practiced at home, they were well matched, and twirled merrily round and round, feeling more friendly than ever after their small tiff.[8]

"Laurie, I want you to do me a favor, will you?" said Meg, as he stood fanning her when her breath gave out, which it did very soon.

"Of course!" said Laurie.

"Please don't tell them at home about my dress tonight. It will worry Mother . . . and I want to confess to her myself about how silly I've been. So you'll not tell, will you?"

"I give you my word I won't, only what shall I say when they ask me?"

---

[8] **tiff.** Disagreement, fight

112

"Just say I looked pretty well and was having a good time."

"I'll say the first with all my heart, but how about the other? You don't look as if you were having a good time. Are you?" And Laurie looked at her with an expression that made her answer in a whisper . . .

"No, not just now. I only wanted a little fun, but this sort doesn't pay, I find, and I'm getting tired of it."

"Here comes Ned Moffat. What does he want?" said Laurie, knitting his black brows as if he did not regard his young host in the light of a pleasant addition to the party.

How does Laurie feel about Ned Moffat?

"He put his name down for three dances, and I suppose he's coming for them. What a bore!" said Meg, assuming a **languid** air that amused Laurie immensely.

He did not speak to her again till suppertime, when he saw her drinking champagne with Ned and his friend Fisher, who were behaving "like a pair of fools," as Laurie said to himself, for he felt a brotherly sort of right to watch over the Marches and fight their battles whenever a defender was needed.

"You'll have a splitting headache tomorrow, if you drink much of that. I wouldn't, Meg, your mother doesn't like it, you know," he whispered, leaning over her chair, as Ned turned to refill her glass and Fisher stooped to pick up her fan.

"I'm not Meg tonight, I'm 'a doll' who does all sorts of crazy things. Tomorrow I shall put away my 'fuss and feathers' and be desperately good again," she answered with an affected little laugh.

"Wish tomorrow was here, then," muttered Laurie, walking off, ill-pleased at the change he saw in her.

Meg danced and flirted, chattered and giggled, as the other girls did. After supper she undertook the German,[9] and blundered through

---

[9] **the German.** A type of dance

Vocabulary in Place
languid, *adj.* Showing little spirit or energy; weak

it, nearly upsetting her partner with her long skirt, and romping in a way that scandalized Laurie, who looked on and meditated a lecture. But he got no chance to deliver it, for Meg kept away from him till he came to say good night.

"Remember!" she said, trying to smile, for the champagne had already brought on a splitting headache.

"Silence à la mort,"[10] replied Laurie, with a **melodramatic** flourish, as he went away.

Meg was sick all the next day, and on Saturday went home feeling that she had "sat in the lap of luxury" long enough.

"It does seem pleasant to be quiet, and not have company manners on all the time. Home is a nice place, though it isn't splendid," said Meg, looking about her with a restful expression, as she sat with her mother and Jo on the Sunday evening.

"I'm glad to hear you say so, dear, for I was afraid home would seem dull and poor to you after your fine quarters," replied her mother, with an anxious look.

Meg had told her adventures gaily and said over and over what a charming time she had had, but something still seemed to weigh upon her spirits. When the younger girls were gone to bed, she sat on Beth's stool and leaned her elbows on her mother's knee, saying bravely . . .

What does Meg confess to her mother?

"Marmee, I want to 'fess.'"

"I thought so. What is it, dear?"

"I was ashamed to speak of it before the younger children, but I want you to know all the dreadful things I did at the Moffats'."

"We are prepared," said Mrs. March, smiling but looking a little nervous.

---

10 **Silence à la mort.** A French phrase meaning "silence until death"

Vocabulary in Place
melodramatic, *adj.* Elaborate or exaggerated; overly emotional

"I told you they dressed me up, but I didn't tell you that they powdered and squeezed and frizzled, and made me look like a fashion-plate. Laurie thought I wasn't proper, and one man called me 'a doll'. I knew it was silly, but they flattered me and said I was a beauty, so I let them make a fool of me."

"Is that all?" asked Jo, as Mrs. March looked silently at the downcast face of her pretty daughter, and could not find it in her heart to blame her little follies.

"No, I drank champagne and romped and tried to flirt, and was altogether abominable," said Meg self-reproachfully.

"There is something more, I think." And Mrs. March smoothed the soft cheek, as Meg answered slowly . . .

"Yes. It's very silly, but I want to tell it, because I hate to have people say and think such things about us and Laurie."

Then she told the various bits of gossip she had heard at the Moffats', and as she spoke, Jo saw her mother fold her lips tightly.

"Well, if that isn't the greatest rubbish I ever heard," cried Jo indignantly. "The idea of having 'plans' and being kind to Laurie because he's rich and may marry us by-and-by! Won't he shout when I tell him about it." And Jo laughed, as if on second thoughts the thing struck her as a good joke.

"If you tell Laurie, I'll never forgive you! She mustn't, must she, Mother?" said Meg, looking distressed.

"No, never repeat that foolish gossip, and forget it as soon as you can," said Mrs. March gravely. "I was very unwise to let you go among people of whom I know so little. Though kind, they are vain and **vulgar**, and I am more sorry than I can express for the mischief this visit may have done you, Meg."

"Don't be sorry, I won't let it hurt me. I'll forget all the bad and remember only the good, for I did enjoy a great deal. It is nice to

Why does Mrs. March regret having allowed Meg to go to the Moffats'?

Vocabulary in Place

vulgar, *adj.* Rude or offensive

be praised and admired, and I can't help saying I like it," said Meg, looking half ashamed of the confession.

"That is perfectly natural, and quite harmless, if the liking does not lead one to do foolish or unmaidenly things. Learn to know and value the praise that is worth having and to excite the admiration of excellent people by being modest as well as pretty, Meg."

Meg sat thinking a moment, while Jo stood with her hands behind her, looking a little **perplexed**. Jo felt as if her sister had grown up amazingly, and was drifting away from her into a world where she could not follow.

"Mother, do you have 'plans,' as Mrs. Moffat said?" asked Meg bashfully.

"Yes, my dear, I have a great many, all mothers do, but mine differ somewhat from Mrs. Moffat's, I suspect. I will tell you some of them, for the time has come when a word may set this romantic little head and heart of yours right, on a very serious subject. You are young, Meg, but not too young to understand me, and mothers' lips are the fittest to speak of such things to girls like you. Jo, your turn will come in time, perhaps, so listen to my 'plans' and help me carry them out, if they are good."

Jo went and sat on one arm of the chair, looking as if she thought they were about to join in some very solemn affair. Holding a hand of each, and watching the two young faces wistfully, Mrs. March said, in her serious yet cheery way . . .

How do Mrs. March's "plans" differ from Mrs. Moffat's?

"I want my daughters to be beautiful, accomplished, and good. To be admired, loved, and respected. To have a happy youth, to be well and wisely married, and to lead useful, pleasant lives, with as little care and sorrow to try them as God sees fit to send. To be loved and chosen by a good man is the best and sweetest thing that can happen to a woman, and I sincerely hope my girls may know this beautiful

---

Vocabulary in Place

perplexed, *adj.* Confused or puzzled

experience. It is natural to think of it, Meg, right to hope and wait for it, and wise to prepare for it, so that when the happy time comes, you may feel ready for the duties and worthy of the joy. My dear girls, I am ambitious for you, but not to have you make a dash in the world, marry rich men merely because they are rich, or have splendid houses, which are not homes because love is wanting. Money is a needful and precious thing, and when well used, a noble thing, but I never want you to think it is the first or only prize to strive for. I'd rather see you poor men's wives, if you were happy, beloved, contented, than queens on thrones, without self-respect and peace."

"Poor girls don't stand any chance, Belle says, unless they put themselves forward," sighed Meg.

"Then we'll be old maids," said Jo stoutly.

"Right, Jo. Better be happy old maids than unhappy wives, or unmaidenly girls, running about to find husbands," said Mrs. March decidedly. "Don't be troubled, Meg, poverty seldom daunts a sincere lover. Some of the best and most honored women I know were poor girls, but so love-worthy that they were not allowed to be old maids. Leave these things to time. Make this home happy, so that you may be fit for homes of your own, if they are offered you, and contented here if they are not. One thing to remember, my girls: Mother is always ready to be your confidante, Father to be your friend, and both are of hope and trust that our daughters, whether married or single, will be the pride and comfort of our lives."

"We will, Marmee, we will!" cried both, with all their hearts, as she bade them good night.

What does Mrs. March think about the importance of money?

CHAPTER 10

The P.C. and the P.O.

As spring came on, the lengthening days gave long afternoons for work and play of all sorts. Gardening, walks, rows on the river, and flower hunts employed the fine days, and for rainy ones, they had house **diversions**, some old, some new, all more or less original. One of these was the "P.C." As secret societies were the fashion, it was thought proper to have one, and as all of the girls admired Dickens, they called themselves the Pickwick Club.[1] With a few interruptions, they had kept this up for a year, and met every Saturday evening in the big garret to read the society's weekly newspaper, *The Pickwick Portfolio*, to which all contributed something, while Jo, who **reveled** in pens and ink, was the editor.

At seven o'clock, the four members ascended to the clubroom and took their seats with great **solemnity**. Meg, as the eldest, was Samuel Pickwick; Jo, being the literary type, Augustus Snodgrass; Beth, because she was round and rosy, Tracy Tupman; and Amy, who was always trying to do what she couldn't, was Nathaniel Winkle. Pickwick, the president, read the paper, which was filled with original tales, poetry, local news, funny advertisements, and hints,

Who belongs to the P.C. and what do the members do? Is it a serious club or just for fun?

---

[1] **Pickwick Club.** Named in honor of *Pickwick Papers,* a novel by the nineteenth-century English author, Charles Dickens, about a group of newspapermen. The girls' "P.C." names are those of characters in the book.

Vocabulary in Place
diversion, *n.* A game or pastime; leisure activity
revel, *v.* To thoroughly enjoy or immerse oneself in
solemnity, *n.* The quality or condition of being serious and sober

in which they good-naturedly reminded each other of their faults and shortcomings.

On one occasion, Mr. Pickwick put on a pair of spectacles without any glass, rapped upon the table, hemmed, and began to read:

THE PICKWICK PORTFOLIO
MAY 20, 18—
Poet's Corner
Anniversary Ode

Again we meet to celebrate
With badge and solemn rite,
Our fifty-second anniversary,
In Pickwick Hall, tonight

We all are here in perfect health,
None gone from our small band:
Again we see each well-known face,
And press each friendly hand.

Our Pickwick, always at his post,
With reverence we greet,
As, spectacles on nose, he reads
Our well-filled weekly sheet.

Although he suffers from a cold,
We joy to hear him speak,
For words of wisdom from him fall,
In spite of croak or squeak.
Old six-foot Snodgrass looms on high,
With elephantine[2] grace,
And beams upon the company,

Who is reading this poem aloud?

What is meant by the phrase "elephantine grace"? Is this meant to be humorous?

---

[2] **elephantine.** Of or related to an elephant

With brown and jovial face.

Poetic fire lights up his eye,
He struggles 'gainst his lot.
Behold ambition on his brow,
And on his nose, a blot.[3]

Next our peaceful Tupman comes,
So rosy, plump, and sweet,
Who chokes with laughter at the puns,[4]
And tumbles off his seat.

Prim little Winkle too is here,
With every hair in place,
 A model of propriety,
Though he hates to wash his face.

What do they hope to gain by reading literature?

The year is gone, we still unite
To joke and laugh and read,
And tread the path of literature
That doth to glory lead.

Long may our paper prosper well,
Our club unbroken be,
And coming years their blessings pour
On the useful, gay "P.C.".

Which March sister wrote this poem?

A. SNODGRASS

---

[3] **blot.** Spot or stain

[4] **pun.** A play on words. The poet Robert Frost used a pun in "Mending Wall" when he wrote, "Before I built a wall I'd ask to know . . . to whom I was like to give offense." This is a play on words because someone might receive *offense* (be offended) by the wall, which serves the same purpose as *a fence*.

[*The second submission, entitled "The Masked Marriage (A Tale of Venice)," is a brief romance by Mr. Pickwick, featuring a poor but gallant young man who gains his fortune and his true love. In a dramatic ending fit for a romantic novel, the hero dons a mask and marries his love in place of the man her parents have chosen for her to wed.*

Beth's contribution, called "The History of a Squash," is a narrative detailing its author's experience fetching and preparing the said vegetable for supper. It ends with a nice little recipe for a squash soufflé.

Amy's literary effort consists of an elegantly worded but grammatically flawed letter, begging pardon for not composing an original piece and lamenting the demands of schoolwork which left her little time for such tasks.

These great works of literature are followed by the news of the week, consisting of a report of a fall Mr. Pickwick had taken, which gave everyone quite a scare but luckily turned out to produce no lasting injury. Next there is the sad announcement of the mysterious disappearance of the beloved family cat, Mrs. Snowball Pat Paw, followed by a poem of lament by A. Snodgrass for the cherished pet.

The final page of the paper is devoted entirely to practical matters: advertisements, announcements, and the weekly report, which that week read . . .]

—*The editors have here abridged the original text.*

WEEKLY REPORT

Meg—Good.
Jo—Bad.
Beth—Very Good.
Amy—Middling.

What is this Weekly Report about?

As the President finished reading the paper, a round of applause followed, and then Mr. Snodgrass rose to make a proposition.

"Mr. President and gentlemen," he began, in a distinguished tone, "I wish to propose the admission of a new member—one who highly deserves the honor, would be deeply grateful for it, and would add immensely to the spirit of the club and the literary value of the paper. I propose Mr. Theodore Laurence as an honorary member of the P.C. Come now, do have him."

Jo's sudden change of tone made the girls laugh, but all looked rather anxious, and no one said a word as Snodgrass took his seat.

"We'll put it to a vote," said the President. "All in favor of this motion please say, 'Aye.'"

A loud response from Snodgrass, followed, to everybody's surprise, by a timid one from Beth.

"**Contrary**-minded say, 'No.'"

Meg and Amy were contrary-minded, and Mr. Winkle rose to say with great elegance, "We don't wish any boys, they only joke and bounce about. This is a ladies' club, and we wish to be private and proper."

"I'm afraid he'll laugh at our paper, and make fun of us afterward," observed Pickwick, pulling the little curl on her forehead, as she always did when doubtful.

Up rose Snodgrass, very much in earnest. "Sir, I give you my word as a gentleman, Laurie won't do anything of the sort. He likes to write, and he'll give a tone to our contributions and keep us from being sentimental, don't you see? We can do so little for him, and he does so much for us, I think the least we can do is to offer him a place here, and make him welcome if he comes."

This artful **allusion** to benefits conferred brought Tupman to his feet, looking as if he had quite made up his mind.

"Yes, we ought to do it, even if we are afraid. I say he may come, and his grandpa, too, if he likes."

This spirited burst from Beth electrified the club, and Jo left her seat to shake hands approvingly. "Now then, vote again. Everybody remember it's our Laurie, and say, 'Aye!'" cried Snodgrass excitedly.

"Aye! Aye! Aye!" replied three voices at once.

Vocabulary in Place

contrary, *adj.* Opposed or opposite

allusion, *n.* Reference to something else; a vague or indirect mention of something (See Language Alive!, page 94.)

"Good! Bless you! Now, allow me to present the new member." And, to the dismay of the rest of the club, Jo threw open the door of the closet, and displayed Laurie sitting on a rag bag, flushed and twinkling with suppressed laughter.

"You rogue! You traitor! Jo, how could you?" cried the three girls, as Snodgrass led her friend triumphantly forth, and, producing a chair, installed him in a jiffy.

"The coolness of you two rascals is amazing," began Mr. Pickwick, trying to get up an awful frown and only succeeding in producing a friendly smile. But the new member rose to the occasion, and said in the most engaging manner, "Mr. President and ladies— I beg pardon, gentlemen—allow me to introduce myself as Sam Weller, the very humble servant of the club."

"Good! Good!" cried Jo, pounding with the handle of the old warming pan on which she leaned.

"My faithful friend and noble patron," continued Laurie with a wave of the hand, "who has so flatteringly presented me, is not to be blamed for the **stratagem**. I planned it, and she only gave in after lots of teasing."

"Come now, don't lay it all on yourself. You know I proposed the cupboard," broke in Snodgrass, who was enjoying the joke amazingly.

"Never mind what she says. I'm the wretch that did it, sir," said the new member, with a nod to Mr. Pickwick. "But on my honor, I never will do so again, and henceforth devote myself to the interest of this immortal club."

"Hear! Hear!" cried Jo, clashing the lid of the warming pan like a cymbal.

"Go on, go on!" added Winkle and Tupman, while the President bowed.

"I merely wish to say, that as a slight token of my gratitude for the honor done me, and as a means of promoting friendly relations

> What trick do Laurie and Jo play on the other members of the club?

Vocabulary in Place
stratagem, *n.* Clever plan or scheme

among members, I have set up a post office in the hedge in the lower corner of the garden. It's the old birdhouse, but I've stopped up the door and made the roof open, so it will hold all sorts of things, and save our valuable time. Letters, manuscripts, books, and bundles can be passed in there, and it will be uncommonly nice, I fancy. Allow me to present the club key, and with many thanks for your favor, take my seat."

Great applause as Mr. Weller deposited a little key on the table and sat down. The warming pan clashed and waved wildly, and it was some time before order could be restored. A long discussion followed. It was an unusually lively meeting, which did not adjourn till a late hour, when it broke up with three shrill cheers for the new

member. No one ever regretted the admittance of Sam Weller, for a more devoted, well-behaved, and jovial member no club could have. He certainly did add "spirit" to the meetings, and his contributions were excellent, but never sentimental. Jo regarded them as worthy of Bacon, Milton, or Shakespeare,[5] and remodeled her own works with good effect, she thought.

The P.O. flourished wonderfully, for nearly as many queer things passed through it as through the real post office. Tragedies, poetry and pickles, garden seeds, music and gingerbread, invitations, scoldings, and puppies. The old gentleman liked the fun, and amused himself by sending odd bundles, mysterious messages, and funny telegrams. And his gardener, who was **smitten** with Hannah's charms, actually sent a love letter to Jo's care. How they laughed when the secret came out, never dreaming how many love letters that little post office would hold in the years to come.

Who might use the P.O. for love letters in the future?

---

[5] **Bacon, Milton, or Shakespeare.** Refers to Francis Bacon (1561–1626), John Milton (1608–1674), and William Shakespeare (1564–1616), three of the most influential authors and thinkers of their time

Vocabulary in Place
smitten, *past part.* Affected sharply with great feeling; afflicted. (From *smite,* to strike down.)

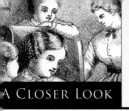

A Closer Look

Understanding the Selection

Recalling (just the facts)

1. Why is Meg so excited about her trip?
2. What do the Moffat sisters and other girls do to alter Meg's appearance?
3. Remember the ratings in the Weekly Report. Who got the worst mark for behavior in the Weekly Report? Who got the best mark? What are these ratings for?
4. Who objects to having Laurie in the club, and what are their objections? Who speaks up on his behalf as his sponsor, or patron?

Interpreting (delving deeper)

1. How does Meg feel about her new appearance? What is Laurie's reaction when he sees her?
2. At the end of Chapter 9, Marmee describes her hopes and dreams for her daughters. What are her ambitions for them? Does she want her daughters to marry rich men, as the gossips at the party claimed?
3. Are the girls likely to try harder to be good if they know their marks in the Weekly Report will be read aloud each week?
4. How does Jo convince the other club members to accept Laurie? Will he be a good addition to the club?

Synthesizing (putting it all together)

1. Did Meg enjoy sitting "in the lap of luxury" and being popular at the ball? What did she learn from her visit to the Moffats'? Is Meg likely to be less envious of rich girls in the future?
2. The *Pickwick Portfolio,* the P.O., and the girls' interest in writing and producing plays all reflect their deep enjoyment of all things literary and creative. What affect do such projects have on the general mood and community spirit? What affect do they have on other characters, like Mr. Laurence? Use examples from the text to support your answer.

Writing

EXTENSIONS

Newspaper. Given Jo's fondness for reading literature and writing short stories, it is not surprising that one of the favorite activities of the March girls' Pickwick Club is to read aloud from their homemade newspaper. Although Jo takes the lead, the paper is comprised of submissions from each of the girls.

Dividing into groups of four to six students, create your own newspapers that describe life within your school or community.

- First, create a **masthead**; this includes the newspaper's title, as it appears on the front page, and information about the paper's publisher and staff, which normally appears on the editorial page. Refer to your local newspaper for ideas.
- Choose one student to be the **editor-in-chief**—the person who will compile all the entries and bind them together. Everyone in the group will be responsible for editing articles, but the editor-in-chief must approve everything before printing.
- Other group members will be reporters or staff writers. Each student (including the editor-in-chief) will have two writing assignments—one from each of the following categories. Brainstorm story ideas as a group; then the editor-in-chief will assign stories at random or according to each reporter's interests.

    Feature Stories. Newspapers and journals of the 1800s contained fictional stories and poetry in addition to news events. Include at least one of each of the following entries in your newspaper: short story; poem; a report on a current local news event within your school or community; and an editorial providing an opinion on a school-related issue.

    Extras. Include some or all of the following: movie or music reviews; fashion column; crossword puzzle; horoscopes; advice column; comics or political cartoons; recipe; interview; announcements and classified ads.

- You may also want to enhance your paper with artwork or photography.
- Drafts of the stories should be distributed for editing to all group members. Use the Revision and Proofreading checklists in the back of the book. Submit all final stories to the editor-in-chief, who will staple them together into a single newspaper.

EXTENSIONS

History Alive!

Victorian America. In Chapter 9, Meg finally gets the long-awaited opportunity to visit the Moffat family and participate in their lavish social events. Embarassed by her "poverty," she allows the Moffat sisters to replace her ordinary tarlatan dress and slippers with a tight-fitting silk gown and lace-up boots. They frizzle her hair and apply make-up, transforming her into a porcelain doll—a look that Laurie disapprovingly calls "fuss and feathers." Using the details of this dressing ritual, Alcott signals to the reader that Meg ultimately is disappointed by the rich life she had previously glamorized. Alcott also conveys the fact that following certain standards of dress and behavior were imporant elements of high-society life in the Victorian era in which the March girls lived.

The **Victorian era** refers to the reign of Queen Victoria of England (1837–1901). During this period of history the world welcomed major new ideas and developments in the arts, sciences, architecture, medicine, industry, and more. Today, we use the term  "Victorian" to refer to the events and customs that developed during this period in both Britain and America. (Despite having gained their independence, Americans were still greatly influenced by British culture.)

The "Victorians" of the U.S. primarily were members of the middle and upper classes who shared particular values and beliefs. Of central importance was the idea of strict morality. The majority of Victorians were Protestant Christians who believed that moral conduct brought one closer to God. It is with this spirit that the March girls, armed with their Christmas bibles as their guide books, journey toward womanhood, an inner pilgrimage requiring personal moral "bundles." Along with this sense of personal moral conduct, Victorians also valued civic-mindedness, or caring for those less fortunate, with much the same spirit as the March family brings firewood and food to the Hummel family or knits socks for soldiers.

Whether deeply religious or not, however, all Victorians felt that people should strive to conduct themselves with great self control; they should maintain their homes and appearances in a tidy fashion, never use improper language,

History Alive!

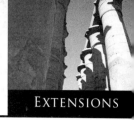

EXTENSIONS

always work hard, and remain modest about their achievements. Viewing the expression of strong emotions as undignified, they developed alternative means of communicating feelings. For example, a bouquet of red roses suggested romantic love, whereas yellow roses signified friendly devotion. The Victorian emphasis on proper conduct is apparent in *Little Women*; Jo, for instance, struggles with her rough speech, hot temper, and untidy appearance, and she reports in their *Pickwick Portfolio* that she has been bad again this week.

Exercising self-restraint was an important element of the overall emphasis on **etiquette,** or the rules for social behavior. In addition to academic subjects, Victorians schooled their children in proper social graces. For women, proper social behavior meant attending to home and family with diligence and patience. Victorians regarded their homes as retreats from the business of public life, and women—increasingly viewed as separate from the world of business and labor— were responsible for all aspects of domestic life. Women's fashions reflected this separation from the public realm. **Corsets** (close-fitting undergarments designed to cinch the waste) suggested restraint, while large flowing skirts resembling interior fabrics emphasized their association with the home.

Given the seriousness of their attention to strict etiquette and upright moral behavior, one might think that the Victorians never had any fun. However, they did enjoy a number of pastimes. In this pre-television era, Victorians were extremely literary. They loved going to libraries, attending public lectures, joining reading groups, and devouring literature of all kinds. They entertained guests and played board games in their parlors. They went to plays and musical performances in theaters. And, as you have seen, those of social standing wore their finest attire to formal parties and dances.

Are manners and social etiquette still important today? Do you think children are expected to behave in the same way today as they were one hundred years ago? What "holdovers" from the Victorian era are present in today's society?

CHAPTER 11

Experiments

"The first of June! The Kings are off to the seashore tomorrow, and I'm free. Three months' vacation—how I shall enjoy it!" exclaimed Meg, coming home one warm day to find Jo lying upon the sofa in an unusual state of exhaustion. Beth took off her dusty boots, while Amy made lemonade for the refreshment of the whole party.

"Aunt March went today, for which, oh, be joyful!" said Jo. "I had a fright every time she spoke to me, for I was in such a hurry to be through that I was uncommonly helpful and sweet. I quaked till she was in the carriage, and had a final fright, for as it drove off, she popped out her head, saying, 'Josyphine, won't you—?' I didn't hear any more, for I turned and fled."

"Poor old Jo! She came in looking as if bears were after her," said Beth, as she cuddled her sister's feet with a motherly air.

"What shall you do with all your vacation?" asked Amy, changing the subject with tact.

"I shall lie in bed late, and do nothing," replied Meg, from the depths of the rocking chair. "I've been woken up early all winter and had to spend my days working for other people, so now I'm going to rest and revel to my heart's content."

"No," said Jo, "that dozy way wouldn't suit me. I have a heap of books, and I'm going to improve my shining hours reading on my perch in the old apple tree."

"Let's not do any lessons, Beth, but play all the time and rest," proposed Amy.

"Well, I will, if Mother doesn't mind. I want to learn some new songs, and my children need fitting up for the summer. They are dreadfully out of order and really suffering for clothes."

"May we, Mother?" asked Meg, turning to Mrs. March, who sat sewing in what they called "Marmee's corner."

"You may try your experiment for a week and see how you like it. I think by Saturday night you will find that all play and no work is as bad as all work and no play."

"Oh, dear, no! It will be delicious, I'm sure," said Meg **complacently.**

"I now propose a toast. Fun forever, and no grubbing!"[1] cried Jo, rising, glass in hand, as the lemonade went round.

They all drank it merrily, and began the experiment by lounging for the rest of the day. Next morning, Meg did not appear till ten o'clock. Her solitary breakfast did not taste nice, and the room seemed lonely and untidy, for Jo had not filled the vases, Beth had not dusted, and Amy's books lay scattered about. Nothing was neat and pleasant but "Marmee's corner," which looked as usual. And there Meg sat, to "rest and read," which meant to yawn and imagine what pretty summer dresses she would get with her salary. Jo spent the morning on the river with Laurie and the afternoon reading. Beth began by rummaging everything out of the big closet where she kept her dolls, but soon left things topsy-turvy and went to her music, rejoicing that she had no dishes to wash. Amy put on her best white frock and sat down to draw, hoping someone would see and inquire who the young artist was. As no one appeared but an inquisitive daddy-longlegs, she went for a walk, got caught in a shower, and came home dripping.

It was astonishing what a peculiar and uncomfortable state of things was produced by the "resting and reveling" process. The days kept getting longer, the weather was unusually variable and so were tempers, and Satan found plenty of mischief for the idle hands to do.[2] Feeling time hang so heavily, Meg fell to snipping and spoiling her

Why would "all play and no work" be as bad as "all work and no play"?

What happens to the house while the girls are "resting"?

---

[1] **grubbing.** Toiling; doing difficult work
[2] **Satan . . . idle hands to do.** From the saying, "Idle hands are the devil's playground," which means that people are often tempted to do bad things when they are feeling bored or lazy

Vocabulary in Place
complacently, *adv.* With satisfaction; contentedly

clothes in her attempts to supply them. Jo read till her eyes gave out and got so fidgety that even good-natured Laurie had a quarrel with her. Beth's tranquility was much disturbed, and she actually shook poor dear Joanna, telling her she was a "fright." Amy fared worst of all, for when her sisters left her to amuse herself, she soon found that she didn't like dolls, fairy tales were childish, and one couldn't draw all the time. "If one could have a fine house, full of nice girls, or go traveling, the summer would be delightful," she complained, after several days devoted to pleasure, fretting, and **ennui**. "But to stay at home with three selfish sisters and a grown-up boy is enough to try one's patience."

How does Mrs. March "impress the lesson more deeply"?

No one would own that they were tired of the experiment, but by Friday night each acknowledged to herself that she was glad the week was nearly done. Hoping to impress the lesson more deeply, Mrs. March, who had a good deal of humor, resolved to finish off the trial in an appropriate manner, so she gave Hannah a holiday and let the girls enjoy the full effect of the play system. When they got up on Saturday morning, there was no fire in the kitchen, no breakfast in the dining room, and no mother anywhere to be seen.

"Mercy on us! What has happened?" cried Jo, staring about her in dismay.

Meg ran upstairs and soon came back again, looking relieved but rather bewildered.

"Mother isn't sick, only very tired, and she says she is going to stay quietly in her room all day and let us do the best we can to take care of ourselves."

"That's easy enough, and I like the idea. I'm aching for some new amusement, you know," added Jo quickly.

In fact it was an immense relief to them all to have a little work. There was plenty of food in the cupboard, and while Beth and Amy set the table, Meg and Jo got breakfast, wondering as they did why servants ever talked about hard work.

Vocabulary in Place

ennui, *n.* Boredom; dissatisfaction resulting from lack of interest

"I shall take some up to Mother, though she said we were not to think of her, for she'd take care of herself," said Meg, who felt quite matronly[3] behind the teapot.

So a tray was fitted out before anyone began, and taken up with the cook's compliments. The boiled tea was very bitter, the omelet scorched, and the biscuits speckled with baking soda, but Mrs. March received her repast with thanks and laughed heartily over it after Jo was gone.

"Poor little souls, they will have a hard time, I'm afraid, but they won't suffer, and it will do them good," she said, producing the more palatable viands[4] with which she had provided herself. So that their feelings might not be hurt, she disposed of the bad breakfast—a motherly little deception for which they were grateful.

Many were the complaints below, and great the **chagrin** of the head cook at her failures. "Never mind, I'll get the dinner and be servant, you be mistress, keep your hands nice, see company, and give orders," said Jo, who knew still less than Meg about **culinary** affairs. With perfect faith in her own powers, she immediately put a note in the post office, inviting Laurie to dinner.

"You'd better see what you have got before you think of having company," said Meg, when informed of the hospitable but **rash** act.

"Oh, there's corned beef and plenty of potatoes, and I shall get some asparagus and a lobster, 'for a relish,' as Hannah says. We'll have lettuce and make a salad. I don't know how, but the book tells. I'll have blancmange and strawberries for dessert, and coffee too, if you want to be elegant."

Are the girls able to take care of themselves?

---

[3] **matronly.** Motherly
[4] **palatable viands.** Better-tasting foods

Vocabulary in Place
chagrin, *n.* Annoyance or disappointment
culinary, *adj.* Of or relating to the kitchen
rash, *adj.* Reckless; performed hastily, without forethought

Does Meg have confidence in Jo's ability as a chef?

"Don't try too many messes, Jo, for you can't make anything but gingerbread and molasses candy fit to eat. I wash my hands of the dinner party, and since you have asked Laurie on your own responsibility, you may just take care of him."

"You'll give me your advice if I make a mess, won't you?" asked Jo, rather hurt.

"Yes, but I don't know much. You had better ask Mother's leave before you order anything," returned Meg **prudently.**

"Of course I shall. I'm not a fool." And Jo went off in a huff at the doubts expressed of her powers.

"Get what you like, and don't disturb me. I'm going out to dinner and can't worry about things at home," said Mrs. March, when Jo spoke to her. "I never enjoyed housekeeping, and I'm going to take a vacation today, and read, write, go visiting, and amuse myself."

Is Marmee behaving in her usual manner?

The unusual spectacle of her busy mother rocking comfortably and reading early in the morning made Jo feel as if some unnatural phenomenon had occurred, for an eclipse, an earthquake, or a volcanic eruption would hardly have seemed stranger. Feeling very much out of sorts herself, Jo hurried into the parlor to find Beth sobbing over Pip, the canary, who lay dead in the cage with his little claws pathetically extended.

"It's all my fault, I forgot him, there isn't a seed or a drop left. Oh, Pip! How could I be so cruel to you?" cried Beth, taking the poor thing in her hands and trying to restore him.

Jo peeped into his half-open eye, felt his little heart, and finding him stiff and cold, shook her head, and offered her domino box for a coffin.

"I'll make him a shroud,[5] and he shall be buried in the garden," murmured Beth, sitting on the floor with her pet folded in her hands. "I'll never have another bird, never, my Pip! For I am too bad to own one."

---

[5] **shroud.** A cloth used to wrap a body for burial

Vocabulary in Place
prudently, *adv.* With good judgement or common sense

"The funeral shall be this afternoon, and we will all go. Now, don't cry, Bethy. It's a pity, but nothing goes right this week, and Pip has had the worst of the experiment. Make the shroud, and lay him in my box, and after the dinner party, we'll have a nice little funeral," said Jo, beginning to feel as if she had undertaken a good deal.

Mrs. March went out, after peeping here and there to see how matters went, also saying a word of comfort to Beth, who sat making a shroud, while the dear departed lay in the domino box. A strange sense of helplessness fell upon the girls as the gray bonnet vanished round the corner, and despair seized them when a few minutes later Miss Crocker appeared, and said she'd come to dinner. Now this lady was a thin spinster, with a sharp nose and inquisitive eyes, who saw everything and gossiped about all she saw. They disliked her, but had been taught to be kind to her, simply because she was old and poor and had few friends. So Meg gave her the easy chair and tried to entertain her, while she asked questions, criticized everything, and told stories of the people whom she knew.

Language cannot describe the anxieties, experiences, and **exertions** that Jo underwent that morning, and the dinner she served up became a standing joke. Fearing to ask any more advice, she did her best alone, and discovered that something more than energy and good will is necessary to make a cook. She boiled the asparagus for an hour and was grieved to find the heads cooked off and the stalks harder than ever. The lobster was a scarlet mystery to her, but she hammered and poked till it was unshelled and its meager proportions concealed in a grove of lettuce leaves. The potatoes had to be hurried, not to keep the asparagus waiting, and were not done at the last. The blancmange was lumpy, and the strawberries not as ripe as they looked.

Vocabulary in Place

exertion, *n.* The act of putting great effort into something

Why would Jo want to go under the table?

"Well, they can eat beef and bread and butter, if they are hungry," thought Jo, as she rang the bell half an hour later than usual, and stood, hot, tired, and dispirited, surveying the feast spread before Laurie and Miss Crocker, whose tattling tongue would report them far and wide.

Poor Jo would gladly have gone under the table, as one thing after another was tasted and left, while Amy giggled, Meg looked distressed, Miss Crocker pursed her lips, and Laurie talked and laughed with all his might to give a cheerful tone to the festive scene. Jo's one strong point was the fruit, for she had sugared it well, and had a pitcher of rich cream to eat with it. Miss Crocker tasted first, made a wry face, and drank some water hastily. Jo glanced at Laurie, but he was eating away manfully, though there was a slight pucker[6] about his mouth. Amy, who was fond of delicate fare, took a heaping spoonful, choked, hid her face in her napkin, and left the table.

"Oh, what is it?" exclaimed Jo, trembling.

"Salt instead of sugar, and the cream is sour," replied Meg with a tragic gesture.

Jo uttered a groan and fell back in her chair, remembering that she had given a last hasty powdering to the berries out of one of the two boxes on the kitchen table, and had neglected to put the milk in the refrigerator. She turned scarlet and was on the verge of crying, when she met Laurie's eyes, which would look merry in spite of his heroic efforts. The comical side of the affair suddenly struck her, and she laughed till the tears ran down her cheeks. So did everyone else, even "Croaker" as the girls called the old lady, and the unfortunate dinner ended gaily, with bread and butter, olives and fun.

"I haven't strength of mind enough to clear up now, so we will sober ourselves with a funeral," said Jo, as they rose, and Miss Crocker made ready to go, being eager to tell the new story at another friend's dinner table.

They did sober themselves for Beth's sake. Laurie dug a grave under the ferns, and little Pip was laid in and covered with moss,

---

[6] **pucker.** A facial expression in which the lips are pulled tightly together and pushed outward, as if tasting something sour or kissing

while a wreath of flowers was hung on his tombstone. At the conclusion of the ceremonies, Beth retired to her room, and found her grief much **assuaged** by beating up the pillows and putting things in order. Meg helped Jo clear away the remains of the feast, which took half the afternoon and left them so tired that they agreed to be contented with tea and toast for supper.

Before the housewives could rest, tea must be got, errands done, and one or two necessary bits of sewing neglected until the last minute. As twilight fell, one by one they gathered on the porch where the June roses were budding beautifully, and each groaned or sighed as she sat down, as if tired or troubled.

"What a dreadful day this has been!" began Jo, usually the first to speak.

"It has seemed shorter than usual, but so uncomfortable," said Meg.

"Not a bit like home," added Amy.

"It can't seem so without Marmee and little Pip," sighed Beth, glancing with full eyes at the empty cage above her head.

"Here's Mother, dear, and you shall have another bird tomorrow, if you want it."

As she spoke, Mrs. March came and took her place among them, looking as if her holiday had not been much pleasanter than theirs.

"Are you satisfied with your experiment, girls, or do you want another week of it?" she asked, as Beth nestled up to her and the rest turned toward her with brightening faces, as flowers turn toward the sun.

"I don't!" cried Jo decidedly.

"Nor I," echoed the others.

"You think then, that it is better to have a few duties and live a little for others, do you?"

How does Mrs. March look at the end of the day?

Vocabulary in Place

assuage, *v.* To calm or pacify

"Lounging and **larking** doesn't pay," observed Jo, shaking her head.

"Suppose you learn plain cooking. That's a useful accomplishment, which no woman should be without," said Mrs. March, laughing at the recollection of Jo's dinner party, for she had met Miss Crocker and heard her account of it.

"Mother, did you go away and let everything be, just to see how we'd get on?" cried Meg, who had had suspicions all day.

"Yes, I wanted you to see how the comfort of all depends on each doing her share faithfully. I thought, as a little lesson, I would show you what happens when everyone thinks only of herself. Don't you feel that it is pleasanter to help one another, to have daily duties that make leisure sweet when it comes, and home comfortable and lovely to us all?"

How do daily duties make leisure time "sweet"?

"We do, Mother, we do!" cried the girls.

"Then let me advise you to take up your little burdens again, for though they seem heavy sometimes, they are good for us, and lighten as we learn to carry them. Work is wholesome, and there is plenty for everyone. It keeps us from ennui and mischief, is good for health and spirits, and gives us a sense of power and independence better than money or fashion."

According to Mrs. March, why are the girls' "burdens" good for them?

"We'll work like bees and love it too, see if we don't," said Jo. "I'll learn plain cooking for my holiday task, and the dinner party I have shall be a success."

"I'll make the set of shirts for Father," said Meg. "Though I'm not fond of sewing, it will be better than fussing over my own things, which are plenty nice enough as they are."

"I'll do my lessons every day, and not spend so much time with my music and dolls. I ought to be studying, not playing," was Beth's resolution, while Amy followed their example by heroically declaring, "I shall learn to make buttonholes, and attend to my parts of speech."

Vocabulary in Place

lark, *v.* To engage in spirited fun or pranks

"Very good! Then I am quite satisfied with the experiment and fancy that we shall not have to repeat it, only don't go to the other extreme and delve like slaves," Mrs. March advised. "Have regular hours for work and play, make each day both useful and pleasant, and prove that you understand the worth of time by employing it well."

"We'll remember, Mother!" And they did.

Words to Keep

The following sentences contain important words from the Vocabulary in Place boxes in Chapters 8–11 of *Little Women*. In your notebook, or on a separate sheet of paper, write the part of speech of each boldface word, a synonym (or a short definition in your own words), and a new sentence of your own.

1. Rather than ending the feud, the meeting **kindled** more hostility between the groups.
2. The flight attendant gave the passengers free drinks to **pacify** them during the delay.
3. The oil spill was an environmental **calamity**.
4. The conditions inside the prison were **abominable**.
5. Careful! This road is **treacherous** when it is icy.
6. The criminal seemed quite **penitent** when he confessed to the crime.
7. The museum was full of **relics** from ancient Egyptian tombs.
8. The unruly crowd was becoming more **agitated** by the minute.
9. "Please quiet down and listen to our guest speaker!" yelled the teacher **indignantly**.
10. Spitting in public is not only **vulgar**, it is a health hazard.
11. They knew he was a nice man, so they were **perplexed** by his aggravating behavior.
12. My little sister **reveled** in being the center of attention on her birthday.
13. **Contrary** to what most people think, cats actually can be trained to do things.
14. Bernard was **smitten** by grief after his pet parakeet escaped.
15. During the Revolutionary War, the colonies **prudently** sought an alliance with France.
16. In mountain climbing, the reward of reaching the summit far outweighs the pain and **exertion** required to get there.

CHAPTER 12

Camp Laurence

Beth was postmistress and dearly liked the daily task of unlocking the little door and distributing the mail. One July day she came in with her hands full and went about the house leaving letters and parcels like the penny post.

"Here's your posy, Mother! Laurie never forgets that," she said, putting the fresh flower in Marmee's vase.

"Miss Meg March, one letter and a glove," continued Beth, delivering the articles to her sister, who sat stitching wristbands.

"Why, I left a pair over there, and here is only one," said Meg. "Never mind, the other may be found. My letter is only a translation of the German song I wanted. I think Mr. Brooke did it, for this isn't Laurie's writing."

Mrs. March glanced at Meg, who was looking very pretty in her morning gown, and very womanly, as she sat sewing at her little worktable, and singing. Her thoughts were busied with innocent, girlish fancies, and Mrs. March smiled and was satisfied.

"Two letters for Doctor Jo, a book, and a funny old hat, which covered the whole post office and stuck outside," said Beth, laughing as she went into the study where Jo sat writing.

"What a sly fellow Laurie is! I said I wished bigger hats were the fashion, because I burn my face every hot day. He said, 'Why mind the fashion? Wear a big hat, and be comfortable!' I said I would if I had one, and he has sent me this to try me. I'll wear it for fun and show him I don't care for the fashion." And hanging the broad-brim hat on a bust,[1] Jo read her letters.

One from her mother made her eyes fill, for it reassured her that her efforts to tame her temper had been noticed and were progressing

Why do Jo's eyes fill with tears when she reads Marmee's letter?

---

[1] **bust.** A sculpture of a person's head, shoulders, and upper chest

nicely. Those few words of love and encouragement from Marmee were worth millions of money to Jo.

"Oh, Marmee, I do try! I will keep on trying, since I have you to help me."

Feeling stronger than ever, she pinned the note inside her frock, as a shield and a reminder. Her other letter was written in Laurie's big, dashing hand . . .

Dear Jo,

What ho! Some English girls and boys are coming to see me tomorrow and I want to have a jolly time. If it's fine, I'm going to pitch my tent in Longmeadow, and row up the whole crew to lunch and croquet,[2] *and all sorts of larks. They are nice people, and like such things. Brooke will go to keep us boys steady, and Kate Vaughn will look after the girls. I want you all to come, can't let Beth off at any price, and nobody shall worry her. I'll see to everything, only do come, there's a good fellow!*

In a tearing hurry,
Yours ever, Laurie.

"Here's richness!" cried Jo, flying in to tell the news to Meg. "Of course we can go, Mother? It will be such a help to Laurie, for we will all be useful in some way."

"I hope the Vaughns are not fine grown-up people. Do you know anything about them, Jo?" asked Meg.

"Only that there are four of them. Kate is older than you, Fred and Frank (twins) about my age, and a little girl (Grace), who is nine or ten. Laurie knew them abroad, and liked the boys. I fancied, from the way he primmed up his mouth in speaking of her, that he didn't admire Kate much."

"I'm so glad my French print is clean, it's just the thing and so becoming!" observed Meg complacently. "Have you anything decent, Jo?"

"Scarlet and gray boating suit, good enough for me. I shall row and tramp about, so I don't want any starch to think of. You'll come, Bethy?"

---

[2] **croquet.** A game, played on a lawn, in which players use mallets to hit balls through wickets

"If you won't let any boys talk to me," replied Beth.

"Not a boy!" teased Jo.

"I like to please Laurie, and I'm not afraid of Mr. Brooke, he is so kind. But I don't want to play, or sing, or say anything. I'll work hard and not trouble anyone, and you'll take care of me, Jo, so I'll go."

"That's my good girl. You do try to fight off your shyness, and I love you for it. Fighting faults isn't easy, as I know, and a cheery word kind of gives a lift. Thank you, Mother." And Jo gave the thin cheek a grateful kiss, more precious to Mrs. March than if it had given back the rosy roundness of her youth.

"I had a box of chocolate drops, and the picture I wanted to copy," said Amy, showing her mail.

"And I got a note from Mr. Laurence, asking me to come over and play to him tonight, before the lamps are lighted, and I shall go," added Beth, whose friendship with the old gentleman prospered finely.

"Now let's fly round, and do double duty today, so that we can play tomorrow with free minds," said Jo, preparing to replace her pen with a broom.

The sun peeped into the girls' room early next morning to promise them a fine day. Sunshine and laughter were good omens for a pleasure party, and soon a lively bustle began in both houses. Beth, who was ready first, kept reporting what went on next door, and enlivened her sisters' toilets[3] by frequent telegrams from the window.

"There goes the man with the tent! I see Mrs. Barker doing up the lunch in a hamper and a great basket. There's Laurie, looking like a sailor, nice boy! Oh, mercy me! Here's a carriage full of people, a tall lady, a little girl, and two dreadful boys. One is **lame,** poor thing, he's got a crutch. Laurie didn't tell us that. Be quick, girls! It's getting late.

---

[3] **toilet.** The act or process of dressing and grooming oneself

Vocabulary in Place
lame, *adj.* Disabled so that movement, especially walking, is difficult or impossible

Why, there is Ned Moffat, I do declare. Meg, isn't that the man who bowed to you one day when we were shopping?"

"So it is. I thought he was at the mountains. There is Sallie. I'm glad she got back in time. Am I all right, Jo?" cried Meg in a flutter.

"A regular daisy. Now then, come on!"

"Oh, Jo, you are not going to wear that awful hat? It's too absurd! You shall not make a guy[4] of yourself," scolded Meg, as Jo tied down with a red ribbon the broad-brimmed, old-fashioned hat Laurie had sent for a joke.

"I just will, though, for it's capital, so shady, light, and big. It will make fun, and I don't mind being a guy if I'm comfortable." With that Jo marched straight away and the rest followed, a bright little band of sisters, all looking their best in summer suits, with happy faces under their hatbrims.

Laurie ran to meet and present them to his friends in the most **cordial** manner. Meg was grateful to see that Miss Kate, though twenty, was dressed with elegant simplicity. Jo understood why Laurie didn't fancy Kate, for that young lady had a standoff don't-touch-me air, which contrasted strongly with the free and easy **demeanor** of the other girls. Beth decided that Frank, the lame boy, was not "dreadful," but gentle, and she would be kind to him on that account. Amy found Grace a well-mannered, merry, little person and they soon became very good friends.

Tents, lunch, and croquet utensils having been sent on beforehand, the party boarded, and the two boats pushed off together. Laurie and Jo rowed one boat, Mr. Brooke and Ned the other. Jo's funny hat deserved a vote of thanks, for it broke the ice in the beginning by producing a laugh. It created quite a refreshing breeze, flapping to and fro as she rowed, and would make an excellent umbrella for the whole party, if

Why is Jo determined to wear her new hat on the picnic? Why doesn't Meg like the hat?

---

[4] **guy.** (British.) A person of odd appearance or dress.

Vocabulary in Place
cordial, *adj.* Warm and friendly
demeanor, *n.* Way of behaving or carrying oneself

a shower came up, she said. Miss Kate decided that Jo was "odd," but rather clever, and smiled upon her from afar.

Meg, in the other boat, was delightfully situated, face to face with the rowers, who both manned their oars with uncommon "skill and **dexterity**." Mr. Brooke was a grave, silent young man, with handsome brown eyes and a pleasant voice. Meg liked his quiet manners and his wealth of useful knowledge. He never talked to her much, but he looked at her a good deal. Ned, being in college, put on all sorts of airs. He was not very wise, but very good-natured, and altogether an excellent person to carry on a picnic. Sallie Gardiner chatted with Fred, who kept Beth in constant terror by his pranks.

It was not far to Longmeadow, but the tent was already pitched on a pleasant green field, with three wide-spreading oaks in the middle and a smooth strip of turf for croquet.

"Welcome to Camp Laurence!" said the young host, as they landed with exclamations of delight. "Now, let's have a game before it gets hot, and then we'll see about dinner."

Frank, Beth, Amy, and Grace sat down to watch the game played by the other eight. Mr. Brooke chose Meg, Kate, and Fred. Laurie took Sallie, Jo, and Ned. The English played well, but the Americans played better, and contested every inch of the ground as strongly as if the Spirit of '76[5] inspired them. Jo and Fred had several **skirmishes** and once narrowly escaped high words. Fred's ball had stopped an inch on the wrong side of a wicket, and, thinking no one could see, he gave it a sly nudge with his toe, which put it just an inch on the right side.

"I'm through! Now, Miss Jo, I'll settle you, and get in first," cried the young gentleman, swinging his mallet for another blow.

---

[5] **Spirit of '76.** Refers to the enthusiasm and determination that sparked the American Revolution (1776–1783)

> **Vocabulary in Place**
>
> **dexterity,** *n.* Coordination, efficiency, and skill, especially involving use of the hands
>
> **skirmish,** *n.* A small conflict or battle

"You pushed it. I saw you. It's my turn now," said Jo sharply.

"Upon my word, I didn't move it. It rolled a bit, perhaps, but that is allowed. So, stand off please, and let me have a go at the stake."

"We don't cheat in America, but you can, if you choose," said Jo angrily.

"Yankees are a deal the most tricky, everybody knows. There you go!" returned Fred, croqueting her ball far away.

Jo opened her lips to say something rude, but checked herself in time, and stood a minute, hammering down a wicket with all her might, while Fred hit the stake and declared himself out with much **exultation.** She went off to get her ball, and was a long time finding it among the bushes, but she came back, looking cool and quiet, and waited her turn patiently. It took several strokes to regain the place she had lost, and when she got there, the other side had nearly won, for Kate's was the last ball.

"Well, it's all up with us! Goodbye, Kate. Miss Jo owes me one, so you are finished," cried Fred excitedly, as they all drew near to see the finish.

"Yankees have a trick of being generous to their enemies," said Jo, with a look that made the lad redden, "especially when they beat them," she added, as, leaving Kate's ball untouched, she won the game by a clever stroke.

Laurie threw up his hat, then remembering his manners, whispered to his friend, "Good for you, Jo! He did cheat, I saw him. We can't tell him so, but he won't do it again, take my word for it."

Meg drew her aside and said approvingly, "It was dreadfully **provoking**, but you kept your temper, and I'm so glad, Jo."

"Don't praise me, Meg, for I could box his ears this minute. I had to stay among the nettles till I got my rage under control. It's simmering now, so I hope he'll keep out of my way," returned Jo, biting her lips as she glowered at Fred from under her big hat.

What does Fred do to infuriate Jo?

Why does Meg praise Jo for keeping her temper in check? Is this easy for Jo?

Vocabulary in Place

exultation, *n.* The act of rejoicing greatly; celebration

provoking, *adj.* Baiting or stirring up anger; aggravating or irritating

"Time for lunch," said Mr. Brooke, looking at his watch.

A very merry lunch it was, for everything seemed fresh and funny, and frequent peals of laughter wafted across the meadow.

"What shall we do when we can't eat anymore?" asked Laurie.

"Have games till it's cooler," said Jo. "Who knows a good game?"

Soon someone suggested one, and while the rest played, the three elders sat apart, talking. Miss Kate took out her sketch again, and Meg watched her, while Mr. Brooke lay on the grass with a book, which he did not read.

"How beautifully you do it! I wish I could draw," said Meg, with mingled admiration and regret in her voice.

"Why don't you learn? I should think you had taste and talent for it," replied Miss Kate graciously.

"I haven't time."

"Your mamma prefers other accomplishments? Mine did too, but I convinced my governess to let me take lessons privately, and when Mother saw I had talent she was quite willing I should go on. Can't you do the same with your governess?"

"I have none."

"I forgot young ladies in America go to school more than with us. You go to a private one, I suppose?"

"I don't go at all. I am a governess myself."

"Oh, indeed!" said Miss Kate, but she might as well have said, "Dear me, how dreadful!" for her tone implied it, and something in her face made Meg blush.

Mr. Brooke looked up and said quickly, "Young ladies in America love independence and are admired and respected for supporting themselves."

"Oh, yes, of course it's very nice and proper in them to do so. We have many most respectable and worthy young women who are employed by the nobility," said Miss Kate in a **patronizing** tone that

> *Does Meg go to private school or have a governess? Why is she so embarrassed about the type of work she does?*

Vocabulary in Place

patronizing, *adj.* Belittling or condescending, as if one is better than others, even if well-intended

hurt Meg's pride, and made her work seem not only more distasteful, but degrading.

"Did the German song suit, Miss March?" inquired Mr. Brooke, breaking an awkward pause.

"Oh, yes! It was very sweet, and I'm much obliged to whoever translated it for me." And Meg's downcast face brightened as she spoke.

"Don't you read German?" asked Miss Kate with a look of surprise.

"Not very well. My father, who taught me, is away, and I've no one to correct my pronunciation."

"Try a little now. Here is Schiller's *Mary Stuart*[6] and a tutor who loves to teach." And Mr. Brooke laid his book on her lap with an inviting smile.

"It's so hard I'm afraid to try," said Meg, grateful, but bashful in the presence of the accomplished young lady beside her.

"I'll read a bit to encourage you." And Miss Kate read one of the most beautiful passages in a perfectly correct but perfectly expressionless manner.

Mr. Brooke made no comment as she returned the book to Meg, who said innocently, "I thought it was poetry."

"Some of it is. Try this passage."

There was a queer smile about Mr. Brooke's mouth as he opened at poor Mary's **lament**.

Meg, following the long grass-blade which her new tutor used to point with, read slowly and timidly, unconsciously making poetry of the hard words by the soft intonation of her musical voice. Presently, forgetting her listener in the beauty of the sad scene, Meg read as if alone, giving a little touch of tragedy to the words of the unhappy

---

[6] *Mary Stuart*. A novel about Mary, Queen of Scots, by German author Friedrich Schiller (1759–1805)

Vocabulary in Place
lament, *n.* Expression of sorrow or grief

queen. If she had seen the brown eyes then, she would have stopped short, but she never looked up.

"Very well indeed!" said Mr. Brooke, as she paused, quite ignoring her many mistakes, and looking as if he did indeed love to teach.

Miss Kate put up her glass, and, having taken a survey of the little scene before her, shut her sketch book, saying with condescension, "You've a nice accent and in time will be a clever reader. I must look after Grace, she is romping." And Miss Kate strolled away, adding to herself with a shrug, "What odd people these Yankees are. I'm afraid Laurie will be quite spoiled among them."

"I forgot that English people rather turn up their noses at governesses and don't treat them as we do," said Meg, looking after the retreating figure with an annoyed expression.

"There's no place like America for us workers, Miss Margaret." And Mr. Brooke looked so contented and cheerful that Meg was ashamed to lament her hard lot.

> What does Mr. Brooke mean by this statement about America?

They talked of teaching and Mr. Brooke said he was able to enjoy it because he had such a talented pupil. "I shall be very sorry to lose him next year," said Mr. Brooke, busily punching holes in the turf.

"Going to college, I suppose?" Meg's lips asked the question, but her eyes added, "And what becomes of you?"

"Yes, it's high time he went, for he is ready, and as soon as he is off, I shall turn soldier. I am needed."

"I am glad of that!" exclaimed Meg. "I should think every young man would want to go, though it is hard for the mothers and sisters who stay at home," she added sorrowfully.

> What will Mr. Brooke do after Laurie goes to college? What does Meg think of this?

"I have neither, and very few friends to care whether I live or die," said Mr. Brooke rather bitterly.

"Laurie and his grandfather would care a great deal, and we should all be very sorry to have any harm happen to you," said Meg heartily.

"Thank you, that sounds pleasant," began Mr. Brooke, looking cheerful again, but before he could finish his speech, Ned, mounted on the old horse, came lumbering up to display his equestrian[7] skill

---

[7] **equestrian.** Of or relating to horseback riding

before the young ladies, and there was no more quiet that day, as the afternoon was taken up with riding and racing.

An **impromptu** circus, fox and geese, and an **amicable** game of croquet finished the afternoon. At sunset the tent was struck,[8] hampers packed, wickets pulled up, boats loaded, and the whole party floated down the river, singing at the tops of their voices.

Ned tried a serenade for Meg, but he looked so sentimental that she couldn't hold back her laughter. Ned was offended and turned to Sallie for consolation, saying to her rather pettishly, "There isn't a bit of flirt in that girl, is there?"

Why does Meg laugh at Ned? How does he react?

"Not a particle, but she's a dear," returned Sallie, defending her friend.

On the lawn where it had gathered, the little party separated with cordial good-nights and good-byes. As the four sisters went home through the garden, Miss Kate looked after them, saying, without the patronizing tone in her voice, "In spite of their **demonstrative** manners, American girls are very nice when one knows them."

"I quite agree with you," said Mr. Brooke.

---

[8] **struck.** Dismantled; taken down and packed

Vocabulary in Place
impromptu, *adj.* Not planned in advance
amicable, *adj.* Friendly
demonstrative, *adj.* Marked by the open expression of emotions

Understanding the Selection

Recalling (just the facts)

1. What experiment does Marmee agree to let the girls try? What does each sister plan to do?
2. Who comes to Jo's dinner party? What kind of meal do they have?
3. Do most of Miss Kate's friends have to work? What kind of school do they go to?
4. Did Fred get away with cheating at croquet? Who won the match after all?

Interpreting (delving deeper)

1. Do the girls enjoy their experiment? What happens to each of them?
2. What happens to Beth's parrot? Why does this take place? How do Jo and the others comfort her?
3. When Meg explains that she works as a governess, does Kate make her feel better or worse?
4. Why is there tension between Laurie's old friends from England and his new ones from America?

Synthesizing (putting it all together)

1. At the end of the "experiment," what kind of day does Marmee have in contrast to her girls? Has she taught them a valuable lesson? What do they learn? What kind of resolutions do they make in the end?
2. What happens during the croquet game between the British and the Yankees? Who wins? Why is the rivalry between Laurie's old friends and his new ones so intense? Discuss, using examples from the story to support your answer.

Writing

EXTENSIONS

Persuasive Essay. At the beginning of Chapter 11, Meg is thrilled to have "three months' vacation" from work, and the sisters plan how they would best like to spend their time. Meg would like to do nothing, Amy and Beth want to "play all the time and rest," and Jo wants to read a stack of books to pass the time. Sitting in her corner, Marmee offers her opinion on the girls' plans. She says "You may try your experiment for a week and see how you like it. I think by Saturday night you will find that all play and no work is as bad as all work and no play."

What is your take on work and play? If you had your choice, would you spend all your time playing? Do you, or anyone you know, seem to be working on one thing or another all the time? Should you balance work and play or do just enough work to get by? Consider how either playing or working all the time might impact important areas of your life such as your relationships with friends and family. Write a persuasive essay to convince others of your opinion about work and play.

— Use the questions above to determine your opinion about work and play.
— In the opening paragraph, clearly state your opinion and hint at the ideas you will use to convince your audience. Think of these hints as the "coming attractions" you see before a movie in a movie theater—don't give everything away!
— In the main body of your essay, use as much evidence and as many examples you can think of to convince your readers of your argument. If you think that only playing is the best way to pass time, you can say that work can be tedious and boring, and then make the argument stronger by talking about specific examples from your life experiences.
— Try to foresee ways in which your audience might disagree with your beliefs and to argue against those points in the body of your essay. If you are going to try to pursuade others that not working to clean your room is a good thing, you need to come up with a good argument to support this view, because your audience probably knows better.
— After you complete your body paragraphs, write a conclusion that summarizes the most important things you have said.
— Be sure to refer to the Resources for Writers on page 253–256.

SpeakUp!

EXTENSIONS

Vocal Expression. At Camp Laurence, Miss Kate—after making Meg feel uncomfortable not only in her position as governess but also in her ability to speak German—encourages Meg to read a bit of Schiller's *Mary Stuart*. Though Miss Kate read the passages aloud in perfect German, her reading was boring and expressionless, and her voice lacked pleasant inflection. When it was Meg's turn to read, her German pronunciation was far from perfect, but she tried to make poetry and create emotion with her musical voice despite the difficulty of the passage.

When speaking—whether in everyday conversation or in front of a group of any size—using expressive, emotive speech is very important. It will engage your listeners and make them want to hear what you have to say. Reading passages from stories and poems expressively can also make understanding easier. With a partner, read the poem below once in a very boring, expressionless way and then read it again with lots of expression and variety in your voice.

"Sing me a song" by Christina Rossetti

>Sing me a song—
> What shall I sing?—
>Three merry sisters
> Dancing in a ring,
>Light and fleet upon their feet
> As birds upon the wing.
>
>Tell me a tale—
> What shall I tell?
>Two mournful sisters,
> And a tolling knell,
>Tolling ding and tolling dong,
> Ding dong bell.

How does expression change the poem? Does it make the poem easier to understand? Did you listen more intently when the poem was spoken with feeling? Was it more fun to recite the poem the first or second time?

CHAPTER 13

Castles in the Air

Laurie lay swinging to and fro in his hammock one warm September afternoon. He was in one of his moods, for the day had been both unprofitable and unsatisfactory. He was staring up into the horse-chestnut trees above him, daydreaming about an ocean voyage round the world, when the sound of voices brought him ashore in a flash. Peeping through the meshes of the hammock, he saw the Marches coming out, as if bound on some expedition.

"What in the world are those girls about now?" thought Laurie, opening his sleepy eyes to take a good look, for their appearance was rather peculiar. Each wore a large, flapping hat, a brown linen pouch slung over one shoulder, and carried a long staff. Meg had a cushion, Jo a book, Beth a basket, and Amy a portfolio. All walked quietly through the garden, out at the little back gate, and began to climb the hill that lay between the house and river.

"Well, that's cool," said Laurie to himself, "to have a picnic and never ask me! I'll take after them, and see what's going on."

It took him some time to find a hat, so that the girls were quite out of sight when he leaped the fence and ran after them. He ran to the boathouse, but no one was there, and he went up the hill to take an observation. Peeping through the bushes, Laurie saw a rather pretty little picture. The sisters sat together in the shady nook. Meg was upon her cushion, sewing daintily with her white hands, and looking as fresh and sweet as a rose in her pink dress. Beth was sorting the cones that lay thick under the hemlock near by, for she made pretty things with them. Amy was sketching a group of ferns, and Jo was knitting socks as she read aloud.

A shadow passed over the boy's face as he watched them, feeling that he ought to go away because he was uninvited. Suddenly Beth

Where are the girls going? Do they know that Laurie is coming too?

looked up, spied the wistful face behind the birches, and **beckoned** with a reassuring smile.

"May I come in, please? Or shall I be a bother?" he asked, advancing slowly.

Meg lifted her eyebrows, but Jo scowled at her and said at once, "Of course you may. We should have asked you before, only we thought you wouldn't care for such a girl's game as this."

"I always like your games, but if Meg doesn't want me, I'll go away."

"I've no objection, if you do something. It's against the rules to be idle here," replied Meg gravely but graciously.

"Much obliged. Shall I sew, read, cone, draw, or do all at once? I'm ready." And Laurie sat down with a **submissive** expression that delighted the girls.

"Finish this story while I knit the heel," said Jo, handing him the book.

"Yes'm," he answered meekly, and did his best to prove his gratitude for the favor of admission into the "Busy Bee Society."

The story was not a long one, and when it was finished, he ventured to ask a few questions.

"Please, ma'am, could I inquire if this highly instructive and charming institution is a new one?"

"Oh, didn't we tell you about this new plan of ours?" asked Jo. "Well, we have tried not to waste our holiday, but each has worked at a task. The vacation is nearly over, and we are ever so glad that we didn't **dawdle**."

"Yes, I should think so," and Laurie thought regretfully of his own idle days.

"Mother likes to have us out-of-doors as much as possible, so we bring our work here and have nice times. For the fun of it, we bring

What kind of projects are the girls doing? What are the rules of this new "Busy Bee Society"?

Vocabulary in Place

beckon, *v.* To call over or invite, usually with a hand motion

submissive, *adj.* Willing to acknowledge or give in to someone else's authority or control

dawdle, *v.* To poke along or waste time

our things in these bags, wear old hats, use poles to climb the hill, play pilgrims, as we used to do years ago," Jo explained. "We call this hill the **Delectable** Mountain, for we can look far away and see the country where we hope to live some time."

Jo pointed, and Laurie sat up to examine, for through an opening in the wood one could look cross the wide, blue river, far over the outskirts of the great city, to the green hills that rose to meet the gold and purple splendor of an autumn sunset. Rising high into the ruddy light were silvery white peaks that shone like the airy spires of some Celestial City.

"How beautiful that is!" said Laurie softly, for he was quick to see and feel beauty of any kind.

"We like to watch it, for it is never the same, but always splendid," replied Amy, wishing she could paint it.

"Jo talks about the country where we hope to live some time—the real country, with pigs and chickens and haymaking. It would be nice, but I wish the beautiful country up there was real, and we could ever go to it," said Beth musingly, looking up at the sky.

"Wouldn't it be fun if all the castles in the air which we make could come true, and we could live in them?" said Jo, after a little pause.

"I've made such quantities it would be hard to choose which I'd have," said Laurie, lying flat and throwing cones.

"What is your favorite one?" asked Meg.

"After I'd seen as much of the world as I want to, I'd like to settle in Germany and be a famous musician, and all creation will rush to hear me. And I'm never to be bothered about money or business, but just enjoy myself and live for what I like. That's my favorite castle. What's yours, Meg?"

Meg seemed to find it a little hard to tell hers, and waved a fan before her face as she said slowly, "I should like a lovely house, full of all sorts of luxurious things—nice food, pretty clothes, handsome

Where do the girls "hope to live some time"? What does Jo point out to Laurie?

Is Jo talking about real castles here?

Vocabulary in Place

delectable, *adj.* Extremely tasty; also highly pleasing or delightful

furniture, pleasant people, and heaps of money. I'd like to have plenty of servants, so I never need work a bit. How I should enjoy it! For I wouldn't be idle, but do good, and make everyone love me dearly."

"Wouldn't you have a master for your castle in the air?" asked Laurie slyly.

"I said 'pleasant people,'" and Meg carefully tied up her shoe as she spoke, so that no one saw her face.

"Why don't you say you'd have a splendid, wise, good husband and some angelic little children? You know your castle wouldn't be perfect without," said blunt Jo, who scorned romance, except in books.

"You'd have nothing but horses, inkstands, and novels in yours," answered Meg **petulantly**.

"Wouldn't I though? I'd have a stable full of Arabian steeds, rooms piled high with books, and I'd write out of a magic inkstand, so that my works should be as famous as Laurie's music. I want to do something splendid, something heroic or wonderful that won't be forgotten after I'm dead. I don't know what, but I'm on the watch for it, and mean to astonish you all some day. I think I shall write books, and get rich and famous, that would suit me, so that is my favorite dream."

"Mine is to stay at home safe with Father and Mother and help take care of the family," said Beth contentedly.

"Don't you wish for anything else?" asked Laurie.

"Since I had my little piano, I am perfectly satisfied. I only wish we may all keep well and be together, nothing else."

"I have ever so many wishes, but the pet one is to be an artist, and go to Rome, and do fine pictures, and be the best artist in the whole world," was Amy's modest desire.

"We're an **ambitious** set, aren't we? Every one of us, but Beth, wants to be rich and famous, and gorgeous in every respect. I do

Is Amy's wish really a "modest" one?

Vocabulary in Place

petulantly, *adv.* With a pout; in an unreasonably irritated manner

ambitious, *adj.* Full of high hopes or dreams of success

wonder if any of us will ever get our wishes," said Laurie, chewing a blade of grass.

"If we are all alive ten years hence, let's meet, and see how many of us have got our wishes, or how much nearer to them we are than now," said Jo, always ready with a plan.

"Bless me! How old I shall be, twenty-seven!" exclaimed Meg, who felt grown up already, having just reached seventeen.

"You and I will be twenty-six, Teddy,[2] Beth twenty-four, and Amy twenty-two," said Jo.

"I hope I shall have done something to be proud of by that time, but I'm such a lazy dog, I'm afraid I shall dawdle, Jo."

"You need a motive, Mother says, and when you get it, she is sure you'll work splendidly."

"Is she? By Jupiter, I will, if I only get the chance!" cried Laurie, sitting up with sudden energy. "I ought to be satisfied to please Grandfather, and I do try, but he wants me to be an India merchant,[3] as he was, and I'd rather be shot. I hate tea and silk and spices, and every sort of rubbish his old ships bring. Going to college ought to satisfy him. But he's set, and I've got to do just as he did. If there was anyone left to stay with the old gentleman, I'd break away and please myself, as my father did."

What does Laurie's grandfather want him to be when he grows up? What does Laurie think of this idea?

Laurie spoke excitedly, and looked ready to carry out his threat, for he had a young man's restless longing to try the world for himself.

"I advise you to sail away in one of your ships, and never come home again till you have tried your own way," said Jo, whose imagination was fired by the thought of such a daring **exploit**.

What does Jo tell Laurie to do? Does Meg agree with her?

"That's not right, Jo. You mustn't talk in that way, and Laurie mustn't take your bad advice. You should do just what your

---

[2] **Teddy.** A nickname for Laurie, whose real name is Theodore

[3] **India merchant.** One who buys and resells goods from India

Vocabulary in Place
exploit, *n.* Adventure, usually involving bravery or daring

grandfather wishes, my dear boy," said Meg in her most maternal tone. "As you say, there is no one else to stay with and love him, and you'd never forgive yourself if you left him. Don't fret, but do your duty and you'll get your reward, as good Mr. Brooke has, by being respected and loved."

"What do you know about him?" asked Laurie, grateful for the good advice but objecting to the lecture.

"Only what your grandpa told us about him, how he took good care of his own mother till she died, and wouldn't go abroad as a tutor because he wouldn't leave her. And how he provides now for an old woman who nursed his mother, and never tells anyone, but is just as generous and patient and good as he can be."

"So he is, dear old fellow!" said Laurie heartily, as Meg paused, looking flushed and earnest with her story. "It's like Grandpa to tell all his goodness to others, so that they might like him. If ever I do get my wish, you see what I'll do for Brooke."

"Begin to do something now by not plaguing his life out," said Meg sharply.

"How do you know I do, Miss?"

"I can always tell by his face when he goes away. If you have been good, he looks satisfied and walks briskly. If you have plagued him, he's sober and walks slowly, as if he wanted to go back and do his work better."

"So you keep an account of my good and bad marks in Brooke's face, do you? I see him bow and smile as he passes your window, but I didn't know you'd got up a telegraph."

"We haven't. Don't be angry, and oh, don't tell him I said anything! What is said here is said in confidence, you know," cried Meg, much alarmed.

"I don't tell tales," replied Laurie, with his "high and mighty" air, as Jo called it.

"Please don't be offended. We feel as if you were our brother and say just what we think. Forgive me, I meant it kindly." And Meg offered her hand with a gesture both affectionate and timid.

Ashamed of his momentary **pique**, Laurie squeezed the kind little hand, and said frankly, "I'm the one to be forgiven. I've been out of sorts all day. I like to have you tell me my faults and be sisterly, so don't mind if I am grumpy sometimes. I thank you all the same."

Bent on showing that he was not offended, he made himself as agreeable as possible, until the faint sound of a bell warned the party that it was time to get home to supper.

"May I come again?" asked Laurie.

"Yes, if you are good, and attend to your books," said Meg, smiling.

"I'll try."

That night, when Beth played to Mr. Laurence in the twilight, Laurie, standing in the shadow of the curtain, listened and watched the old man, who sat with his gray head on his hand, thinking tender thoughts of the dead child he had loved so much. Remembering the conversation of the afternoon, the boy said to himself, "I'll let my castle go, and stay with the dear old gentleman while he needs me, for I am all he has."

Why does Laurie decide to put his dream on hold? Who needs him?

Vocabulary in Place

pique, *n.* Slight temper tantrum or feeling of resentment or wounded pride, often in response to something that seems like an insult

CHAPTER 14

Secrets

Jo was very busy in the garret, for the October days began to grow chilly, and the afternoons were short. For two or three hours the sun lay warmly in the high window, showing Jo seated on the old sofa, writing busily, with her papers spread out upon a trunk before her, while Scrabble, the pet rat, promenaded the beams overhead, accompanied by his oldest son, a fine young fellow, who was evidently very proud of his whiskers. Quite absorbed in her work, Jo scribbled away till the last page was filled, when she signed her name with a flourish and threw down her pen, exclaiming . . .

"There, I've done my best! If this won't suit I shall have to wait till I can do better."

Lying back on the sofa, she read the manuscript[1] carefully through, making dashes here and there, and putting in many exclamation points. Then she tied it up with a smart red ribbon, and sat a minute looking at it with a serious, wistful expression, which plainly showed how earnest her work had been. Then she retrieved another manuscript from a tin cabinet that she used to store her books, paper, and ink.

As noiselessly as possible, she put on her hat and jacket, crept down the stairs, climbed out the back entry window and swung herself down to the grassy bank. Once she got to the road, she smoothed her dress, hailed a passing omnibus, and rolled away to town, looking very merry and mysterious.

What is Jo preparing in the garret?

---

[1] **manuscript.** An original draft or copy of an author's work, prepared and submitted for publication

Upon **alighting**, she went off at a great pace till she reached a certain number in a certain busy street. She went into the doorway, looked up the dirty stairs, and stood stock still a minute. Suddenly, she dived into the street and walked away as rapidly as she came. She repeated this **maneuver** several times, to the great amusement of a dark-eyed young gentleman lounging in the window of a building

> **Vocabulary in Place**
>
> **alight,** *v.* To step down from
>
> **maneuver,** *n.* A skillful or strategic movement, sometimes a bit tricky

opposite. On returning for the third time, Jo gave herself a shake, pulled her hat over her eyes, and walked up the stairs, looking as if she were going to have all her teeth out.

There was a dentist's sign, among others, above the entrance. The young gentleman put on his coat, took his hat, and went down to post himself beneath it, saying with a smile and a shiver, "It's like her to come alone, but if she has a bad time she'll need someone to help her home."

In ten minutes, Jo came running downstairs with a very red face, looking as if she had just passed through a trying ordeal of some sort. When she saw the young gentleman she looked displeased, and passed him with a nod. But he followed, asking with sympathy, "Did you have a bad time?"

"Not very."

"Why did you go alone?"

"Didn't want anyone to know."

"You're the oddest fellow I ever saw. How many did you have out?"

Jo looked at her friend as if she did not understand him, then began to laugh mightily.

"There are two which I want to have come out, but I must wait a week."

"What are you laughing at? You are up to some mischief, Jo," said Laurie, looking **mystified.**

"So are you. What were you doing, sir, up in that billiard saloon?"

"Begging your pardon, ma'am, it wasn't a billiard saloon, but a gymnasium, and I was taking a lesson in fencing."

"I'm glad of that."

"Why?"

"I'm glad that you were not in the saloon, because I hope you never go to such places. Do you?"

"Not often."

"I wish you wouldn't."

Who is waiting outside for Jo? Where does he think that she has been?

Vocabulary in Place

mystify, *v.* To confuse or puzzle; to make mysterious

"It's no harm, Jo. I have billiards at home, but it's no fun unless you have good players, so I come sometimes and have a game with Ned Moffat or some of the other fellows."

"Oh, dear, I'm so sorry, for you will waste time and money, and grow like those dreadful boys. I did hope you'd stay respectable and be a satisfaction to your friends," said Jo, shaking her head.

Laurie walked in silence a few minutes, and Jo watched him, wishing she had held her tongue, for his eyes looked angry, though his lips smiled as if at her warnings.

"Are you going to deliver lectures all the way home?" he asked presently.

"Of course not. Why?"

"If you're not, I'd like to walk with you and tell you something very interesting."

"I won't preach any more, and I'd like to hear the news immensely."

"Very well, then. It's a secret, and if I tell you, you must tell me yours."

"I haven't got any," began Jo, but stopped suddenly, remembering that she had.

"You know you have—you can't hide anything, so up and 'fess, or I won't tell," cried Laurie.

"You'll not say anything about it at home, will you?"

"Not a word."

What is Jo's secret?

"Well, I've left two stories with a newspaperman, and he's to give his answer next week," whispered Jo, in her confidant's ear.

"Hurrah for Miss March, the celebrated American authoress!" cried Laurie, throwing up his hat and catching it again.

"Hush! It won't come to anything, I dare say, but I couldn't rest till I had tried. I said nothing about it because I didn't want anyone else to be disappointed."

Why hasn't she told anyone about it?

"It won't fail. Why, Jo, your stories are works of Shakespeare compared to half the rubbish that is published every day. Won't it be fun to see them in print?"

Jo's eyes sparkled, for it is always pleasant to be believed in.

"Where's your secret, Teddy?" she said, trying to extinguish the brilliant hopes that blazed up at a word of encouragement.

"I may get into a scrape for telling, but . . . I know where Meg's glove is."

"Is that all?" said Jo, looking disappointed, as Laurie nodded and his eyes twinkled mysteriously. "Tell, then."

Laurie bent, and whispered three words in Jo's ear. She stood and stared at him for a minute, looking both surprised and displeased, then walked on, saying sharply, "How do you know?"

"Saw it."

"Where?"

"Pocket."

"All this time?"

"Yes, isn't that romantic?"

"No, it's horrid. It's ridiculous. My patience! What would Meg say? I wish you hadn't told me."

"I thought you'd be pleased."

"At the idea of anybody coming to take Meg away? No, thank you."

"You'll feel better about it when somebody comes to take you away."

"I'd like to see anyone try it," cried Jo fiercely.

"So should I!" and Laurie chuckled at the idea.

To help cure Jo's bad temper, Laurie challenged her to a race. As no one was in sight and the smooth road sloped so invitingly before her, she darted away, scattering hat, comb and hairpins as she ran. Laurie reached the goal first and Jo came panting up behind with flying hair, bright eyes, and ruddy cheeks. Laurie went to recover the lost property, and Jo bundled up her braids, hoping no one would pass by till she was tidy again, but someone did pass. And who should it be but Meg, looking particularly ladylike in her best suit.

"What in the world are you doing here?" she asked, regarding her **disheveled** sister with surprise. "You have been running, Jo.

How does Jo react to Laurie's secret?

What does Jo mean in saying that someone might "take Meg away"?

Vocabulary in Place
disheveled, *adj.* Untidy or sloppy; out of order

Why is Meg scolding Jo this time? Will Jo ever grow up to be a lady?

How could you? When will you stop such romping ways?" said Meg reprovingly.

"Never till I'm stiff and old and have to use a crutch. Don't try to make me grow up before my time, Meg," said Jo, thinking just how grown up her sister was becoming.

Drawing Meg's attention from Jo's troubled face, Laurie asked quickly, "Where have you been calling, all so fine?"

"At the Gardiners'. Sallie has been telling me all about Belle Moffat's splendid wedding. They have gone to spend the winter in Paris. Just think how delightful that must be! I'm afraid I envy her terribly."

"I'm glad of it!" muttered Jo, tying on her hat with a jerk.

"Why?" asked Meg, looking surprised.

"Because if you care about riches, you will never go and marry a poor man," said Jo, frowning at Laurie, whose expression warned her to mind what she said.

"I shall never 'go and marry' anyone," observed Meg, walking on with great dignity while the others followed, laughing, skipping stones, and "behaving like children," as Meg said to herself.

For a week or two, Jo behaved so strangely that her sisters were quite bewildered. She rushed to the door when the postman rang, was rude to Mr. Brooke whenever they met, and stared sadly at Meg, who, as she sat sewing at her window, was scandalized by the sight of Laurie chasing Jo all over the garden and finally capturing her. What went on there, Meg could not see, but shrieks of laughter were heard, followed by the murmur of voices and a great flapping of newspapers.

"What shall we do with that girl? She never will behave like a young lady," sighed Meg, as she watched the race with a disapproving face.

"I hope she won't. She is so funny and dear as she is," said Beth, who had never betrayed that she was a little hurt at Jo's having secrets with anyone but her.

"It's very trying, but we never can make her *commy la fo*,"[2] added Amy, who sat making some new frills for herself, with her curls tied

---

2 **commy la fo.** Amy's attempt at the French phrase *comme il faut,* meaning "as it should be"

up in a very becoming way, two agreeable things that made her feel unusually elegant and ladylike.

In a few minutes Jo bounced in, laid herself on the sofa, and pretended to read.

"Have you anything interesting there?" asked Meg, with **condescension.**

"Nothing but a story," returned Jo, carefully keeping the name of the paper out of sight.

"What's the name?" asked Beth, wondering why Jo kept her face behind the sheet.

"The Rival Painters."

"That sounds well. Read it," said Meg.

With a loud "Hem!" and a long breath, Jo began to read very fast. The girls listened with interest, for the tale was romantic and tragic.

"I like that about the splendid picture," was Amy's approving remark, as Jo paused.

"I prefer the 'lovering' part.[3] Viola and Angelo are two of our favorite names, isn't that queer?" said Meg, wiping her eyes, for the lovering part was quite sad.

"Who wrote it?" asked Beth, who had caught a glimpse of Jo's face.

Who wrote the story?

The reader suddenly sat up, cast away the paper, displaying a flushed face, and replied in a loud voice, "Your sister."

"You?" cried Meg, dropping her work.

"It's very good," said Amy critically.

"I knew it! I knew it! Oh, my Jo, I am so proud!" and Beth ran to hug her sister.

Dear me, how delighted they all were, to be sure! How proud Mrs. March was when she knew it. Hannah came in to exclaim,

---

[3] **lovering part.** The part of the story involving love

Vocabulary in Place
condescension, *n.* The act of descending to the level of an inferior or looking down upon someone

"Sakes alive, well I never!" in great astonishment. Jo laughed, with tears in her eyes, as she declared she might as well be a peacock.

"Tell us about it."

"Stop jabbering, girls, and I'll tell you everything," said Jo. Having told how she disposed of her tales, Jo added, "And when I went to get my answer, the man said he liked them both, but didn't pay beginners, only let them print in his paper. It was good practice, he said, and when the beginners improved, anyone would pay. So I let him have the two stories, and today this was sent to me, and Laurie caught me with it and insisted on seeing it, so I let him. And he said it was good, and I shall write more, and he's going to get the next paid for. I am so happy, for in time I may be able to support myself and help the girls."

Jo's breath gave out here, and wrapping her head in the paper, she wet her little story with a few tears, for to be independent and earn the praise of those she loved were the dearest wishes of her heart, and this seemed to be the first step toward that happy end.

What did the newspaper editor say about Jo's work, and why is she so happy about it?

Understanding the Selection

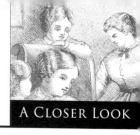

A CLOSER LOOK

Recalling (just the facts)

1. What must one do to join the "Busy Bee Society"? What kind of project is each sister doing when Laurie arrives?
2. What is each sister's favorite dream, or "castle in the air"? What would each one like to be doing ten years from now?
3. Is Jo nervous when she takes her work to the newspaper editor? What is the editor's opinion of her work?
4. How does Jo react when Laurie tells her that Mr. Brooke has Meg's other glove?

Interpreting (delving deeper)

1. Why does Beth say that the real countryside is nice, but she wishes that "the beautiful country up there" were real, and that they could go to it?
2. What do the distant mountains glowing in the sunset represent? Why does Jo say that they hope to live there someday?
3. What is Laurie's favorite "castle in the air"? Why does he say that he would "rather be shot" than go into the family business when he grows up?
4. Is Jo happy that her sister has a boyfriend? Why or why not?

Synthesizing (putting it all together)

1. After graduating college, what would Laurie rather do in place of going into the family business? What does this tell you about the way he feels about Mr. Laurence?
2. What is Jo's dream? Is she willing to put her dream on hold, or is she already on her way to accomplishing her goals? Use examples from the story to support your answer.

Writing

Reflection. In Chapter 13, Jo, her sisters, and Laurie talk about their hopes and dreams for the future as they gaze at a beautiful mountain range in the sunset. Alcott describes the mountains on the horizon as "silvery white peaks that shone like the airy spires of some Celestial City." This lofty image echoes Jo's wish that someday all their "castles in the air" will come to life.

Everyone has hopes and dreams. Some of these hopes and dreams relate to the short term—things you hope to achieve or accomplish in the next month or year. But how do you think about life ten or even twenty years from now? In Chapter 14, Jo complains about Meg's criticism of her supposed unladylike behavior by saying "Don't try to make me grow up before my time, Meg." On the other hand, Jo has a very clear vision of at least one of her dreams: she wants to be a published writer, and she takes decisive steps in Chapter 14 toward achieving this goal.

What are your hopes and dreams? In a journal or diary, describe your favorite "castle in the air." What do you wish you could be doing ten years from now? What do you think you need to do in order to reach those "castles"?

These are your personal thoughts, so there is no need to share them with anyone else unless you wish to do so. It might be fun, however, to look back at the thoughts in your journal in a few years, as Jo suggests. Where do you think you might be by then?

Language Alive!

EXTENSIONS

Prefixes, Suffixes, and Roots. Has anyone ever suggested to you that taking vitamins is vital to revitalizing your vitality? Probably not! However, if one did, he or she would be using no less than four words containing the same root: *vita*. In Latin, *vita* means *life*. If you add *re-* (which means *back* or *again* in Latin) to the beginning of the root, you get *revitalize*, or "bring back to life." When you add *-ity—the state of*—then you get *vitality*, or the state of having (or being full of) life.

A **root** is the smallest unit of a word, and it carries the word's main meaning. In the examples given in the paragraph above, *re-* and *-ity* are known as **affixes**, which are things you attach to the root. Specifically *re-* is a **prefix**, which comes at the beginning of a word. (*Prefix* starts with the prefix **pre-**, or "before," which is a common prefix in the English language; just remember, before kindergarten, some children attend *pre*-kindergarten.) A **suffix**, such as *-ity*, is an affix at the end of a word.

Root, affix, prefix, suffix—these words may seem strange or confusing, but their meanings are very important. If you learn to recognize common roots and affixes then you will have a much easier time figuring out the meanings of unfamiliar words when you are reading or taking tests.

Often, the roots of English words come from other languages, particularly Greek and Latin. For example, the Latin root *spirare*, meaning "to breathe," comes into English as *spir*, a root within such words as *inspire*, *expire*, and *perspire*. When you in**spir**e someone, you "breathe life" into them. When something ex**spir**es, its breath has gone out, meaning that it has ended. When you per**spir**e, you breathe through your skin, or sweat. So, the basic meanings of root words and affixes do not change, but—depending on which prefixes and suffixes are attached to the root—there are many ways to use and interpret those meanings.

Consider the word *condescension*, which appears on page 159 of *Little Women*. This word is composed of a definite prefix, root, and suffix, all of which are common in English. The prefix *con-* means "with"; the root *scend* means "climb"; and the suffix *-sion* is "an action or instance of something." (The suffixes *-sion* and *-tion* have the same meaning and are among the most common suffixes in English; examples include *demonstration, cancellation, expansion, admission,* and *infection*.)

171

Language Alive!

The following are some important prefixes and their meanings. You should know or commit these to memory. Copy each prefix onto a separate sheet of paper and write at least one word that begins with that prefix. (Try to think of a word on your own; if you are unable to think of a word, use a dictionary.)

anti-	opposing		co-	together, jointly
dis-	not, apart		en-	to put into
fore-	earlier or in front of		il-	not
in-	not		inter-	between, among
mid-	middle		mis-	bad, wrong
non-	not		post-	after or behind
pre-	before		re-	again or back
semi-	partial		un-	reverse or undo

The following are some important suffixes and their meanings. Again, copy each suffix onto a separate sheet of paper and write at least one word that ends with that suffix.

-able	capable of		-er	shows comparison
-ful	full of		-ible	inclined to
-ily	makes a word an adverb		-ish	characteristic of
-ist	one that performs an action		-less	without, lacking
-ly	like, resembling		-ment	action
-ness	state or degree of		-tion	expresses action or meaning

Also on a separate sheet of paper, identify and define the prefixes and or suffixes used in the list of words below. Make an educated guess as to the meaning of the roots.

contentedly
discontented
sociable
enticement
delectable

resolve
remorseful
indignantly
exultation
artfully

CHAPTER 15

A Telegram

"November is the most disagreeable month in the whole year," said Meg, standing at the window one dull afternoon, looking out at the frostbitten garden.

"That's the reason I was born in it," observed Jo pensively, quite unconscious of the blot on her nose.

"If something very pleasant should happen now, we should think it a delightful month," said Beth, who took a hopeful view of everything, even November. "And two pleasant things are going to happen right away. Marmee is coming down the street, and Laurie is tramping through the garden as if he had something nice to tell."

In they both came, Mrs. March with her usual question, "Any letter from Father, girls?" and Laurie to say in his persuasive way, "Won't some of you come for a drive? It's a dull day, but the air isn't bad, and I'm going to take Brooke home."

"Much obliged, but I'm busy." And Meg whisked out her workbasket, for she had agreed with her mother that it was best, for her at least, not to drive too often with the young gentleman.

"Come, Jo, you and Beth will go, won't you?"

"Of course we will."

"We three will be ready in a minute," cried Amy, running to get ready.

"Can I do anything for you, Madam Mother?" asked Laurie, leaning over Mrs. March's chair with the affectionate look and tone he always gave her.

"No, thank you, except call at the post office, if you'll be so kind, dear. Father's letter hasn't arrived and they're usually as regular as the sun, but there's some delay on the way, perhaps."

A sharp ring interrupted her, and a minute after Hannah came in with a letter.

Why is it best for Meg that she not go for a ride with Laurie?

"It's one of them horrid telegraph things, mum," she said, handling it as if she was afraid it would explode and do some damage.

At the word "telegraph," Mrs. March snatched it, read the two lines it contained, and dropped back into her chair as white as if the little paper had sent a bullet to her heart. Laurie dashed for water, while Meg and Hannah supported her, and Jo read aloud, in a frightened voice . . .

> Mrs. March:
> Your husband is very ill. Come at once.
> S. HALE
> Blank Hospital, Washington.

How does Mrs. March react to the telegram?

How still the room was as they listened breathlessly, how strangely the day darkened outside, and how suddenly the whole world seemed to change. The girls gathered about their mother, feeling as if all the happiness and support of their lives was about to be taken from them.

Mrs. March read the message over, and stretched out her arms to her daughters, saying, in a tone they never forgot, "I shall go at once, but it may be too late. Oh, children, children, help me to bear it!"

In what tone does Mrs. March speak? What will she do?

For several minutes there was nothing but the sound of sobbing in the room, mingled with broken words of comfort, tender assurances, and hopeful whispers that died away in tears. Poor Hannah was the first to recover. She set all the rest a good example, for with her, work was the cure for most afflictions.

"The Lord keep the dear man! I won't waste no time a-cryin', but git your things ready right away, mum," she said heartily, as she wiped her face on her apron and went away to work like three women in one.

"She's right, there's no time for tears now. Be calm, girls, and let me think."

They tried to be calm as their mother sat up, looking pale but steady, and put away her grief to think and plan for them.

"Where's Laurie?" she asked presently, when she had collected her thoughts.

"Here, ma'am. Oh, let me do something!" cried the boy, hurrying from the next room whither he had withdrawn, feeling that their first sorrow was too sacred for even his friendly eyes to see.

"Send a telegram saying I will come at once. The next train goes early in the morning. I'll take that."

"What else? The horses are ready. I can go anywhere, do anything," he said, looking ready to fly to the ends of the earth.

"Leave a note at Aunt March's. Jo, give me that pen and paper."

Tearing off the blank side of one of her newly copied pages, Jo drew the table before her mother, well knowing that money for the long, sad journey must be borrowed, and feeling as if she could do anything to add a little to the sum for her father.

"Now go, dear, but don't kill yourself driving at a desperate pace; there is no need of that."

Mrs. March's warning was evidently thrown away, for five minutes later Laurie tore by the window on his own swift horse, riding as if for his life.

Why does Mrs. March need a pen and paper? Where will they get money for the journey?

"Jo, run to the rooms, and tell Mrs. King that I won't be coming to help for a while. On the way, get these things. I must go prepared for nursing. Hospital stores are not always good. Beth, go and ask Mr. Laurence for a couple of bottles of old wine. I'm not too proud to beg for Father. Amy, tell Hannah to get down the black trunk, and Meg, come and help me find my things."

Writing, thinking, and directing all at once left the poor lady a bit bewildered, and Meg begged her to sit quietly in her room for a little while, and let them work. Everyone scattered like leaves before a gust of wind, and the quiet, happy household was broken up as suddenly as if the paper had been an evil spell.

Mr. Laurence came hurrying back with Beth, bringing every comfort the kind old gentleman could think of for the invalid, from his own dressing gown to himself as escort. But the last was impossible; Mrs. March would not hear of the old gentleman's undertaking the long journey, yet a look of relief crossed her face when he mentioned it, making it clear what comfort a companion would be. He saw the look, knit his heavy eyebrows, and marched abruptly away, saying he'd be back directly. No one had time to think

Would Mrs. March like to have a companion?

of him again till, as Meg ran through the entry, a cup of tea in hand, she came suddenly upon Mr. Brooke.

"I'm very sorry to hear of this, Miss March," he said, in the kind, quiet tone that soothed her **perturbed** spirit. "I came to offer myself as escort to your mother. Mr. Laurence has commissions for me in Washington, and it will give me real satisfaction to be of service to her there."

> Who will escort Mrs. March?

The tea nearly dropped to the floor, as Meg put out her hand, with a face so full of gratitude that Mr. Brooke would have felt repaid for a much greater sacrifice than the one he was about to take.

"How kind you all are! Mother will accept, I'm sure, and it will be such a relief to know that she has someone to take care of her. Thank you very, very much!" Meg spoke earnestly, and forgot herself entirely till she remembered the cooling tea, and led the way into the parlor.

Soon Laurie returned with a note from Aunt March, enclosing the requested sum, and a few lines repeating what she had often said before, that it was absurd for March to go into the army and she hoped they would take her advice the next time. Mrs. March put the note in the fire, the money in her purse, and went on with her preparations, with her lips folded tightly.

> Why does Mrs. March burn the note from Aunt March?

The short afternoon wore away. All other errands were done, but still Jo did not come. They began to get anxious, and Laurie went off to find her, for no one knew what freak idea Jo might take into her head. He missed her, however, and she came walking in with a very queer expression. There was a mixture of fun and fear, satisfaction and regret in it, which puzzled the family as much as did the roll of bills she laid before her mother. With a little choke in her voice she said, "That's my contribution toward making Father comfortable and bringing him home!"

Vocabulary in Place

perturbed, *adj.* Troubled or upset

"My dear, where did you get it? Twenty-five dollars! Jo, I hope you haven't done anything **rash**?"

"No, it's mine honestly. I didn't beg, borrow, or steal it. I earned it, for I only sold what was my own."

As she spoke, Jo took off her bonnet, and a general outcry arose, for all her abundant hair was cut short.

"Your hair! Your beautiful hair! Oh, Jo, how could you? Your one beauty. My dear girl, there was no need of this!" cried Mrs. March.

How did Jo earn the money?

Everyone exclaimed, and Beth hugged the cropped head tenderly. Jo assumed an **indifferent** air which did not deceive anyone a particle, and said, rumpling up the brown bush and trying to look as if she liked it, "It doesn't affect the fate of the nation, so don't wail, Beth. It will be good for my vanity, I was getting too proud of my mane. My head feels deliciously light and cool, and the barber said I could soon have a curly crop, which will be boyish, **becoming,** and easy to keep in order. I'm satisfied, so please take the money and let's have supper."

"I am not quite satisfied, Jo, but I can't blame you, for I know you willingly sacrificed your vanity, as you call it, out of love. But, my dear, it was not necessary, and I'm afraid you will regret it one of these days," said Mrs. March.

"No, I won't!" returned Jo stoutly, feeling much relieved that she was not entirely condemned.

"What made you do it?" asked Amy, who would as soon have thought of cutting off her head as her pretty hair.

"Well, I was wild to do something for Father," replied Jo, as they gathered about the table. "I passed by a barber's window and saw tails of hair with the prices marked, and one black tail, not so thick as mine, was forty dollars. It came to me all of a sudden that I had

---

Vocabulary in Place

rash, *adj.* Reckless or done in a hurry, without much thought; impulsive or foolish

indifferent, *adj.* Without care or concern

becoming, *adj.* Appropriately attractive

one thing to make money out of, so I walked in, asked if they bought hair, and what they would give for mine."

"I don't see how you dared to do it," said Beth in a tone of awe.

"At first he expressed no interest. He said my hair wasn't the fashionable color, and he never paid much for it in the first place. The work put into it made it dear, and so on. So I begged him to take it, and told him why I was in such a hurry. It was silly, I dare say, but it changed his mind, for his wife heard, and said so kindly, 'Take it, Thomas, and oblige the young lady. I'd do as much for our Jimmy any day if I had a spire of hair worth selling.'"

"Who was Jimmy?" asked Amy.

"Her son, she said, who was in the army. How friendly such things make strangers feel, don't they? She talked away all the time the man clipped, to distract my mind."

"Didn't you feel dreadfully when the first cut came?" asked Meg, with a shiver.

"I took a last look at my hair while the man got his things, and that was the end of it. I never snivel over trifles like that. I will confess, though, I felt queer when I saw the dear old hair laid out on the table—as if I'd an arm or leg off. The woman saw me look at it, and picked out a long lock for me to keep. I'll give it to you, Marmee, just to remember past glories by, for a crop is so comfortable I don't think I shall ever have a mane again."

Mrs. March folded the wavy chestnut lock, and laid it away with a short gray one in her desk. She only said, "Thank you, deary," but something in her face made the girls change the subject, and talk as cheerfully as they could about Mr. Brooke's kindness, and the happy times they would have when Father came home to be nursed.

When the last job was finished, Mrs. March said, "Come girls." Beth went to the piano and played Father's favorite hymn. All began bravely but broke down one by one till Beth was left alone, singing with all her heart.

"Go to bed and don't talk, for we must be up early and shall need all the sleep we can get. Good night, my darlings," said Mrs. March, as the hymn ended, for no one cared to try another.

What changed the barber's mind?

Does Jo regret her decision?

They kissed her quietly and went to bed. Beth and Amy soon fell asleep in spite of the great trouble, but Meg lay awake, thinking the most serious thoughts she had ever known in her short life. Jo lay motionless and seemed to be asleep, till a stifled sob made Meg exclaim,

"Jo, dear, what is it? Are you crying about Father?"

"No, not now."

"What then?"

"My . . . My hair!" burst out poor Jo, trying vainly to smother her emotion in the pillow.

Meg kissed and caressed the afflicted heroine in the tenderest manner.

"I'd do it again tomorrow, if I could," protested Jo, with a choke. "It's only the vain part of me that cries in this silly way. Don't tell anyone. I thought you were asleep, so I just made a little private moan for my one beauty. How came you to be awake?"

"I can't sleep, I'm so anxious," said Meg.

"Think about something pleasant, and you'll soon drop off."

"I tried it but felt wider awake than ever."

"What did you think of?"

"Handsome faces—eyes particularly," answered Meg, smiling to herself in the dark.

Jo laughed, and Meg sharply ordered her not to talk, then amiably promised to make her hair curl, and fell asleep to dream of living in her castle in the air.

The clocks were striking midnight as Mrs. March glided quietly from bed to bed, smoothing a coverlet here, settling a pillow there, and pausing to look long and tenderly at each unconscious face, to kiss each with lips that silently blessed, and to pray the fervent prayers that only mothers utter. As she lifted the curtain to look out into the dreary night, the moon broke suddenly from behind the clouds and shone upon her like a bright, benignant[1] face, which seemed to whisper in the silence, "Be comforted, dear soul! There is always light behind the clouds."

---

[1] **benignant.** Kind and gracious

Why is Jo crying?

What does Marmee see when she looks out the window?

Words to Keep

The following sentences contain important words from the Vocabulary in Place boxes in Chapters 12–15 of *Little Women*. In your notebook, or on a separate sheet of paper, write the part of speech of each boldface word, a synonym (or a short definition in your own words), and a new sentence of your own.

1. The newborn calf appeared **lame** at first, but he soon gained his feet.
2. They put everyone at ease by giving them a **cordial** welcome at the door.
3. As they were twins, Amy and Mike had many **skirmishes** over small matters, like who would sit in the front seat of the car.
4. The team accepted the championship trophy amidst wild cheering and **exultation** from their fans.
5. Now that she wasn't a little girl anymore, she found her older brother's **patronizing** tone hard to take.
6. The tragic story began with the main character's **lament** about the loss of a loved one.
7. After saying a few **impromptu** remarks, she began her prepared speech.
8. Fortunately, it was only an **amicable** game, because our team was utterly beaten.
9. "Come on over when you get a chance," **beckoned** her neighbor from the garden.
10. The big puppy jumped up on everyone and had not yet learned to be **submissive** to his owner.
11. We had to go somewhere after school, so my mother asked me not to **dawdle** on the way home.
12. Napoleon's invasion of Russia was too **ambitious**, and it proved to be his undoing.
13. We always enjoyed hearing about his daring **exploit** climbing Mt. Everest.
14. Jill was **mystified** by the many buttons on the remote control, but she finally figured out how to turn the power off.
15. Her hair always looked a bit **disheveled** after she rode in the convertible.
16. When he got to the unmarked fork in the trail for the second time in an hour, he stopped, **bewildered** about where to go next.
17. Although she hadn't finished her story, he turned and **abruptly** walked away.
18. She was **perturbed** that she hadn't heard from him for a while.

CHAPTER 16

Letters

Everything seemed very strange the next morning, when the girls went down for an early breakfast. It was so dim and still outside, so full of light and bustle within. Breakfast at that early hour seemed odd, and even Hannah's familiar face looked unnatural as she flew about her kitchen with her nightcap on. The big trunk stood ready in the hall, Marmee's cloak and bonnet lay on the sofa, and Marmee herself sat trying to eat but looking so pale and worn with sleeplessness and anxiety that the girls found it very hard to keep their resolution to give her a cheerful send off. Meg's eyes kept filling in spite of herself, Jo had to hide her face more than once, and the little girls wore grave, troubled expressions.

Nobody talked much as the time for Marmee's departure drew near. The girls busied themselves, one folding her shawl, another smoothing out the strings of her bonnet, a third putting on her overshoes, and a fourth fastening up her travelling bag. When all was ready and they sat waiting for the carriage, Mrs. March said to the girls . . .

"Children, I leave you to Hannah's care and Mr. Laurence's protection. Don't grieve and fret when I am gone. Go on with your work as usual, for work is a blessed **solace**. Hope and keep busy, and whatever happens, remember that you never can be fatherless."

"Yes, Mother."

"Meg, dear, watch over your sisters, consult Hannah, and if you have any troubles, go to Mr. Laurence. Be patient, Jo, don't get **despondent**, write to me often, and be my brave girl, ready to

---

Vocabulary in Place

solace, *n.* Source of comfort, especially in difficult circumstances

despondent, *adj.* Hopeless or very depressed

> **What are Marmee's instructions to her daughters right before she leaves?**

help and cheer all. Beth, comfort yourself with your music, and be faithful to the little home duties; And you, Amy, help all you can, be obedient, and keep happy and safe at home."

"We will, Mother! We will!"

When the carriage approached, no one cried or ran away, though their hearts were very heavy. They sent loving messages to Father, remembering as they spoke that it might be too late to deliver them. They kissed their mother quietly, clung about her tenderly, and tried to wave their hands cheerfully when she drove away.

Laurie and his grandfather came over to see her off, and Mr. Brooke looked so strong and sensible and kind that the girls christened him "Mr. Greatheart"[1] on the spot.

"Goodbye, my darlings! God bless and keep us all!" whispered Mrs. March, as she kissed the dear little faces and hurried into the carriage.

As she rolled away, the sun came out, and looking back, she saw it shining on the group at the gate like a good **omen**. They saw it also, and smiled and waved their hands. The last thing Mrs. March **beheld** as she turned the corner was the four bright faces, and behind them like a bodyguard, old Mr. Laurence, faithful Hannah, and devoted Laurie.

"How kind everyone is to us!" she said, turning to find fresh proof of it in the young man's sympathetic face.

"I don't see how they can help it," returned Mr. Brooke, laughing so that Mrs. March could not help smiling.

> **What are the signs that Marmee's journey will go well?**

And so the journey began with the good omens of sunshine, smiles, and cheerful words.

---

[1] **Mr. Greatheart.** A character in *Pilgrim's Progress* who serves as a guide for Christian's wife, Christiana, their children, and a neighbor

Vocabulary in Place
omen, *n.* Sign of the outcome of future events
behold, *v.* To see or view something

"I feel as if there had been an earthquake," said Jo, as their neighbors went home to breakfast, leaving them to rest and refresh themselves.

"It seems as if half the house was gone," added Meg sadly.

Beth opened her lips to say something, but could only point to the pile of nicely mended stockings which lay on Mother's table, showing that even in her last hurried moments she had thought and worked for them. It was a little thing, but it went straight to their hearts, and in spite of their brave resolutions, they all broke down and cried bitterly.

When the tears showed signs of clearing up, Hannah came to the rescue, armed with a coffeepot. "Now, my dear young ladies, remember what your ma said, and don't fret. Come and have a cup of coffee all round, and then let's fall to work and be a credit to the family."

Coffee was a treat, and they drew up to the table, exchanged their handkerchiefs for napkins, and in ten minutes were all right again.

"'Hope and keep busy,' that's the motto for us, so let's see who will remember it best. I shall go to Aunt March, as usual. Oh, won't she lecture though!" said Jo.

"I shall go to my Kings," said Meg, wishing she hadn't made her eyes so red.

"Hannah will tell us what to do, and we'll have everything nice when you come home," added Beth, getting out her mop and dish tub without delay.

When the older two went out to their daily tasks, they looked sorrowfully back at the window where they were accustomed to see their mother's face. It was gone, but Beth's was there, nodding away at them faithfully.

"That's so like my Beth!" said Jo, waving her hat, with a grateful face. "Goodbye, Meggy, I hope the Kings won't strain today," she added, as they parted.

"And I hope Aunt March won't trouble you. Your hair is becoming, and it looks very boyish and nice," returned Meg, trying not to smile at the curly head.

Soon the girls received news that comforted them very much, for though dangerously ill, their father was already much improved.

What does Hannah want them to do? Why?

Mr. Brooke sent a **bulletin** every day, which grew more cheerful as the weeks passed. At first, everyone was eager to write, and plump envelopes were carefully poked into the letter box by one or other of the sisters, who felt rather important with their Washington correspondence.

As one of these packets contained characteristic notes from the party, we will rob an imaginary mail, and read them.

My dearest Mother:

It is impossible to tell you how happy your last letter made us, for the news was so good we couldn't help laughing and crying over it. How very kind Mr. Brooke is, and how fortunate that Mr. Laurence's business keeps him near you so long, since he is so useful to you and Father. The girls are all as good as gold. Jo helps me with the sewing, and insists on doing all sorts of hard jobs. I should be afraid she might overdo, if I didn't know that this burst of acting wouldn't last long. Beth is as regular about her tasks as a clock, and never forgets what you told her. She grieves about Father, and looks serious except when she is at her little piano. Amy minds me nicely, and I take great care of her. She does her own hair, and I am teaching her to make buttonholes and mend her stockings. She tries very hard, and I know you will be pleased with her improvement when you come home. Mr. Laurence watches over us like a motherly old hen, as Jo says, and Laurie is very kind and neighborly. He and Jo keep us merry, for we get pretty blue sometimes, and feel like orphans, with you so far away. Hannah is a perfect saint. She does not scold at all, and always calls me Miss Margaret, which is quite proper, you know, and treats me with respect. We are all well and busy, but we long, day and night, to have you back. Give my dearest love to Father, and believe me, ever your own . . .

MEG

Vocabulary in Place

bulletin, *n.* A brief report or update of current news

This note, prettily written on scented paper, was a great contrast to the next, which was scribbled on a big sheet of thin foreign paper, ornamented with blots and all manner of stylish curly-tailed letters.

My precious Marmee:

Three cheers for dear Father! Brooke was a trump to telegraph right off, and let us know the minute he was better. I rushed up to the garret when the letter came, and tried to thank God for being so good to us, but I could only cry, and say, "I'm glad! I'm glad!" Didn't that do as well as a regular prayer? For I felt a great many in my heart. We have such funny times, and now I can enjoy them, for everyone is so desperately good, it's like living in a nest of turtledoves. You'd laugh to see Meg head the table and try to be motherish. She gets prettier every day and the children are regular archangels, and I—well, I'm Jo, and never shall be anything else. Oh, I must tell you that I came near having a quarrel with Laurie. I freed my mind about a silly little thing, and he was offended. I was right, but didn't speak as I ought, and he marched home, saying he wouldn't come again till I begged pardon. I declared I wouldn't and got mad. It lasted all day. I felt bad and wanted you very much. Laurie and I are both so proud, it's hard to beg pardon. But I thought he'd come to it, for I was in the right. He didn't come, and just at night I remembered what you said when Amy fell into the river. I read my little book, felt better, resolved not to let the sun set on my anger, and ran over to tell Laurie I was sorry. I met him at the gate, coming for the same thing. We both laughed, begged each other's pardon, and felt all good and comfortable again.

I made a "pome" yesterday, when I was helping Hannah wash, and as Father likes my silly little things, I put it in to amuse him. Give him my lovingest hug that ever was, and kiss yourself a dozen times for your . . .

TOPSY-TURVY JO
A SONG FROM THE SUDS

Queen of my tub, I merrily sing,
While the white foam rises high,
And sturdily wash and rinse and wring,
And fasten the clothes to dry.
Then out in the free fresh air they swing,
Under the sunny sky.

What trait do Laurie and Jo share?

> *What activity provides the basis for Jo's poem?*

I wish we could wash from out hearts and souls
The stains of the week away,
And let water and air by their magic make
Ourselves as pure as they.
Then on the earth there would be indeed,
A glorious washing day!

Along the path of a useful life,
Will heart's ease ever bloom.
The busy mind has no time to think
Of sorrow or care or gloom.
And anxious thoughts may be swept away,
As we bravely wield a broom.

I am glad a task to me is given,
To labor at day by day,
For it brings me health and strength and hope,
And I cheerfully learn to say,
"Head, you may think, Heart, you may feel,
But, Hand, you shall work alway!"

Dear Mother,

There is only room for me to send my love, and some pressed pansies from the root I have been keeping safe in the house for Father to see. I read every morning, try to be good all day, and sing myself to sleep with Father's tune. I can't sing "Land of the Leal" now, it makes me cry. Everyone is very kind, and we are as happy as we can be without you. Amy wants the rest of the page, so I must stop. I didn't forget to cover the holders, and I wind the clock and air the rooms every day.

Kiss dear Father on the cheek he calls mine. Oh, do come soon to your loving . . .

LITTLE BETH

Ma Chère Mamma,

We are all well. I do my lessons always and never corroborate *the girls*—*Meg says I mean* contradikt *so I put in both words and you can take the properest. Meg is a great comfort to me and lets me have jelly every night at tea. Its so good for me, Jo says, because it keeps me sweet tempered. Laurie is not as* respeckful *as he ought to be now I am almost in my teens. He calls me Chick and hurts my feelings by talking French to me very fast when I say Merci or Bon jour as Hattie King does. The sleeves of my blue dress were all worn out, and Meg put in new ones, but the full front came wrong and they are more blue than the dress. I felt bad but did not fret I bear my troubles well but I do wish Hannah would put more starch in my aprons and have buckwheats every day. Can't she? Didn't I make that interrogation point[2] nice? Meg says my punchtuation and spelling are disgraceful and I am* mortyfied[3] *but dear me I have so many things to do, I can't stop. Adieu, I send heaps of love to Papa. Your affectionate daughter . . .*

AMY CURTIS MARCH

[*Hannah also included a note at times, to report on how well the girls were holding up and managing their duties. Even Laurie and Mr. Laurence dropped in a line or two to reassure Mr. and Mrs. March that all was well at home and the girls were being guarded carefully.*]

> What two things does Meg claim that Amy needs to improve?

> —The editors have here abridged the original text

---

[2] **interrogation point.** Amy means to write *interrogative mark,* which is the same as a question mark.

[3] **mortyfied.** Amy's attempt to say *mortified,* which means "extremely embarrassed"

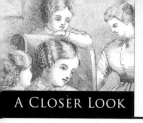

A Closer Look

Understanding the Selection

Recalling (just the facts)

1. Where does the money come from for Marmee's trip? What does Jo do to help?
2. Name two ways Laurie has helped the March family when they needed it.
3. When Marmee is leaving for Washington, who is standing behind her daughters "like a bodyguard"? (Name all three people.)
4. What is the girls' motto, or words to live by, according to Jo?

Interpreting (delving deeper)

1. Why is Hannah so afraid of the telegram? Does a telegram always mean bad news?
2. Why is Marmee so upset when she gets the telegram? What does she do in response to this news?
3. What is an affliction? Would Jo agree with Hannah that work is "the cure for most afflictions"?
4. How could you tell which sister wrote each letter to Mr. and Mrs. March, even if she had not signed the letter? Why is Jo's letter so different from Meg's?

Synthesizing (putting it all together)

1. How have the Marches and the Laurences helped each other in the past? Is Laurie grateful that he can help the Marches in a crisis, or is he just being a good neighbor and a gentleman?
2. What does each letter reveal about how its writer is coping with the weight of her "bundle"?

Writing

EXTENSIONS

Writing a Short Story. (If students are unfamiliar with the terms *omen* and *foreshadowing,* please refer to the Language Alive! activity on page 182) Foreshadowing and omens are common in theater and cinema. Countless directors of suspense movies have relied on a well-timed thunderclap to accent an actor's statement, allowing the audience to guess that things might not go as planned for the characters. Changes in the weather and the appearance of animals are some of the types of omens that frequently crop up in folktales; everyone knows that a black cat in the path is an omen of bad luck. Strong use of foreshadowing can set the tone for a story. If a story begins with a dark or scary omen, the reader begins to imagine the bad or frightening things that will possibly occur to the characters as the story advances. Foreshadowing and omens are also important tools in fiction writing, particularly in novels such as *Little Women.*

    Write your own short story that makes good use of at least one strong omen. The short story can be anything from an adventure story to a silly story about a kitchen fly watching a glass of milk balance precariously on a counter.

    Before you write, brainstorm what types of characters you will use and whether you'd like to write your story from the first-person point of view (using pronouns like "I" and "we") or from the third-person point of view (using pronouns like "he," "she," and "they"). Plan the beginning, middle, and end of your story to establish how the plot will progress.

    The story should have a significant change in tone or action from beginning to end so that you can include an omen that will foreshadow that change. Make sure that the omen appropriately reflects the change that takes place. For example, if you write a story about a sick person getting better, you will want to use an omen that reflects growth and health, such as a flower blooming. As you write, think carefully about the placement of your omen. If you put the omen too early or too late in the action of the story, the reader may not understand the significance. And remember, conflict is one of the most important elements of a good short story; whether the conflict is internal (such as a feeling of guilt) or external (such as a natural disaster or economic hardship), the main character should have to overcome—or be overcome by—some kind of conflict.

EXTENSIONS

Language Alive!

Omens and Foreshadowing. In Chapter 15, the author tells us that, when Marmee left for Washington, "the sun came out . . . shining on the group at the gate like a good omen." As you know from your vocabulary list for this chapter, an **omen** is a sign of what might happen in the future. In stories, authors often have the sun come out as a sign that all is well or that things are going to get better soon. Omens are not just images that contribute to the mood of a story; they are symbols that forecast future events in the plot. When an author drops hints about what will happen to the characters in the future, this is called **foreshadowing.**

Notice how the mood of this story has changed from the sense of gloom (about winter coming) at the beginning of Chapter 15—right before the bad news comes—to the sense of optimism in Chapter 16 when the sun shines on the girls as they wave to their mother. Although everyone is concerned about Mr. March's health and about how the girls will get along without their parents, the author doesn't want us to worry too much about them. If she did, she might have had the carriage pull away into the darkness on a dreary night in the pouring rain or sleet, with the girls huddled together miserably at the door. However, the author spells out the omen clearly by saying, "And so the journey began with the good omens of sunshine, smiles, and cheerful words."

These are not the only signs that Marmee's journey likely will have a good outcome. At the end of Chapter 15, the moon breaks out suddenly from behind the clouds and shines on Marmee as she peers into the darkness. Again, the author spells out how she wants us to interpret this omen. She tells us that the moon seems "to whisper [to Marmee] in the silence, 'Be comforted, dear soul! There is always light behind the clouds.'"

As you read *Little Women,* notice how the author often uses little signs or hints like these at the end of a chapter to create a sense of expectations about what will happen next. On a separate sheet of paper, make a chart with three columns. Label the first column "Good Omens," the second (middle) column "Bad Omens," and the third column "What Happens Later." As you read the rest of *Little Women,* keep your chart handy and fill it out whenever you come across an example of foreshadowing. Save your chart for use in future writing exercises.

CHAPTER 17

Little Faithful

For a week the amount of virtue in the old house was really amazing. Everyone seemed in a heavenly frame of mind, and self-denial was all the fashion. Relieved of their first anxiety about their father, the girls relaxed their praiseworthy efforts a little, and began to fall back into old ways. They did not forget their motto, but hoping and keeping busy seemed to grow easier, and after such tremendous exertions, they felt that their efforts deserved a holiday.

Jo caught a bad cold through neglect to cover the shorn head enough, and was ordered to stay at home till she was better, for Aunt March didn't like to hear people read with colds in their heads. Jo liked this and subsided on the sofa to nurse her cold with books. Amy found that housework and art did not go well together and returned to her mud pies. Meg went daily to her pupils, and sewed, or thought she did, at home, but much time was spent in writing long letters to her mother, or reading the Washington dispatches over and over. Beth kept on with all the little duties, and many of the sisters' also, for they were forgetful, and the house seemed like a clock whose pendulum[1] was gone a-visiting. When her heart got heavy with longings for Mother or fears for Father, she went away into a certain closet, hid her face in the folds of a dear gown, and made her little moan and prayed her little prayer quietly by herself. Nobody knew what cheered her up after a fit, but everyone felt how sweet and helpful Beth was, and fell into a way of going to her for comfort or advice in their small affairs.

All were unconscious that this experience was a test of character, and when the first excitement was over, felt that they had done well

Which member of the March family represents the pendulum "gone a-visiting"?

---

[1] **pendulum.** A weight or other object hung from a fixed point so that it swings freely back and forth, used to determine the rate of movement in a clock

and deserved praise. So they did, but their mistake was in **ceasing** to do well, and they learned this lesson through much anxiety and regret.

"Meg, I wish you'd go and see the Hummels. You know Mother told us not to forget them," said Beth, ten days after Mrs. March's departure.

"I'm too tired to go this afternoon," replied Meg, rocking comfortably as she sewed.

"Can't you, Jo?" asked Beth.

"Too stormy for me with my cold," replied Jo.

"I thought it was almost well."

"It's well enough for me to go out with Laurie, but not well enough to go to the Hummels'," said Jo, laughing, but looking a little ashamed of her inconsistency.

Why does Jo feel ashamed?

"Why don't you go yourself?" asked Meg.

"I have been every day, but the baby is sick, and I don't know what to do for it. I think you or Hannah ought to go." Beth spoke earnestly, and Meg promised she would go tomorrow.

"Ask Hannah for some nice little mess,[2] and take it round, Beth, the air will do you good," said Jo, adding apologetically, "I'd go but I want to finish my writing."

"My head aches and I'm tired, so I thought maybe some of you would go," said Beth.

"Amy will be in presently, and she will run down for us," suggested Meg.

So Beth lay down on the sofa, the others returned to their work, and the Hummels were forgotten. An hour passed. Amy did not come, Meg went to her room to try on a new dress, Jo was absorbed in her story, and Hannah was sound asleep before the kitchen fire, when Beth quietly put on her hood, filled her basket with odds and

---

[2] **mess.** Food, a meal

Vocabulary in Place
cease, *v.* To stop

ends for the poor children, and went out into the chilly air with a heavy head and a grieved look in her patient eyes.

It was late when she came back, and no one saw her creep upstairs and shut herself into her mother's room. Half an hour after, Jo went to "Mother's closet" for something, and there found little Beth, sitting on the medicine chest, looking very grave, with red eyes and a medicine bottle in her hand.

Who does Jo find in "Mother's closet"?

"Christopher Columbus! What's the matter?" cried Jo.

Beth put out her hand as if to warn her off, and asked quickly, "You've had the scarlet fever, haven't you?"

"Years ago, when Meg did. Why?"

"Then I'll tell you. Oh, Jo, the baby's dead!"

"What baby?"

"Mrs. Hummel's. It died in my lap before she got home," cried Beth with a sob.

"My poor dear, how dreadful for you! I ought to have gone," said Jo, taking her sister in her arms as she sat down in her mother's big chair, with a remorseful face.

"It wasn't dreadful, Jo, only so sad! I saw in a minute it was sicker, but Lottchen said her mother had gone for a doctor, so I took Baby and let Lotty rest. It seemed asleep, but all of a sudden it gave a little cry and trembled, and then lay very still. I tried to warm its feet, and Lotty gave it some milk, but it didn't stir, and I knew it was dead."

"Don't cry, dear! What did you do?"

"I just sat and held it softly till Mrs. Hummel came with the doctor. He said it was dead, and looked at Heinrich and Minna, who have sore throats. 'Scarlet fever, ma'am. Ought to have called me before,' he said crossly. Mrs. Hummel told him she was poor, and had tried to cure baby herself, but now it was too late, and she could only ask him to help the others and trust to charity for his pay. He smiled then, and was kinder, but it was very sad, and I cried with them till he turned round all of a sudden, and told me to go home right away, or I'd have the fever."

Why did the doctor order Beth to go home?

"No, you won't!" cried Jo, hugging her close, with a frightened look. "Oh, Beth, if you should be sick, I never could forgive myself! What shall we do?"

193

"Don't be frightened, I guess I shan't have it badly. I looked in Mother's book and saw that it begins with a headache, sore throat, and queer feelings like mine, so I did take some medicine, and I feel a little better," said Beth, laying her cold hands on her hot forehead and trying to look well.

"If Mother was only at home!" exclaimed Jo, seizing the book, and feeling that Washington was an immense way off. She read a page, felt Beth's head, peeped into her throat, and then said gravely, "You've been over the baby every day for more than a week, and among the others who are going to have it, so I'm afraid you are going to have it, Beth. I'll call Hannah, she knows all about sickness."

"Don't let Amy come. She never had it, and I should hate to give it to her. Can't you and Meg have it over again?" asked Beth, anxiously.

"I guess not. Don't care if I do. Serve me right, selfish pig, to let you go, and stay writing rubbish myself!" muttered Jo, as she went to consult Hannah.

The good soul was wide awake in a minute, and took the lead at once, assuring that there was no need to worry; everyone had scarlet fever, and if rightly treated, nobody died, all of which Jo believed, and felt much relieved as they went up to call Meg.

"Now I'll tell you what we'll do," said Hannah, when she had examined and questioned Beth. "We will have Dr. Bangs take a look at you, dear, and see that we start right. Then we'll send Amy off to Aunt March's for a spell, to keep her out of harm's way, and one of you girls can stay at home and amuse Beth for a day or two."

"I shall stay, of course, I'm oldest," began Meg, looking anxious and **self-reproachful.**

"I shall, because it's my fault she is sick. I told Mother I'd do the errands, and I haven't," said Jo decidedly.

Why do Meg and Jo feel guilty when Beth gets sick with "the fever"?

Vocabulary in Place
self-reproachful, *adj.* Full of blame for oneself

"Which will you have, Beth? There ain't no need of but one," said Hannah.

"Jo, please." And Beth leaned her head against her sister with a contented look, which **effectually** settled that point.

"I'll go and tell Amy," said Meg, feeling a little hurt, yet rather relieved on the whole, for she did not like nursing, and Jo did.

Amy rebelled outright, passionately declaring that she had rather have the fever than go to Aunt March's, and Meg left her in despair to ask Hannah what should be done. Before she came back, Laurie walked into the parlor to find Amy sobbing, with her head in the sofa cushions. She told her story, expecting to be consoled, but Laurie only said, in his most wheedlesome[3] tone,

"Now be a sensible little woman, and do as they say. No, don't cry, but hear what a jolly plan I've got. You go to Aunt March's, and I'll come and take you out every day, driving or walking, and we'll have capital times. Won't that be better than moping here?"

"I don't wish to be sent off as if I was in the way," began Amy, in an injured voice.

"Bless your heart, child, it's to keep you well. You don't want to be sick, do you?"

"No, I'm sure I don't, but it's dull at Aunt March's, and she is so cross," said Amy, looking rather frightened.

"It won't be dull with me popping in every day to tell you how Beth is, and take you out **gallivanting.** The old lady likes me, and I'll be as sweet as possible to her, so she won't peck at us, whatever we do."

"Will you take me out in the trotting wagon with Puck?"

"On my honor as a gentleman."

"And come every single day?"

"See if I don't!"

What does Laurie say to make Amy less upset about going to Aunt March's?

---

[3] **wheedlesome.** Attempting to persuade, especially through flattery

Vocabulary in Place
effectually, *adv.* Adequately; producing the desired effect
gallivant, *v.* To roam about in search of a good time

"And bring me back the minute Beth is well?"

"The identical minute."

"Well—I guess I will," said Amy slowly.

"Good girl! Call Meg, and tell her you'll give in," said Laurie, with an approving pat, which annoyed Amy more than the "giving in."

Meg and Jo came running down to behold the miracle that had been **wrought**, and Amy, feeling very precious and self-sacrificing, promised to go, if the doctor said Beth was going to be ill.

"How is the little dear?" asked Laurie, for Beth was his especial pet, and he felt more anxious about her than he liked to show.

"She is lying down on Mother's bed and feels better. The baby's death troubled her, but I dare say she has only got cold. Hannah says she thinks so, but she looks worried and that makes me fidgety," answered Meg.

"What a trying world it is!" said Jo, rumpling up her hair in a fretful way. "No sooner do we get out of one trouble than down comes another."

"Well, don't make a porcupine of yourself, it isn't becoming. Settle your wig, Jo, and tell me if I shall telegraph to your mother, or do anything?" asked Laurie, who never had been **reconciled** to the loss of his friend's one beauty.

"That is what troubles me," said Meg. "I think we ought to tell her if Beth is really ill, but Hannah says we mustn't, for Mother can't leave Father, and it will only make them anxious. Beth won't be sick long, and Hannah knows just what to do, and Mother said we were to mind her, so I suppose we must, but it doesn't seem quite right to me."

"Hum, well, I can't say. Suppose you ask Grandfather after the doctor has been."

"We will. Jo, go and get Dr. Bangs at once," commanded Meg. "We can't decide anything till he has been."

Why shouldn't they tell mother?

Vocabulary in Place

wrought, *v.* Put together, created. (A past tense form of *work*.)

reconcile, *v.* To come to terms with; accept

"Stay where you are, Jo. I'm errand boy to this establishment," said Laurie, taking up his cap.

"I have great hopes for my boy," observed Jo, watching him fly over the fence with an approving smile.

"He does very well, for a boy," was Meg's somewhat ungracious answer, for the subject did not interest her.

Dr. Bangs came, said Beth had symptoms of the fever, but he thought she would have it lightly, though he looked sober over the Hummel story. Amy was ordered off at once, and departed in great state, with Jo and Laurie as escort. Aunt March received them with her usual **hospitality**.

"What do you want now?" she asked, looking sharply over her spectacles, while the parrot, sitting on the back of her chair, called out . . .

"Go away. No boys allowed here."

Laurie retired to the window, and Jo told her story.

"No more than I expected, if you are allowed to go poking about among poor folks. Amy can stay and make herself useful if she isn't sick. Don't cry, child, it worries me to hear people sniff."

Amy was on the point of crying, but Laurie slyly pulled the parrot's tail, which caused Polly to utter an astonished croak and call out, "Bless my boots!" in such a funny way, that she laughed instead.

"What do you hear from your mother?" asked the old lady gruffly.

"Father is much better," replied Jo, trying to keep sober.

"Oh, is he? Well, that won't last long, I fancy. March never had any **stamina**," was the cheerful reply. "Jo, you'd better go at once. It isn't proper to be gadding[4] about so late with a rattlepated[5] boy like . . ."

What kind of welcome do Amy, Jo, and Laurie get when they arrive at Aunt March's?

Is Aunt March's reply really "cheerful"?

---

[4] **gadding.** Moving around restlessly

[5] **rattlepated.** Giddy and talkative; foolish

Vocabulary in Place
hospitality, *n.* Welcome; tending to guests' needs
stamina, *n.* Strength to resist illness or hardships; endurance

"Hold your tongue, you disrespectful old bird!" cried Polly, tumbling off the chair with a bounce, and running to peck the "rattlepated" boy, who was shaking with laughter at the last speech.

"I don't think I can bear it, but I'll try," thought Amy, as she was left alone with Aunt March.

"Get along, you fright!" screamed Polly, and at that rude speech Amy could not restrain a sniff.

Words to Keep

The following sentences contain important words from the Vocabulary in Place boxes in Chapters 16–17 of *Little Women.* In your notebook, or on a separate sheet of paper, write the part of speech of each boldface word, a synonym (or a short definition in your own words), and a new sentence of your own.

1. We did not win, but we took **solace** in having made it to the finals.
2. It was difficult not to feel **despondent** about their neighbor's illness.
3. She considered it an **omen** of bad luck when the black cat crossed her path.
4. They shoveled snow without **ceasing** until the driveway was cleared.
5. The interstate **effectually** connected the two towns and improved life for commuters.
6. They built the recreation center with the hope of keeping teenagers from **gallivanting** around town aimlessly.
7. It was amazing to see the change they had **wrought** in the town after one year.
8. Ed **reconciled** himself to the fact that his arm would be in a cast for six weeks.
9. The President and First Lady were known for their **hospitality** and hosted numerous dignitaries and heads of state at the White House.
10. By training and eating right every day, Tim built up his **stamina** before the city marathon.

CHAPTER 18

Dark Days

Beth did have the fever, and was much sicker than anyone but Hannah and the doctor suspected. Busy Dr. Bangs did his best, but left a good deal to Hannah, who was an excellent nurse. Meg stayed at home to keep house, feeling very anxious and a little guilty when she wrote letters in which no mention was made of Beth's illness. She could not think it right to deceive her mother, but Hannah wouldn't hear of "Mrs. March bein' worried just for sech[1] a trifle."

Jo devoted herself to Beth day and night; not a hard task, for Beth was very patient and bore her pain uncomplainingly. But there came a time when, during the fever fits, she began to sing in a hoarse, broken voice, to play on the bedspread as if on her beloved little piano; a time when she did not know the familiar faces around her and called **imploringly** for her mother. Then Jo grew frightened, Meg begged to be allowed to write the truth, and even Hannah said she "would think of it, though there was no danger yet." A letter from Washington added to their trouble, for Mr. March had had a **relapse**, and could not think of coming home for a long while.

How dark the days seemed now, how sad and lonely the house, and how heavy were the hearts of the sisters as they worked and waited, while the shadow of death hovered over the once happy home. It was then that Meg felt how rich she had been in things more precious than any luxuries money could buy—in love, protection, peace, and health, the real blessings of life. It was then

How sick is Beth? Have the girls told their mother that Beth has scarlet fever?

---

[1] **sech.** Such

Vocabulary in Place
imploringly, *adv.* Pleadingly; with begging
relapse, *n.* Setback in the process of getting well

that Jo learned to see the beauty and the sweetness of Beth's nature and to acknowledge the worth of Beth's unselfish ambition to live for others and of her simple virtues, which all should value more than talent, wealth, or beauty. And Amy, in her **exile**, longed to be at home, that she might work for Beth, remembering, with regret, how many neglected tasks those willing hands had done for her. Laurie haunted the house like a restless ghost, and Mr. Laurence locked the grand piano, because he could not bear to be reminded of his young neighbor. Everyone missed Beth. The milkman, baker, grocer, and butcher inquired how she did, the neighbors sent all sorts of comforts and good wishes, and even those who knew her best were surprised to find how many friends shy little Beth had made.

Why does Mr. Laurence lock the piano?

Meanwhile she lay on her bed with old Joanna at her side, for even in her wanderings she did not forget the ragged little doll. She was full of anxiety about Jo, sent loving messages to Amy, and often begged for pencil and paper to try to say a word to Father and Mother. But soon even these intervals of consciousness ended, and she lay hour after hour, tossing to and fro, mumbling **incoherent** words. Dr. Bangs came twice a day, Hannah sat up at night, Meg kept a telegram in her desk all ready to send off at any minute, and Jo never stirred from Beth's side.

The first of December was a wintry day indeed, and the year seemed getting ready for its death. When Dr. Bangs came that morning, he looked long at Beth, held the hot hand in both his own for a minute, and laid it gently down, saying, in a low voice to Hannah, "If Mrs. March can leave her husband, she'd better be sent for."

Why does the doctor say that they should send for Mrs. March?

Hannah nodded without speaking, for her lips twitched nervously. Meg dropped down into a chair as the strength seemed to go out of her limbs at the sound of those words, and Jo ran to the

---

Vocabulary in Place

exile, *n.* Forced removal from one's home

incoherent, *adj.* Impossible to understand; not making sense

parlor, snatched up the telegram, and throwing on her things, rushed out into the storm. She was soon back, noiselessly taking off her cloak, when Laurie came in with a letter, saying that Mr. March was mending again. Jo read it thankfully, but the heavy weight did not seem lifted off her heart, and her face was so full of misery that Laurie asked quickly,

"What is it? Is Beth worse?"

"I've sent for Mother," said Jo, tugging at her rubber boots with a tragic expression.

"Good for you, Jo! Did you do it on your own responsibility?" asked Laurie, as he seated her in the hall chair and took off the troublesome boots, seeing how her hands shook.

"No. The doctor told us to."

"Oh, Jo, it's not so bad as that?" cried Laurie, with a startled face.

"Yes, it is. She doesn't know us. She doesn't look like my Beth, and there's nobody to help us bear it. Mother and Father both gone, and God seems so far away I can't find Him."

As the tears streamed down her cheeks, Jo stretched out her hand in a helpless sort of way, as if **groping** in the dark. Laurie took it in his, whispering as well as he could with a lump in his throat, "I'm here. Hold on to me, Jo, dear!"

She could not speak, but she did "hold on," and the warm grasp of the friendly human hand comforted her sore heart, and seemed to lead her nearer to the Divine arm which alone could uphold her in her trouble. Laurie longed to say something tender and comfortable, but no fitting words came to him, so he stood silent, gently stroking her bent head as her mother used to do. It was the best thing he could have done, far more soothing than the most **eloquent** words, for Jo felt his unspoken sympathy. Soon she dried the tears which had relieved her, and looked up with a grateful face.

What does Laurie do to try to make Jo feel better?

Vocabulary in Place
grope, *v.* To feel one's way, especially in the dark; also to reach out for support
eloquent, *adj.* Expressive; conveying thoughts vividly in speech

"Thank you, Teddy, I'm better now. I don't feel so forlorn, and will try to bear it if it comes."

"Keep hoping for the best, that will help you, Jo. Soon your mother will be here, and then everything will be all right."

"I'm so glad Father is better. Now she won't feel so bad about leaving him. Oh me! It does seem as if all the troubles came in a heap, and I got the heaviest part on my shoulders," sighed Jo, spreading her wet handkerchief over her knees to dry.

"Doesn't Meg share the burden?" asked Laurie, looking indignant.

"Oh yes, she tries to, but she can't love Bethy as I do, and she won't miss her as I shall. Beth is my **conscience**, and I can't give her up. I can't! I can't!"

Down went Jo's face into the wet handkerchief, and she cried despairingly, for she had kept up bravely till now and never shed a tear. Laurie could not speak till he had **subdued** the choky feeling in his throat and steadied his lips. It might be unmanly, but he couldn't help it, and I am glad of it. Presently, as Jo's sobs quieted, he said hopefully, "I don't think she will die. She's so good, and we all love her so much, I don't believe God will take her away yet."

"The good and dear people always do die," groaned Jo, but she stopped crying, for her friend's words cheered her up in spite of her own doubts and fears.

"Poor girl, you're worn out. Stop a bit. I'll hearten you up in a jiffy."

Laurie went off two stairs at a time, and Jo laid her wearied head down on Beth's little brown hood, which was still on the table where she left it. When Laurie came running down with a glass of wine, she took it with a smile, and said bravely, "I drink—Health to my Beth! You are a good doctor, Teddy. How can I ever pay you?" she added.

Why is the narrator glad that Laurie feels emotional?

Vocabulary in Place

conscience, *n.* Sense of right and wrong; moral or spiritual guide

subdue, *v.* To suppress or fight down; to overcome

"I'll send my bill, by-and-by, and tonight I'll give you something that will warm the cockles of your heart,"[2] said Laurie, beaming at her.

"What is it?" cried Jo, forgetting her woes for a minute in her wonder.

"I telegraphed to your mother yesterday. She'll be here tonight, and everything will be all right. Aren't you glad I did it?" Laurie spoke very fast, and turned red and excited all in a minute, for he had kept his plot a secret.

Jo grew quite white, flew out of her chair, and amazed him by throwing her arms round his neck, and crying out joyfully, "Oh, Laurie! Oh, Mother! I am so glad!" She did not weep again, but laughed hysterically, and trembled and clung to her friend, bewildered by the sudden news.

Laurie patted her back soothingly and followed it up by a bashful kiss or two, which brought Jo round at once. She put him gently away, saying breathlessly, "Oh, don't! I didn't mean to . . . it was dreadful of me, but you were such a dear to do it that I couldn't help flying at you. Tell me all about it."

"I don't mind," laughed Laurie, as he settled his tie. "Why, you see, Grandpa and I got fidgety, for we thought Hannah was overdoing the authority business, and your mother ought to know. She'd never forgive us if Beth . . . Well, if anything happened, you know. So off I pelted to the office yesterday, for the doctor looked sober. Your mother will come, I know, and the late train is in at two A.M. I shall go for her, and you've only got to keep Beth quiet till that blessed lady gets here."

"Laurie, you're an angel! How shall I ever thank you?"

"Fly at me again. I rather liked it," said Laurie, looking mischievous.

"No, thank you. Don't tease, but go home and rest, for you'll be up half the night. Bless you, Teddy, bless you!" Jo said as Laurie departed.

"That's the *interferingest* chap I ever see, but I forgive him," said Hannah, with an air of relief, when Jo told the good news.

What has Laurie decided to do on his own?

---

2 **cockles of your heart.** Innermost feelings

> *Why is the budding rose important here?*

Meg had a quiet **rapture,** while Jo set the sickroom in order, and Hannah "knocked up a couple of pies." A breath of fresh air seemed to blow through the house, and everything appeared to feel the hopeful change. Beth's bird began to chirp again, and a budding rose was discovered in the window. Every time the girls met, their pale faces broke into smiles as they hugged one another, whispering, "Mother's coming, dear! Mother's coming!"

Every one rejoiced but Beth. She lay in that heavy stupor, as if unconscious of hope and joy, doubt and danger. It was a **piteous** sight, the once rosy face so changed and empty, the once busy hands so weak and wasted, and the once pretty, well-kept hair scattered rough and tangled on the pillow. All day she lay so, only rousing now and then to mutter, "Water!" with lips so dry, they could hardly shape the word. All day Jo and Meg hovered over her, waiting, hoping, and trusting in God and Mother. All day the snow fell, the wind raged, and the hours dragged by, but night came at last, and the sisters looked at each other with brightening eyes. The doctor had said that some change, for better or worse, would probably take place about midnight, at which time he would return.

> *What is the overall mood of the March household on this night?*

Hannah, quite worn out, fell fast asleep at the foot of the bed. Mr. Laurence marched to and fro in the parlor, feeling that he would rather face rebels than Mrs. March's face as she entered. Laurie lay on the rug, pretending to rest, but staring into the fire.

The girls never forgot that night, when they kept their watch, with the dreadful sense of powerlessness which comes to us in hours like those.

"If God spares Beth, I never will complain again," whispered Meg earnestly.

"If God spares Beth, I'll try to love and serve Him all my life," answered Jo, with equal determination.

"I wish I had no heart, it aches so," sighed Meg, after a pause.

Vocabulary in Place

rapture, *n.* An experience of ecstasy; a feeling of being carried off

piteous, *adj.* Worthy of pity; pathetic

"If life is often as hard as this, I don't see how we ever shall get through it," added her sister despondently.

Here the clock struck twelve, and both forgot themselves in watching Beth. The house was still as death, and nothing but the wailing of the wind broke the deep hush, as a pale shadow seemed to fall upon the little bed. An hour went by, and nothing happened except Laurie's quiet departure for the station. Another hour, still no one came, and anxious fears of delay in the storm, or accidents by the way, or, worst of all, a great grief at Washington, haunted the girls.

It was past two, when Jo, who stood at the window thinking how dreary the world looked, heard a movement by the bed. A dreadful fear passed coldly over her, as she thought, "Beth is dead."

She was back at her post in an instant, and to her excited eyes a great change seemed to have taken place. The fever flush and the look of pain were gone, and the beloved little face looked so pale and peaceful that Jo felt no desire to weep or to lament. Leaning low over this dearest of her sisters, she kissed the damp forehead, and softly whispered, "Goodbye, my Beth, goodbye!"

Hannah started out of her sleep, hurried to the bed, looked at Beth, felt her hands, listened at her lips, and then exclaimed under her breath, "The fever's turned. She's sleepin' nat'ral, her skin's damp, and she breathes easy. Praise be given! Oh, my goodness me!"

Before the girls could believe the happy truth, the doctor came to confirm it. "Yes, my dears, I think the little girl will pull through this time. Keep the house quiet, let her sleep, and when she wakes, give her . . ."

What they were to give, neither heard, for both crept into the dark hall, and, sitting on the stairs, held each other close, rejoicing with hearts too full for words. When they went back to be kissed and cuddled by faithful Hannah, they found Beth lying, as she used to do, with her cheek pillowed on her hand, the dreadful **pallor** gone, and breathing quietly, as if just fallen asleep.

What happens to Beth in the middle of the night?

Vocabulary in Place

pallor, *n.* Extreme or unnatural paleness

> What has happened to the rose in the middle of the night? How is this like the change that has taken place in Beth?

"If Mother would only come now!" said Jo, as the winter night began to wane.

"See," said Meg, coming up with a white, half-opened rose, "I thought this would hardly be ready to lay in Beth's hand tomorrow if she went away from us. But it has blossomed in the night, and now I mean to put it in my vase here, so that when the darling wakes, the first thing she sees will be the little rose, and Mother's face."

Never had the sun risen so beautifully, and never had the world seemed so lovely as it did to the heavy eyes of Meg and Jo, as they looked out in the early morning, when their long, sad **vigil** was done.

"It looks like a fairy world," said Meg, smiling to herself, as she stood behind the curtain, watching the dazzling sight.

"Hark!" cried Jo, starting to her feet.

Yes, there was a sound of bells at the door below, a cry from Hannah, and then Laurie's voice saying in a joyful whisper, "Girls, she's come! She's come!"

Vocabulary in Place

vigil, *n.* A watch kept during normal sleeping hours

Understanding the Selection

A Closer Look

Recalling (just the facts)

1. How well do the girls follow through on their efforts to help at home and elsewhere while Marmee is gone?
2. Who ends up going to see the Hummels by herself?
3. Who took the initiative to send for Marmee when Beth's fever seemed to be getting worse?
4. Does Beth take a turn for the better or the worse in the middle of the night? Has her fever broken by the time Marmee arrives?

Interpreting (delving deeper)

1. How does Beth get sick? What does the way in which she became sick reveal about her personality?
2. Why do Meg and Jo feel guilty when Beth gets sick with "the fever"?
3. Why does Jo find Beth in Marmee's closet? What is she doing there? What has she experienced that day?
4. How did the girls react when they found out Marmee was coming back? Why hadn't they contacted her sooner?

Synthesizing (putting it all together)

1. How did Laurie help Mrs. March go to Washington? How does he help when Amy has to go away? How does he help when Beth is sick? Is he grateful that he can be "the official errand boy" for the March family? Why?
2. Why would Jo never forgive herself if Beth died? What aspects of Beth's personality were revealed in Chapters 17 and 18? How important was Beth to stability and happiness in the family? Use example from the text to support your answer.

EXTENSIONS

Writing

Letters and Telegrams. Before the invention of telephones, computers, and email, there were very few ways to communicate and keep up with friends and family. In the previous chapters, the characters write letters and send telegrams in order to stay in touch with others.

While letter writing is a centuries-old practice, the type of **telegraphy** that would have been utilized by the March girls was only invented in the 1830s with the help of men such as **Samuel Morse**, who created his code of dots and dashes (short and long bursts of electricity) to standardize telegraphic communication. The biggest advantage of sending telegrams was the speed at which a message could travel. While letters had to be physically carried from place to place, words broken down into Morse code and transmitted over electric wires could arrive at their destination in a matter of seconds.

When Laurie sent the telegram to Mrs. March, he probably went to a telegraph office and wrote his message on a blank form provided by that particular company. Then, the message was transmitted over the wires by one operator and—at the receiving location—written down by another operator who was able to translate the Morse code into words just by listening to the clicks of the machine. Finally, assuming the telegram was sent first-class because of its urgency, a messenger would deliver the message to the address communicated in the telegram.

While serving much of the same function, telegrams were extremely different from letters. Telegrams were priced per word—the longer the message, the more it cost. As a result, telegrams became known for their brief yet poetic simplicity. Pronouns (such as *I, me, we, he, she,* and *it*), articles (*the, a,* and *an*), and even punctuation were often omitted. Messages were as concise as possible in order to avoid higher fees and also to ensure that important information was not lost in translation. Examples of actual telegrams include messages such as "No letter from you what is the matter answer," "Plane trip cancelled. Home on train. See you Tuesday," and "Mother needs you wire when leaving."

Writing

EXTENSIONS

Just as you would include an address in a business letter, telegram messages had an introductory line called the "check," which identified the sender, the class of service (regular or express), and how many words it contained. Below the check was the name and address of the recipient.

Try writing a telegram.
- First, write a short letter to a friend or family member that includes at least one piece of important information. This letter can be fictional or include real events that have happened or are happening in your life.
- Then, take one important piece of information from the letter and rewrite it as a telegram.
- Keep in mind that few telegrams were over 15 words long and be sure to avoid unnecessary words.
- Include a check and the name and address of the recipient.

Do you think there are similarities between telegraph writing and the sort of writing people use in email? One possible difference between the two: telegrams were short because people wanted to save money and emails tend to be short because people want to save time. Do some research and try to find some examples of famous telegrams through history. Abe Lincoln sent quite a few during the Civil War.

Science Connections

Advances in Medicine. The March family had good reason to worry about Beth's illness. In the days before antibiotics, an infection or even a sore throat could become very serious. At the time *Little Women* was written, people did not have the "miracle drugs" and vaccines that saved so many lives after they became available in the twentieth century. Epidemics of contagious diseases such as scarlet fever could spread rapidly from one family or community to the next, claiming many lives, and many people died from infections that followed surgery or childbirth. Vaccines against diseases like diphtheria and whooping cough were not available either, so many families lost at least one child to a serious disease before he or she could reach adulthood.

The kind of medical care that we now take for granted at hospitals and doctors' offices is very different from the kind of care the town doctor could provide in the nineteenth century—and that's who your family would call for help (if one was available) when someone had a serious problem.

Fortunately, a number of important scientific discoveries were made in the late nineteenth century that brought great improvements in the quality of medical care. It would take decades, however, for the implications of these discoveries to be understood and even longer for them to result in widespread benefits for most patients.

For example, in the 1860s and 1870s, scientists like Louis Pasteur and Joseph Lister were beginning to figure out how bacteria and other microbes, or "germs," could cause disease and infection. They also learned that antiseptics and sterilization techniques (including heat, or **pasteurization**) could halt the growth of bacteria, and that antiseptics and better hygiene could help prevent infection, especially during surgery. (At one time, doctors didn't know that they needed to wear sterile gloves and masks or even wash their hands before operating on patients.) Pasteur eventually discovered the type of bacteria, **streptococcus**, that causes what we call "strep" throat, tonsillitis, scarlet fever, and many other diseases. But it wasn't until the 1940s, during World War II, that doctors had an effective weapon against streptococcus in the form of an antibiotic called **penicillin** (discovered by **Alexander Fleming** in 1928).

Science Connections

EXTENSIONS

Louisa May Alcott knew what scarlet fever was like because she had a sister who caught it. In the late 1860s, when *Little Women* was published, doctors were literally clueless about how to treat scarlet fever and most infectious diseases, but they did the best they could. Families tried to keep patients comfortable while doctors administered a succession of remedies that seemed to help some patients some of the time. Most doctors mixed up their own potions and skin plasters, and some of these "cures" could be as bad as the disease. **Cathartics** and **emetics**—strong chemicals designed to purge the digestive tract of poisonous toxins that were thought to cause disease—were popular with doctors, if not their patients.

If the patient was strong enough to get through the "purging" part of the treatment without succumbing to the disease, he or she would be given a **tonic** to build up the body's strength again in an effort to speed up the healing process. There was no Food and Drug Administration (FDA) to regulate what went into the tonics and elixirs that were popular remedies at this time. There were no requirements for experimental testing of these remedies to see whether they were safe and effective before they could be used on patients. Ingredients and special formulas were often closely guarded secrets. Some concoctions were widely promoted as **panaceas**, or "cure-alls," for both man and beast.

Unfortunately, one popular medicine from the 1800s (called calomel) contained **mercury,** which is now known to be toxic. The author of *Little Women* is just one person who is known to have suffered later in life from problems associated with taking that medicine. The doctors who gave Alcott calomel when she caught typhoid fever (while she was working as a Civil War nurse) were trying to help her, not hurt her. People just didn't know any better at that time.

EXTENSIONS

Science Connections

Activities: Medical History

1. Working individually or in small groups, choose one of the people listed below and prepare a short report on that individual's contributions to modern medicine. Ask your teacher and librarian to help you with the research. Be prepared to present your findings to the class. In your report, be sure to explain why this person's contribution was so important.
   - Ernst Chain
   - Howard Florey
   - Robert Koch
   - Florence Nightingale
   - Walter Reed
   - Alexander Fleming
   - Percy Lavon Julian
   - Joseph Lister
   - Louis Pasteur
   - Jonas Salk

2. Work together as a class on a timeline of milestones in medicine from the mid-1800s to the late 1900s. Here are some questions to discuss:
   - How did vaccines and antibiotics help make lives better and longer?
   - Why is resistance to antibiotics a serious problem?
   - What diseases are medical researchers still trying to conquer today?

3. Writing Exercise: Write a short report on one of the following topics:
   - The discovery of rabies vaccine, polio vaccine, or anthrax vaccine
   - The discovery of penicillin
   - How the use of antiseptics and sterile techniques improved survival after surgery
   - How the discovery of microbes ("germs") put an end to the theory that diseases could be generated spontaneously in damp air or dirty conditions

212

CHAPTER 19

Amy's Will

While these things were happening at home, Amy was having hard times at Aunt March's. She felt her exile deeply, and for the first time in her life, realized how beloved she was at home. Aunt March had a soft place in her old heart for the girls, though she didn't think it proper to confess it. She meant to be kind, for the well-behaved little girl pleased her very much, and she really did her best to make Amy happy, but, dear me, what mistakes she made!

Some old people keep young at heart in spite of wrinkles and gray hairs, and can sympathize with children and make them feel at home. But Aunt March had not this gift, and she worried Amy very much with her rules and orders, her prim ways, and long, preachy talks. Finding the child more **docile** and friendly than her sister, the old lady felt it her duty to train her in order to **counteract** the bad effects of her home. So she took Amy by the hand, and taught her as she herself had been taught sixty years ago, and made her feel like a fly in the web of a very strict spider.

Amy had to wash the cups every morning, and polish up the silver and glasses till they shone. Then she had to dust the room, and not a speck escaped Aunt March's eye. Then Polly had to be fed, the lap dog combed, and a dozen orders to be carried out for the lame old lady, who rarely left her big chair. After these tiresome labors came her lessons, which were a daily trial of every one of her virtues. Then she was allowed one hour for exercise or play, and didn't she

What does it mean to "keep young at heart"? Does Aunt March do this?

Why does Aunt March make Amy do all those chores every day? What does Amy get to do for fun?

Vocabulary in Place

docile, *adj.* Easy to get along with; easily tamed

counteract, *v.* To attempt to improve, relieve, or replace, often by providing a better option

enjoy it? Laurie came every day, and they walked and rode and had capital times.

After dinner, she had to read aloud and sit still while the old lady slept. The rest of the afternoon was devoted to sewing, which Amy did meekly till dusk, when she was allowed to do as she liked till teatime. The evenings were the worst of all, for Aunt March told long, dull stories about her youth until Amy longed to go to bed, intending to cry over her hard fate, but usually going to sleep before she had squeezed out more than a tear or two.

If it had not been for Laurie and old Esther, the maid, she felt that she never could have got through that dreadful time. Esther was a Frenchwoman, who lived with Aunt March, whom she had called "Madame" for many years. She rather **tyrannized** over the old lady, who couldn't get along without her. She took a fancy to Amy and amused her very much with odd stories of her life in France. She allowed Amy to roam about the great house and examine the curious and pretty things stored away in the big wardrobes and the ancient chests. Amy's chief delight was an Indian cabinet, full of queer drawers, little pigeonholes, and secret places, in which were kept all sorts of ornaments.

Amy loved to examine and arrange these things, especially the velvet cushioned jewel cases that held Aunt March's jewels. There was the garnet set that Aunt March wore when she came out, and the pearls her father gave her on her wedding day. There were diamonds, rings, pins, and lockets with portraits of dead friends, the baby bracelets her one little daughter had worn, and in a box all by itself lay Aunt March's wedding ring, too small now for her fat finger but put carefully away like the most precious jewel of them all.

"Which would Mademoiselle[1] choose if she had her will?" asked Esther, who always sat near to watch over the valuables.

---

[1] **Mademoiselle.** French for "miss"

Vocabulary in Place
tyrannize, *v.* To bully or rule over without question

"I like the diamonds best, but there is no necklace among them, and I'm fond of necklaces. They are so becoming. I should choose this if I might," replied Amy, admiring a string of gold and ebony beads from which hung a heavy cross.

"I, too, **covet** that, but not as a necklace. Ah, no! To me it is a rosary,[2] and I should use it like a good Catholic," said Esther, eyeing the handsome thing wistfully.

"You mean, like you use the string of good-smelling wooden beads hanging over your glass?" asked Amy.

"Truly, yes, to pray with. It would please the saints if one used so fine a rosary as this, instead of wearing it as a *vain bijou*."[3]

"You seem to take a great deal of comfort in your prayers, Esther, and always come down looking quiet and satisfied. I wish I could."

"If Mademoiselle was a Catholic, she would find true comfort, but it would be well if you went apart each day to meditate and pray. Perhaps you should have a little chapel, in which to find solace for trouble."

"Would it be right for me to do so too?" asked Amy, who felt lonely and in need of help of some sort.

"It would be excellent and charming, and I shall gladly arrange the little dressing room for you if you like it. Say nothing to Madame. When she sleeps go you and sit alone a while to think good thoughts, and pray the dear God preserve your sister."

Esther was truly **pious** and quite sincere in her advice, for she felt much for the sisters in their anxiety. Amy liked the idea and asked her to please arrange the room.

Why does Esther want the string of beads?

---

[2] **rosary.** A string of beads used for counting prayers
[3] **vain bijou.** French for "vain jewel"

Vocabulary in Place
covet, *v.* To desire; to wish to possess
pious, *adj.* Deeply religious; devout

Who will get these beautiful things when Aunt March dies?

"I wish I knew where all these pretty things would go when Aunt March dies," she said, as she slowly replaced the shining rosary and shut the jewel cases one by one.

"To you and your sisters. I know it, Madame **confides** in me. I witnessed her will," whispered Esther smiling.

"How nice! But I wish she'd let us have them now. **Procrastination** is not agreeable," observed Amy, taking a last look at the diamonds.

"The first one who is affianced[4] will have the pearls, Madame has said it, and I have a fancy that the little turquoise ring will be given to you, for Madame approves your good behavior and charming manners."

"Do you think so? Oh, I'll be a lamb, if I can only have that lovely ring! It's ever so much prettier than Kitty Bryant's. I do like Aunt March after all." And Amy tried on the blue ring with a delighted face and a firm resolve to earn it.

From that day she was a model of obedience, and the old lady admired the success of her training. Esther fitted up the closet with a little table, a footstool before it, and over it a valuable copy of one of the more famous pictures of the Divine Mother[5] in the world. Amy's beauty-loving eyes were never tired of looking up at the sweet face, while thinking good thoughts, and praying the dear God to preserve her sister. She missed her mother's help and just now, her burden seemed very heavy to bear. She tried to keep cheerful and be satisfied with doing right, though no one praised her for it.

In her effort at being good, she decided to make her will, as Aunt March had done, so that if she did fall ill and die, her possessions might be justly divided. It cost her a pang even to think of giving up her little treasures.

---

[4] **affianced.** Engaged to be married
[5] **Divine Mother.** A name for Mary, mother of Jesus

Vocabulary in Place
confide, *v.* To tell something private
procrastination, *n.* Putting things off or delaying them to an indefinite time in the future

During one of her play hours she wrote out the important document as well as she could, with some help from Esther as to certain legal terms. When the good-natured Frenchwoman had signed her name, Amy laid it by to show Laurie, whom she wanted as a second witness.

When Laurie arrived the next day, he was graciously received. "Please sit down. I want to consult you about a very serious matter," said Amy, as she retrieved the document from her desk and settled herself across from him in a very businesslike manner. "I wrote this yesterday, when Aunt was asleep, and I was trying to be as still as a mouse. I want you to read it, please, and tell me if it is legal and right. I felt I ought to do it, for life is uncertain, and I don't want any ill feeling over my tomb."

Laurie bit his lips to keep from smiling and turned a little from the thoughtful speaker, as he read the document with admirable seriousness, considering the spelling. It began—

Why is Laurie amused? Why does he try to hide his amusement from Amy?

MY LAST WILL AND TESTAMENT

I, Amy Curtis March, being in my sane mind, go give and bequeethe[6] *all my earthly property—viz. to wit:—namely*

To my father, my best pictures, sketches, maps, and works of art, including frames. Also my $100, to do what he likes with.

To my mother, all my clothes, except the blue apron with pockets—also my likeness, and my medal, with much love.

To my dear sister Margaret, I give my turkquoise ring (if I get it), also my green box with the doves on it, also my piece of real lace for her neck, and my sketch of her as a memorial of her "little girl."

To Jo I leave my pin, the one mended with sealing wax, also my bronze inkstand—she lost the cover—and my most precious plaster rabbit, because I am sorry I burned up her story.

To Beth (if she lives after me) I give my dolls and the little bureau, my fan, my linen collars and my new slippers if she can wear them being thin when she gets well. And I herewith also leave her my regret that I ever made fun of old Joanna.

---

[6] **bequeethe.** Bequeath; to leave personal property by will

To my friend and neighbor Theodore Laurence I bequeethe my paper mashay *portfolio*, my clay model of a horse though he did say it hadn't any neck. Also in return for his great kindness in the hour of affliction any one of my artistic works he likes. Noter Dame[7] is the best.

To Mr. Laurence I leave my purple box with a looking glass in the cover which will be nice for his pens and remind him of the departed girl who thanks him for his favors to her family, especially Beth.

I wish my favorite playmate Kitty Bryant to have the blue silk apron and my gold-bead ring with a kiss.

To Hannah I give the bandbox she wanted and all the patchwork I leave hoping she "will remember me, when it you see."

And now having disposed of my most valuable property I hope all will be satisfied and not blame the dead. I forgive everyone and trust we may all meet when the trumpets shall sound. Amen.

To this will and testament I set my hand and seal on this 20th day of Nov. Anni Domino 1861.

Amy Curtis March
Witnesses: Estelle Valnor, Theodore Laurence.

The last name was written in pencil, and Amy explained that he was to rewrite it in ink and seal it up for her properly.

"What put it into your head? Did anyone tell you about Beth's giving away her things?" asked Laurie soberly.

She explained and then asked anxiously, "What about Beth?"

"I'm sorry I spoke, but as I did, I'll tell you. She felt so ill one day that she told Jo she wanted to give her piano to Meg, her cats to you, and the poor old doll to Jo, who would love it for her sake. She was sorry she had so little to give, and left locks of hair to the rest of us, and her best love to Grandpa. She never thought of a will."

Laurie was signing and sealing as he spoke, and did not look up till a great tear dropped on the paper. Amy's face was full of trouble, but she only said, "Don't people put postscripts to their wills, sometimes?"

"Yes, 'codicils,' they call them."

What does Laurie tell Amy about Beth? Why did she give a lock of hair to some people?

[7]**Noter Dame.** Amy's attempt to spell Notre Dame, a cathedral in Paris and the subject of one of her artworks

"Put one in mine then, that I wish all my curls cut off and given round to my friends. I forgot it, but I want it done though it will spoil my looks."

Laurie added it, smiling at Amy's last and greatest sacrifice. Then he amused her for an hour, but when he came to go, Amy whispered with trembling lips, "Is there really any danger about Beth?"

"I'm afraid there is, but we must hope for the best, so don't cry, dear." And Laurie put his arm about her with a brotherly gesture, which was very comforting.

When he had gone, she went to her little chapel, and sitting in the twilight, prayed for Beth, with streaming tears and an aching heart, feeling that a million turquoise rings would not console her for the loss of her gentle little sister.

CHAPTER 20

Confidential

I don't think I have any words in which to tell the beautiful meeting of the mother and daughters, so I will leave it to the imagination of my readers, merely saying that the house was full of genuine happiness. Meg's tender hope was realized, for when Beth woke from that long, healing sleep, the first objects on which her eyes fell were the little rose and Mother's face. She smiled and nestled close in the loving arms about her. Then she slept again, and the girls waited upon their mother, for she would not unclasp the thin hand, which clung to hers even in sleep.

Hannah "dished up" an astonishing breakfast for the traveler, and Meg and Jo fed their mother like dutiful young storks, while they listened to her whispered account of Father's state, Mr. Brooke's promise to stay and nurse him, the long homeward journey, and the unspeakable comfort Laurie's hopeful face had given her when she arrived, worn out with fatigue, anxiety, and cold.

The house was quiet and **reposeful** that day, for everyone slept with a blissful sense of burdens lifted off. Mrs. March would not leave Beth's side, but rested in the big chair, waking often to look at, touch, and **brood** over her child.

Laurie meanwhile went off to comfort Amy, and told his story so well that Aunt March actually "sniffed" herself, and never once said "I told you so." Amy came out so strong on this occasion that I think the good thoughts in the little chapel really began to bear fruit. She dried her tears quickly, restrained her impatience to see her mother, and never even thought of the turquoise ring, when the old lady

Why is everyone able to sleep so soundly now?

Vocabulary in Place
reposeful, *adj.* Calm and peaceful
brood, *v.* To focus attention on; protect; worry over

heartily agreed in Laurie's opinion that she behaved "like a capital little woman." Even Polly seemed impressed, for he called her a good girl, blessed her buttons, and begged her to "come and take a walk, dear," in his most **affable** tone. She would very gladly have gone out to enjoy the bright wintry weather, but discovering that Laurie was dropping with sleep in spite of manful efforts to conceal the fact, she persuaded him to rest on the sofa, while she wrote a note to her mother. She was a long time about it, and when she returned, he was stretched out with both arms under his head, sound asleep, while Aunt March had pulled down the curtains and sat doing nothing in an unusual fit of kindness.

After a while, they began to think he was not going to wake up till night, and I'm not sure that he would, had he not been effectually roused by Amy's cry of joy at the sight of her mother. There probably were a good many happy little girls in and about the city that day, but it is my private opinion that Amy was the happiest of all, when she sat in her mother's lap and told her trials, receiving consolation and compensation in the shape of approving smiles and fond caresses. They were alone together in the chapel, to which her mother did not object when its purpose was explained to her.

"I like it very much, dear," said Marmee, looking from the well-worn little book to the lovely picture. "It is an excellent plan to have some place where we can go to be quiet, when hard times **vex** or grieve us."

"Yes, Mother, and when I go home I mean to have a corner in the big closet to put my books and the copy of that picture which I've tried to make. The woman's face is not good, it's too beautiful for me to draw, but the baby is done better, and I love it very much. I like to think He was a little child once, for then I don't seem so far away, and that helps me."

Vocabulary in Place

affable, *adj.* Gentle and gracious; approachable

vex, *v.* To annoy or upset; aggravate

As Amy pointed to the picture, Mrs. March saw something on the lifted hand that made her smile.

Amy saw the look and said, "Aunt gave me the ring today. She called me to her and kissed me, and put it on my finger, and said I was a credit to her, and she'd like to keep me always. She gave me this guard to keep the turquoise on, as it's too big. I'd like to wear them Mother, can I?"

"They are very pretty, but I think you're rather too young for such ornaments, Amy," said Mrs. March, looking at the band of sky-blue stones on the plump forefinger.

Why does Amy want to wear the ring?

"I'll try not to be vain," said Amy. "I don't think I like it only because it's so pretty; I want to wear it to remind me not to be selfish." Amy looked so earnest and sincere about it that her mother listened respectfully to the little plan.

"I've thought a great deal lately about my 'bundle of naughties,' and being selfish is the largest one in it, so I'm going to try hard to cure it, if I can. Beth isn't selfish, and that's the reason everyone loves her and feels so bad at the thoughts of losing her. People wouldn't feel so bad about me if I was sick, so I'm going to try and be like Beth all I can. It will be hard, but if I had something always about me to remind me, I might do better. May we try this way?"

Why does Amy want to be like Beth now?

"Yes, but I have more faith in the corner of the big closet. Wear your ring, dear, and do your best. Now I must go back to Beth. Keep up your heart, little daughter, and we will soon have you home again."

That evening while Meg was writing to her father to report the traveler's safe arrival, Jo slipped upstairs into Beth's room to talk to her mother. She stood a minute twisting her fingers in her hair, with a worried gesture and an undecided look.

"What is it, deary?" asked Mrs. March, holding out her hand, with an inviting look.

"I want to tell you something, Mother."

"About Meg?"

"How quickly you guessed! Yes, it's about her."

"Beth is asleep. Speak low, and tell me all about it."

Jo settled herself on the floor at her mother's feet. "Last summer Meg left a pair of gloves over at the Laurences' and only one was returned. We forgot about it, till Teddy told me that Mr. Brooke likes Meg but doesn't dare say so, because she is so young and he so poor. Now, isn't it a dreadful state of things?"

"Do you think Meg cares for him?" asked Mrs. March, with an anxious look.

"Mercy me! I don't know anything about love and such nonsense!" cried Jo, with a funny mixture of interest and **contempt**. "In novels, the girls show it by blushing, fainting away, growing thin, and acting like fools. Now Meg does not do anything of the sort. She eats and drinks and sleeps like a sensible creature."

"Then you fancy that Meg is not interested in John?"

"Who?" cried Jo, staring.

"Mr. Brooke. I call him 'John' now, and he likes it."

"Oh, dear! He's been good to Father and I know you'll take his part and let Meg marry him, if she wants to. Mean thing! To go helping you and Papa, just to wheedle you into liking him." And Jo pulled at her hair.

"My dear, don't get angry about it. John went with me at Mr. Laurence's request and was so devoted to poor Father that we couldn't help getting fond of him. He told us he loved Meg but would earn a comfortable home before he asked her to marry him. He only wanted our **leave** to try to make her love him if he could. He is a truly excellent, honorable young man, and we could not refuse to listen to him, but I will not consent to Meg's engaging herself so young."

"Of course not. It would be idiotic! I knew there was mischief brewing. I felt it, and now it's worse than I imagined."

"Jo, I confide in you and don't wish you to say anything to Meg yet. When John comes back, and I see them together, I can judge better of her feelings toward him."

Why is Jo angry at Mr. Brooke?

Vocabulary in Place

contempt, *n.* Scorn, disgust

leave, *n.* Permission

Why isn't Jo pleased that her parents like Mr. Brooke?

"She'll see those handsome eyes that she talks about, and then it will be all up with her. She'll go and fall in love, and there's an end of peace and fun, and cozy times together. I see it all! Brooke will scratch up a fortune somehow, carry her off, and make a hole in the family, and I shall break my heart. Oh, dear me! Why weren't we all boys, then there wouldn't be any bother."

Jo leaned her chin on her knees and shook her fist at the **reprehensible** John.

Mrs. March sighed. "It is natural and right you should all go to homes of your own in time, but Meg is only seventeen and it will be some years before John can make a home for her. Your father and I have agreed that she shall not **bind** herself in any way, nor be married, before twenty. If she and John love one another, they can wait, and test the love by doing so. My pretty, tenderhearted girl! I hope things will go happily with her."

"Hadn't you rather have her marry a rich man?" asked Jo, as her mother's voice **faltered** a little over the last words.

"Money is a good and useful thing, Jo, and I hope you all will never feel the need of it too bitterly, but I'm not ambitious for a splendid fortune for my girls. If rank and money come with love and virtue, also, I should accept them gratefully, and enjoy your good luck, but I am content to see Meg rich in the possession of a good man's heart, for that is better than a fortune."

"I quite agree, Mother, but I'm disappointed about Meg, for I'd planned to have her marry Teddy by-and-by and sit in the lap of luxury all her days. Wouldn't it be nice?" asked Jo, looking up with a brighter face.

Vocabulary in Place

reprehensible, *adj.* Horrible, hateful; worthy of blame or criticism

bind, *v.* To make a definite, lasting commitment or promise

falter, *v.* To be unsteady in action or speak hesitantly from lack of confidence

"I'm afraid Laurie is hardly grown-up enough for Meg. Don't make plans, Jo. We can't **meddle** safely in such matters lest it spoil our friendship."

Just then Meg crept into the room with the finished letter in her hand.

"I'm going to bed," said Jo, unfolding herself and kissing them both goodnight.

"Quite right, and beautifully written," said Mrs. March, as she glanced over the letter and gave it back. "Please add that I send my love to John."

"Do you call him 'John?'" asked Meg, smiling innocently.

"Yes, he has been like a son to us, and we are very fond of him," replied Mrs. March, giving Meg a **keen** look.

"I'm glad of that, he is so lonely. Good night, Mother, dear. It is so comforting to have you here," was Meg's answer.

The kiss her mother gave her was a very tender one, and as she went away, Mrs. March said, with a mixture of satisfaction and regret, "She does not love John yet but will soon learn to."

Does Meg love John yet?

Vocabulary in Place

meddle, *v.* To interfere

keen, *adj.* Sharp or intent

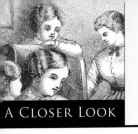

A Closer Look

Understanding the Selection

Recalling (just the facts)

1. What item of jewelry is Amy probably going to inherit from Aunt March? Why? Is she content to wait?
2. What does Amy add to her own will after she hears about Beth's? Why does she do this?
3. Why does everyone sleep "with a blissful sense of sense of burdens lifted off"?
4. Who is "Mr. Greatheart" and how did he get that nickname? What has he done for Mr. and Mrs. March since Mr. March became so ill?

Interpreting (delving deeping)

1. Why does Aunt March like Amy better than Jo? Why does Aunt March think it is her duty to bring up Amy properly?
2. Why does Amy decide to write her own will? Is she afraid she is going to die? Why does Beth tell Jo what to do with all her things?
3. What reason does Amy give for wanting to wear the ring? What lesson has Amy learned from observing Beth's behavior?
4. Is Jo suspicious of Mr. Brooke's motives for helping Father? Explain.

Synthesizing (putting it all together)

1. When Amy hears from Esther that Aunt March is going to give her the little turquoise ring, how does this news affect Amy's behavior? How can you tell that Amy cares about more than just material things?
2. How does Marmee feel about Mr. Brooke? What are her hopes for Meg? Why is Jo so upset by her parents' fondness for Mr. Brooke?

Writing Exercise

EXTENSIONS

Hidden Treasures. For Amy, life with Aunt March—with her strict rules and numerous orders—is tiresome and very lonely. One of her only comforts at this difficult time is to explore the old woman's home. In particular, she enjoys investigating an Indian cabinet filled with jewels that Aunt March has collected at important moments of her life. In one compartment there is the garnet jewelry she wore when she was formally introduced to society, and in another compartment lies her wedding ring, now too small for her "fat finger." Aunt March's treasures provide Amy with hints about the old woman's past.

Write a paragraph in response to one of the following prompts:

- What do the objects that people value say about their lives or their personalities? What kinds of things do you save and why?
- Have you ever come across some treasures from the past in an old trunk or a photograph album? Describe what you found and how you felt about it.
- What are some of your favorite memories? If you could capture those special moments in time, what would you save and how would you save it? Do you save letters, birthday cards, pictures, invitations, or ticket stubs from events as keepsakes?
- Which do you think might bring back some memories more vividly ten or twenty years from now: a handwritten note or an e-mail? A digital photograph or a handmade picture or collage? Explain your reasoning.

History Alive!

EXTENSIONS

Trunks in the Attic: Photographs and Memories. Do you remember the "go abroady" trunk Meg packs at the beginning of Chapter 8 when she goes to visit the Moffats for a couple of weeks? A trip abroad—to Europe—is a luxury beyond the reach of the Marches right now, but the trunk still holds memories of past adventures and dreams of future ones for Meg and her sisters.

While Meg is packing the clothes for her visit, including the clothes she will wear to parties while she is away, Marmee brings out a few surprises of her own—things she had been saving in her own "treasure box." She gives Meg "a few relics" from the past, when she had more fancy clothes, including silk stockings, a "pretty carved fan, and a lovely blue sash." Perhaps Marmee wore these things at a ball when she was younger, and by sharing personal relics from her own past she is expressing her love for her oldest child.

Relics, or items from the past, are also called **keepsakes**, and Victorians were very fond of collecting them, especially if they had sentimental value. One favorite pastime was to keep a scrapbook of pictures and letters of important events or interesting subjects. They filled their scrapbooks with personal notes, meaningful lines of poetry, and pictures of things such as angels, birds, and butterflies.

Victorians also thought it quite romantic to keep a lock of a loved one's hair. In the days when people exchanged handwritten letters instead of emails, most people did not own any images of the people they cared about. Only wealthy patrons had the resources to commission an artist to paint a portrait or create a framed silhouette—a profile in solid black. And, though growing in popularity, photography was a relatively rare art form. In those days, a lock of hair—rather than a photograph—was a common token of love or remembrance of a loved one. Recall that during her illness, Beth requests that, if she should die, her locks should be given to family members. In imitation of her sister, Amy wills her beloved blond curls to her friends, though not without difficulty. Likewise, Jo, after selling her hair to the barber to help raise money for Marmee's trip to Washington, D.C., gives her

History Alive!

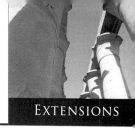

EXTENSIONS

mother a lock of hair "just to remember past glories by." Marmee tucks that lock of hair away into her desk with another "short gray one," presumably one that belonged to her husband, who is now very sick and far away.

Although locks were often tucked away in special drawers or keepsake boxes, Victorians also developed hair art. They wove hair into knot designs to create broaches and other jewelry. One popular kind of hair art involved the arrangement of hair in a pattern, which was glued on mother of pearl and covered with glass. These were often worn as pendants or pins. The zenith of the popularity of hair art and jewelry came after the death of Queen Victoria's husband, Prince Albert. In her mourning, Queen Victoria demanded that all jewelry worn at court could only be mourning and hair jewelry. As a result of this proclamation, hair jewelry soon became fashionable across Europe and in the United States.

People in the Victorian era also liked to keep their relics in special places. For example, elaborately decorated keepsake and jewelry boxes became very popular. Designs on ordinary household items, such as letter openers and hairbrushes, also reflected the Victorians' taste for all things elegant and yet elaborate. Personal relics from the Victorian era are highly collectible these days, and examples (and imitations) can be found in virtually any antique shop or auction.

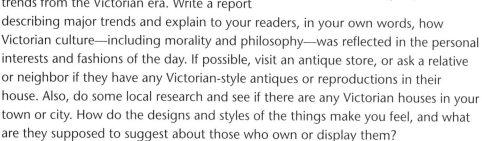

Conduct more research on personal keepsakes and other relics as well as decorative and artistic trends from the Victorian era. Write a report describing major trends and explain to your readers, in your own words, how Victorian culture—including morality and philosophy—was reflected in the personal interests and fashions of the day. If possible, visit an antique store, or ask a relative or neighbor if they have any Victorian-style antiques or reproductions in their house. Also, do some local research and see if there are any Victorian houses in your town or city. How do the designs and styles of the things make you feel, and what are they supposed to suggest about those who own or display them?

CHAPTER 21

Laurie Makes Mischief, and Jo Makes Peace

Jo's face was a study next day, for the secret rather weighed upon her, and she found it hard not to look mysterious and important. Meg observed it, but did not trouble herself to make inquiries, for she had learned that the best way to manage Jo was by the law of contraries, so she felt sure of being told everything if she did not ask. She was rather surprised, therefore, when the silence remained unbroken, and Jo assumed a patronizing air, which decidedly aggravated Meg, who in turn assumed an air of dignified reserve and devoted herself to her mother. This left Jo to her own devices, for Mrs. March had taken her place as nurse, and bade her rest, exercise, and amuse herself after her long confinement. Amy being gone, Laurie was her only refuge, and much as she enjoyed his society, she rather dreaded him just then, for he was an incorrigible tease, and she feared he would **coax** the secret from her.

She was quite right, for the mischief-loving lad no sooner suspected a mystery than he set himself to find it out. He wheedled, bribed, threatened, and scolded; and then he tried to pretend he didn't care to know, which was often the best way to get Jo to reveal a secret. At last, he determined that it concerned Meg and Mr. Brooke, and set his wits to work to devise some proper revenge for not being taken in to his friend's confidence.

Meg meanwhile was absorbed in preparations for her father's return, but all of a sudden a change seemed to come over her, and, for

Vocabulary in Place
coax, *v.* Trick someone into revealing or doing something

a day or two, she was quite unlike herself. She blushed when looked at, was very quiet, and sat over her sewing with a timid, troubled look on her face.

"She feels it in the air—love, I mean. She's got most of the symptoms—is twittery and cross, doesn't eat, lies awake, and mopes in corners. Once she said 'John,' as you do, and then turned as red as a poppy. Whatever shall we do?" said Jo, looking ready for any measures, however violent.

"Nothing but wait. Let her alone and Father's coming will settle everything," replied her mother.

"Here's a note to you, Meg, all sealed up. How odd! Teddy never seals mine," said Jo next day, as she distributed the contents of the little post office.

Mrs. March and Jo were deep in their own affairs, when a sound from Meg made them look up to see her staring at her note with a frightened face.

"My child, what is it?" cried her mother, running to her, while Jo tried to take the paper which had done the mischief.

"Oh, Jo, how could you do it?" and Meg hid her face in her hands, crying as if her heart were quite broken.

"Me! I've done nothing! What's she talking about?" cried Jo, bewildered.

Meg's mild eyes kindled with anger as she pulled a crumpled note from her pocket and threw it at Jo, saying,

"You wrote it, and that bad boy helped you. How could you be so rude, so mean, and cruel to us both?"

Jo hardly heard her, for she and her mother were reading the note, which was written in a peculiar hand.[1]

How can Jo tell that Meg is in love?

---

[1] **hand.** Handwriting

    My Dearest Margaret,

    I can no longer restrain my passion, and must know my fate before I return. I dare not tell your parents yet, but I think they would consent if they knew that we adored one another. Mr. Laurence will help me to some good place, and then, my sweet girl, you will make me happy. I implore you to say nothing to your family yet, but to send one word of hope through Laurie to,

    Your devoted John.

    "Oh, the little villain! He did it to pay me for keeping my word to Mother. I'll give him a hearty scolding and bring him over to beg pardon," cried Jo, burning with fury. But her mother held her back, saying . . .

    "Stop, Jo, you must clear yourself first. You have played so many pranks that I am afraid you have had a hand in this."

    "On my word, Mother, I haven't! I don't know anything about it, as true as I live!" said Jo, so earnestly that they believed her. "If I had taken part, I'd have done it better than this. I should think you'd have known Mr. Brooke wouldn't write such stuff as that," she added, **scornfully** tossing down the paper.

    "It's like his writing," faltered Meg, comparing it with the note in her hand.

    "Oh, Meg, you didn't answer it?" cried Mrs. March quickly.

    "Yes, I did!" and Meg hid her face again, overcome with shame.

    "This is far worse than I thought. Tell me the whole story," commanded Mrs. March, sitting down by Meg and holding on to Jo, lest she fly off after Laurie.

    "I received the first letter from Laurie, who looked very innocent when delivering it," began Meg, without looking up. "I was worried at first and meant to tell you; then I remembered how you liked Mr. Brooke, so I thought you wouldn't mind if I kept my little secret for

Why is Marmee upset that Meg answered the letter?

Vocabulary in Place

scornfully, *adv.* Showing disgust or contempt

a few days. Forgive me, Mother, I'm paid for my silliness now. I never can look him in the face again."

"What did you say to him?" asked Mrs. March.

"I only said I was too young to do anything about it yet, that I didn't wish to have secrets from you, and he must speak to father. I was very grateful for his kindness, and would be his friend, but nothing more, for a long while."

Mrs. March smiled, as if well pleased, and Jo clapped her hands, exclaiming, with a laugh, "You are a model of **prudence!** Tell on, Meg. What did he say to that?"

"He writes in a different way entirely, telling me that he never sent any love letter at all, and is very sorry that my **roguish** sister, Jo, should take liberties with our names. It's very kind and respectful, but think how dreadful for me!"

Meg leaned against her mother, looking the image of despair, and Jo tramped about the room, calling Laurie names. All of a sudden she stopped, examined the two notes, and said decidedly, "I don't believe Brooke ever saw either of these letters. Teddy wrote both."

"You go and get Laurie. I shall sift the matter to the bottom, and put a stop to such pranks at once."

Away ran Jo, and Mrs. March gently told Meg Mr. Brooke's real feelings. "Now, dear, what are your own? Do you love him enough to wait till he can make a home for you, or will you keep yourself quite free for the present?"

"I've been so scared and worried, I don't want to have anything to do with lovers for a long while, perhaps never," answered Meg. "If John doesn't know anything about this nonsense, don't tell him, and make Jo and Laurie hold their tongues. I won't be deceived and made a fool of. It's a shame!"

Why does Marmee send for Laurie?

Vocabulary in Place

prudence, *n.* Self-discipline and carefulness

roguish, *adj.* Naughty or mischievous

discretion, *n.* Restraint or judgment, especially in handling a secret or delicate matter

Seeing Meg's usually gentle temper was roused and her pride hurt by this mischievous joke, Mrs. March soothed her by promises of entire silence and great **discretion** for the future. The instant Laurie's step was heard in the hall, Meg fled into the study, and Mrs. March received the **culprit** alone. Jo had not told him why he was wanted, fearing he wouldn't come, but he knew the minute he saw Mrs. March's face, and stood twirling his hat with a guilty air. Jo was dismissed, but stood in the hall like a sentinel, for fear that the prisoner might bolt. The sound of voices in the parlor rose and fell for half an hour, but what happened during that interview the girls never knew.

When they were called in, Laurie was standing by their mother with such a penitent face that Jo forgave him on the spot, but did not think it wise to betray the fact. Meg received his humble apology, and was much comforted by the assurance that Brooke knew nothing of the joke.

"I'll never tell him to my dying day, wild horses shan't drag it out of me, so you'll forgive me, Meg, and I'll do anything to show how sorry I am," he added, looking very much ashamed of himself.

"I'll try, but it was a very ungentlemanly thing to do. I didn't think you could be so sly and malicious, Laurie," replied Meg, showing her disapproval.

"It was altogether abominable; you will forgive me, though, won't you?" And Laurie folded his hands together with such a pleading look that it was impossible to frown upon him in spite of his scandalous behavior.

Meg pardoned him, and Mrs. March's grave face relaxed, in spite of her efforts to keep sober. Meanwhile, Jo stood **aloof**, trying to harden her heart against him, primming up her face into an

---

Vocabulary in Place

culprit, *n.* The one guilty of wrongdoing; criminal

aloof, *adj.* Off by oneself; not friendly or approachable

relent, *v.* To give in

expression of disapproval. Laurie looked at her once or twice, but as she showed no sign of **relenting**, he made her a low bow and walked off without a word.

As soon as he had gone, she wished she had been more forgiving, and when Meg and her mother went upstairs, she felt lonely and longed for Teddy. After resisting for some time, she yielded to the impulse, and armed with a book to return, went over to the big house.

"Is Mr. Laurence in?" asked Jo, of a housemaid, who was coming downstairs.

"Yes, Miss, but I don't believe he's seeable just yet."

"Why not? Is he ill?"

"No Miss, but he's had a scene with Mr. Laurie, who is in one of his tantrums about something, which vexes the old gentleman."

"Where is Laurie?"

"Shut up in his room, and he won't answer, though I've been a-tapping. I don't know what's to become of the dinner, for it's ready, and there's no one to eat it."

"I'll go and see what the matter is. I'm not afraid of either of them."

Up went Jo, and knocked smartly on the door of Laurie's little study.

"Stop that, or I'll open the door and make you!" called out the young gentleman in a threatening tone.

Jo immediately knocked again. The door flew open, and in she bounced before Laurie could recover from his surprise. Seeing that he really was out of temper, Jo assumed a **contrite** expression, and going dramatically down upon her knees, said meekly, "Please forgive me for being so cross. I came to make it up, and can't go away till I have."

"It's all right. Get up, and don't be a goose, Jo," was the **cavalier** reply to her petition.

Why does Jo apologize to Laurie?

Vocabulary in Place

contrite, *adj.* Genuinely sorry and sincere

cavalier, *adj.* Carefree and nonchalant; casual

"Thank you, I will. Could I ask what's the matter? You don't look exactly easy in your mind."

"I've been shaken by Grandfather, and I won't bear it!" growled Laurie indignantly. "Just because I wouldn't say what your mother wanted me for. I'd promised not to tell, and of course I wasn't going to break my word. I'd have told my part of the scrape, if I could without bringing Meg in. As I couldn't, I held my tongue, and bore the scolding till the old gentleman collared me. Then I bolted, for fear I should forget myself."

"It wasn't nice, but he's sorry, I know, so go down and make up. I'll help you."

"Hanged if I do! I was sorry about Meg, and begged pardon like a man, but I won't do it again, when I wasn't in the wrong."

"He didn't know that."

"He ought to trust me, and not act as if I was a baby."

What does Jo mean when she calls Laurie and Mr. Laurence "pepper pots"?

"What pepper pots you are!" sighed Jo. "How do you mean to settle this affair?"

"Well, he ought to beg pardon, and believe me when I say I can't tell him what the fuss's about."

"Bless you! He won't do that."

"I won't go down till he does."

"Now, Teddy, be sensible. You can't stay here, so what's the use of being melodramatic?"

"I don't intend to stay here long, anyway. I'll slip off and take a journey somewhere, and when Grandpa misses me he'll come round fast enough. I'll go to Washington and see Brooke. It's gay there, and I'll enjoy myself after the troubles."[2]

If Jo went with him, where would they go?

"What fun you'd have! I wish I could run off too," said Jo, forgetting her part of mentor in lively visions of **martial** life at the capital.

---

[2] **troubles.** A reference to the war

Vocabulary in Place

martial, *v.* Relating to an army or to military life

"Come on, then! Why not? You go and surprise your father, and I'll stir up old Brooke. It would be a glorious joke. Let's do it, Jo. We'll leave a letter saying we are all right, and trot off at once. I've got money enough. It will do you good, and no harm, as you go to your father."

For a moment Jo looked as if she would agree, for she was tired of care and confinement and longed for change, liberty, and fun. Her eyes kindled as they turned wistfully toward the window, but they fell on the old house opposite, and she shook her head with sorrowful decision.

"If I was a boy, we'd run away together, and have a capital time, but as I'm a miserable girl, I must be proper and stop at home. Don't tempt me, Teddy, it's a crazy plan."

"That's the fun of it," began Laurie, who was bent on having his own way.

"Bad boy, be quiet! Sit down and think of your own sins, don't go making me add to mine. If I get your grandpa to apologize for the shaking, will you give up running away?" asked Jo seriously.

"Yes, but you won't do it," answered Laurie, who wished to make up, but felt that his outraged dignity must be **appeased** first.

"If I can manage the young one, I can the old one," muttered Jo, as she walked away, leaving Laurie bent over a railroad map.

"Come in!" and Mr. Laurence's gruff voice sounded gruffer than ever, as Jo tapped at his door.

"It's only me, Sir, come to return a book," she said as she entered.

"Want any more?" asked the old gentleman, looking grim but trying not to show it.

"Yes, please. I like this one so well, I think I'll try the second volume," returned Jo, hoping to soften him by praising his recommendations.

The shaggy eyebrows unbent a little as he rolled the steps toward the proper shelf. Jo climbed up, thinking of how to introduce her

Why does Jo say, "Don't tempt me"? Does she really want to go, too? Why can't she go?

Vocabulary in Place

appease, *v.* To soothe or quiet down

subject, but Mr. Laurence seemed to suspect that something was brewing in her mind, for he faced round on her, and said abruptly,

"What has that boy been about? Don't try to shield him. I know he has been in mischief by the way he acted when he came home. I can't get a word from him, and when I threatened to shake the truth out of him he bolted upstairs and locked himself into his room."

"He did wrong, but we forgave him, and all promised not to say a word to anyone," began Jo reluctantly.

"That won't do. He shall not shelter himself behind a promise from you softhearted girls. If he's done anything amiss, he shall confess, beg pardon, and be punished. Out with it, Jo. I won't be kept in the dark."

Mr. Laurence looked so alarming and spoke so sharply that Jo would have gladly run away, if she could, but she was perched aloft on the steps, and could not get past him.

"Indeed, Sir, I cannot tell. Mother forbade it. Laurie has confessed, asked pardon, and been punished quite enough. We don't keep silence to shield him, but someone else, and it will make more trouble if you interfere. Please don't. It was partly my fault, but it's all right now. So let's forget it."

"Come down and give me your word that this harum-scarum[3] boy of mine hasn't done anything ungrateful or **impertinent**. If he has, I'll thrash him with my own hands."

The threat sounded awful, but did not alarm Jo, for she knew the irascible old gentleman would never lift a finger against his grandson. She obediently descended, and made as light of the prank as she could without betraying Meg or forgetting the truth.

"Hum . . . ha . . . well, if the boy held his tongue because he promised, I'll forgive him. He's a stubborn fellow and hard to manage," said Mr. Laurence, smoothing the frown from his brow with an air of relief.

---

[3] **harum-scarum.** Lacking a sense of responsibility; reckless

Vocabulary in Place
impertinent, *adj.* Rude in speech; fresh

"So am I, but a kind word will govern me when all the king's horses and all the king's men couldn't," said Jo, trying to say a good word for her friend.

"You think I'm too hard on the boy. Well, you're right, girl! I love the boy, but he tries my patience past bearing, and I know how it will end, if we go on so."

"He'll run away." Jo was sorry for that speech the minute it was made, for Mr. Laurence's ruddy face changed suddenly, and he sat down, with a troubled glance at the picture of Laurie's father, who had run away in his youth, and married against the old man's will. Jo wished she had held her tongue.

Why does Jo regret what she said?

"He won't do it unless he is very much worried, and only threatens it sometimes, when he gets tired of studying. I often think I should like to, especially since my hair was cut, so if you ever miss us, you may advertise for two boys and look among the ships bound for India."

She laughed as she spoke, and Mr. Laurence looked relieved, evidently taking the whole as a joke.

"You hussy,[4] how dare you talk in that way? Where's your respect for me, and your proper bringing up?" he said, pinching her cheeks good-humoredly. "Go and bring that boy down to his dinner, and tell him it's all right."

"He won't come, Sir. He feels badly because you didn't believe him when he said he couldn't tell. I think the shaking hurt his feelings very much."

Jo tried to look pathetic but must have failed, for Mr. Laurence began to laugh, and she knew the day was won.

"I'm sorry for that, and ought to thank him for not shaking me, I suppose," and the old gentleman looked a trifle ashamed.

"If I were you, I'd write him an apology, Sir. A formal apology will make him see how foolish he is, and bring him down quite amiable. Try it. He likes fun, and this way is better than talking. I'll carry it up."

Mr. Laurence gave her a sharp look, and put on his spectacles, saying slowly, "You're a sly puss. Here, give me a bit of paper, and let us have done with this nonsense."

The note was written in the terms which one gentleman would use to another after offering some deep insult. Jo dropped a kiss on the top of Mr. Laurence's bald head, and ran up to Laurie's room. She called to Laurie to be a good boy and slipped the note under the door. She was going quietly away, when the young gentleman slid down the banister, and waited for her at the bottom, saying, with his most virtuous expression, "What a good fellow you are, Jo! I'm ever so sorry about my temper."

---

[4] **hussy.** A saucy or disrespectful girl

"Go and eat your dinner, you'll feel better after it," said Jo feeling quite satisfied that all was well as she whisked out the front door.

Everyone thought the matter ended and the little cloud blown over, but the mischief was done, for though others forgot it, Meg remembered. She dreamed dreams more than ever, and once as Jo was rummaging her sister's desk for stamps, she found a bit of paper scribbled over with the words, "Mrs. John Brooke." She groaned tragically and cast it into the fire, feeling that Laurie's prank had hastened the evil day for her.

Words to Keep

The following sentences contain important words from the Vocabulary in Place boxes in Chapters 18–21 of *Little Women*. In your notebook, or on a separate sheet of paper, write the part of speech of each boldface word, a synonym (or a short definition in your own words), and a new sentence of your own.

1. When you have a difficult decision to make, let your **conscience** be your guide.
2. **Pallor** overtook Kelley's face when she realized she had forgotten to study for the test.
3. The little boy tried to hold a **vigil** to await Santa on Christmas Eve, but he soon fell asleep by the fireplace.
4. Always be careful around strange dogs no matter how **docile** they appear to be.
5. The ancient Mesopotamians used levees and canals to **counteract** the yearly flooding of the Tigris and Euphrates rivers.
6. Carol never **confides** in me; she doesn't want me to know any of her secrets.
7. Many students learn the hard way that **procrastination** is not the best way to approach a term paper or a research project.
8. The gracious host led her guests into the dining room with an **affable** smile.
9. Fred wanted to ask Emily to dance, but he was afraid that she would reject his offer with **contempt**.
10. Stealing donations from the orphans' fund was **reprehensible**.

CHAPTER 22

Pleasant Meadows

The peaceful weeks which followed were like sunshine after a storm. The invalids improved rapidly, and Mr. March wrote that he would be joining them soon. Beth soon was able to lie on the study sofa all day, amusing herself with her cats and with doll's sewing. Her limbs were so stiff and **feeble** that Jo took her for a daily airing about the house in her strong arms. Meg cheerfully burned her white hands cooking for "the dear," while Amy gave away as many of her treasures as her sisters would accept.

As Christmas approached, Jo and Laurie were clearly plotting some surprise, as there was a good deal of whispering whenever the two got together, and frequent explosions of laughter. Several days of unusually mild weather ushered in a splendid Christmas Day. Beth felt uncommonly well that morning, and, dressed in her mother's gift—a soft crimson wrapper[1]—was carried to the window to behold the offering of Jo and Laurie.

The Unquenchables had worked by night like elves and had created a comical surprise. Out in the garden stood a stately snow maiden, crowned with holly, bearing a basket of fruit and flowers in one hand, a great roll of music in the other, a perfect rainbow afghan[2] round her chilly shoulders, and a Christmas carol **issuing** from her lips on a pink paper streamer.

---

[1] **crimson wrapper.** Red robe

[2] **afghan.** A type of blanket

Vocabulary in Place
feeble, *adj*. Weak
issue, *v*. To come out

THE JUNGFRAU[3] TO BETH

God bless you, dear Queen Bess!
May nothing you dismay,
But health and peace and happiness
Be yours, this Christmas day.
Here's fruit to feed our busy bee,
And flowers for her nose.
Here's music for her pianee,
An afghan for her toes,
Their dearest love my makers laid
Within my breast of snow.
Accept it, and the Alpine maid,
From Laurie and from Jo.

How Beth laughed when she saw it. Laurie ran up and down to bring in the gifts, and Jo made ridiculous speeches as she presented them.

"I'm so full of happiness, that if Father was only here, I couldn't hold one drop more," said Beth, sighing with contentment.

"So am I," added Jo, slapping the pocket which held the long-desired *Undine and Sintram*.

"I'm sure I am," echoed Amy, staring adoringly at her new copy of the *Madonna and Child*, which her mother had given her in a pretty frame.

"Of course I am!" cried Meg, smoothing the silvery folds of her first silk dress, for Mr. Laurence had insisted on giving it.

"How can I be otherwise?" said Mrs. March gratefully, as her eyes went from her husband's letter to Beth's smiling face and her hand carressed the brooch[4] made of gray and golden, chestnut and dark brown hair, which the girls had just fastened on her breast.

Half an hour after everyone had said they were so happy they could only hold one drop more, the drop came. Laurie opened the

---

[3] **Jungfrau.** German for "virgin snow peak;" Swiss for "maiden"

[4] **brooch.** (Also broach.) A large decorative pin.

> **What do the girls and Marmee get for Christmas?**

parlor door and popped his head in very quietly. His face was full of suppressed excitement as he said, in a queer, breathless voice, "Here's another Christmas present for the March family."

Before the words were well out of his mouth, he was whisked away somehow, and in his place appeared a tall man, muffled up to the eyes, leaning on the arm of another tall man. Of course there was a general stampede, and for several minutes everybody seemed to lose their wits.

Mr. March became invisible in the embrace of four pairs of loving arms. Jo nearly fainted away, and had to be doctored by Laurie, to her disgrace. Mr. Brooke kissed Meg entirely by mistake, as he somewhat incoherently explained. And **dignified** Amy tumbled over a stool, and never stopping to get up, hugged and cried over her father's boots in the most touching manner. Mrs. March was the first to recover herself, and held up her hand with a warning, "Hush! Remember Beth." But it was too late. The study door flew open, and Beth ran straight into her father's arms.

The romance of the moment was disrupted when Mr. Brooke suddenly remembered that Mr. March needed rest, and seizing Laurie, he quickly departed. Then the two invalids were ordered to rest, which they did in one big chair, talking hard.

Mr. March told how he had longed to surprise them, and how, when the fine weather came, he was able to make the journey home. He told how devoted Brooke had been, and how he was altogether a most **estimable** and upright young man. Mr. March paused a minute just there to glance at Meg, who was violently poking the fire, and then look at his wife with an inquiring lift of the eyebrows. Mrs. March gently nodded her head and asked, rather abruptly, if he wouldn't like to have something to eat. Jo saw the look and stalked grimly away to get wine and tea, muttering to herself as she slammed the door, "I hate estimable young men with brown eyes!"

Vocabulary in Place

dignified, *adj.* Formal and proper; concerned with appearances

estimable, *adj.* Worthy of praise, esteem, or admiration

There never was such a Christmas dinner as they had that day. The fat turkey was a sight to behold, stuffed, browned, and decorated. So was the plum pudding, which melted in one's mouth, likewise the jellies. Everything turned out well. Mr. Laurence and his grandson dined with them, also Mr. Brooke, at whom Jo glowered darkly, to Laurie's amusement. They drank to healths, told stories, sang songs, "**reminisced**," as the old folks say, and had a thoroughly good time.

As twilight gathered, the guests departed, and the happy family sat together round the fire.

"Just a year ago we were groaning over the dismal Christmas we expected to have. Do you remember?" asked Jo.

"Rather a pleasant year on the whole!" said Meg, smiling at the fire, thinking of Mr. Brooke.

"I think it's been a pretty hard one," observed Amy, watching the light shine on her ring with thoughtful eyes.

"I'm glad it's over, because we've got you back," whispered Beth, who sat on her father's knee.

"Rather a rough road for you to travel, my little pilgrims, especially the latter part of it. But you have got on bravely, and I think the burdens will soon tumble off," said Mr. March, looking with fatherly satisfaction at the four young faces gathered round him.

"How do you know? What did Mother tell you?" asked Jo.

"Not much. I've made several discoveries today."

"Oh, tell us what they are!" cried Meg, who sat beside him.

"Here is one." And taking up her hand, he pointed to the roughened forefinger, a burn on the back, and two or three little hard spots on the palm. "I remember a time when this hand was white and smooth, and your first care was to keep it so. It was very pretty then, but to me it is much prettier now, for this hardened palm has earned something better than blisters, and I'm sure the sewing done by these pricked fingers will last a long time. Meg, my dear, I value the womanly skill which keeps home happy more than the

Why does Mr. March think that Meg's hands are prettier now?

Vocabulary in Place

reminisce, *v.* To share memories; to trade stories and recollections about the past

beauty of white hands. I'm proud to shake this good, **industrious** little hand, and hope I shall not soon be asked to give it away."

If Meg had wanted a reward for hours of patient labor, she received it in the hearty pressure of her father's hand and the approving smile he gave her.

"Please say something nice for Jo. She has been so very, very good to me," said Beth in her father's ear.

He laughed and looked across at the tall girl who sat opposite.

"In spite of the curly crop, I don't see the 'son Jo' whom I left a year ago," said Mr. March. "I see a young lady who pins her collar straight, laces her boots neatly, and neither whistles, talks slang, nor lies on the rug as she used to do. Her face is rather thin and pale just now, with watching and anxiety, but it has grown gentler, and her voice is lower. She doesn't bounce, but moves quietly, and takes care of a certain little person in a delightfully motherly way. I rather miss my wild girl, but if I get a strong, helpful, tenderhearted woman in her place, I shall feel quite satisfied. In all Washington I couldn't find anything beautiful enough to be bought with the five-and-twenty dollars my good girl sent me."

Jo's eyes were rather dim for a minute, and her thin face grew rosy in the firelight as she received her father's praise, feeling that she did deserve a portion of it.

"Now, Beth," said Amy, longing for her turn, but ready to wait.

"There's so little of her, I'm afraid to say much, for fear she will slip away altogether, though she is not so shy as she used to be," began their father cheerfully. But **recollecting** how nearly he had lost her, he held her close, saying tenderly, "I've got you safe, my Beth, and I'll keep you so, please God."

After a minute's silence, he looked down at Amy, who sat at his feet, and said, with a caress of the shining hair . . .

Why doesn't Mr. March mind Jo's short haircut? How has Jo changed since he was gone?

Vocabulary in Place

industrious, *adj.* Hardworking

recollect, *v.* To remember, recall

"I observed that Amy took drumsticks at dinner, ran errands for her mother all the afternoon, gave Meg her place tonight, and has waited on every one with patience and good humor. She does not look in the glass, and has not even mentioned a very pretty ring which she wears. I conclude that she has learned to think of other people more and of herself less, and has decided to mold her character as carefully as she molds her little clay figures. I am glad of this, for I shall be infinitely proud of a lovable daughter with a talent for making life beautiful to herself and others."

"What are you thinking of, Beth?" asked Jo, when Amy had thanked her father and told about her ring.

"I read in *Pilgrim's Progress* today how, after many troubles, Christian and Hopeful came to a pleasant green meadow where lilies bloomed. There they rested happily, as we do now, before they went on to their journey's end," answered Beth, and she slipped out of her father's arms and went to the piano to sing in the sweet voice they had never thought to hear again.

How do Amy's actions indicate a change in her character?

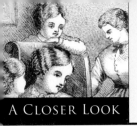

Understanding the Selection

A Closer Look

Recalling (just the facts)

1. What makes Laurie want to run away? Where does he suggest that he and Jo go?
2. How does Jo "make peace" between Laurie and his grandfather?
3. What visible changes does Mr. March notice in Jo when he comes home from the war? What other, less visible changes does he notice?
4. How did Meg's hands used to look before she had to do chores and go to work? How have they changed?

Interpreting (delving deeper)

1. Why does Laurie get in so much trouble with his grandfather after his prank? Why does he refuse to confess what he has done?
2. Why does Jo wish she hadn't told Mr. Laurence that Laurie is ready to run away from home?
3. Is Beth still very weak from her bout with scarlet fever? How can you tell?
4. Is this Christmas much happier than the one a year ago? Why or why not?

Synthesizing (putting it all together)

1. What does Chapter 21 teach about the importance of forgiveness? Find two examples in this chapter in which one character forgave another. Why is forgiveness so important and what would have happened if the characters had remained angry?
2. What changes does Mr. March notice right away when he comes home from the war? How can he tell that the girls he left behind are becoming "little women"?

CHAPTER 23

Aunt March Settles the Question

The next day mother and daughters hovered about Mr. March, neglecting everything to wait upon and listen to the new invalid. As he sat propped up in a big chair by Beth's sofa, with the other three close by, and Hannah popping her head in now and then "to peek at the dear man," nothing seemed needed to complete their happiness. But something was needed, though none confessed the fact. Mr. and Mrs. March looked at one another with an anxious expression, as their eyes followed Meg. Jo was seen to shake her fist at Mr. Brooke's umbrella, which had been left in the hall. Meg was absent-minded, shy, and silent, started when the bell rang, and blushed when John's name was mentioned.

Laurie went by in the afternoon, and seeing Meg at the window, he fell down on one knee in the snow and clasped his hands imploringly. And when Meg told him to go away, he staggered round the corner as if in utter despair.

"What does the goose mean?" said Meg, laughing and trying to look unaware.

"He's showing you how your John will go on by-and-by. Touching, isn't it?" answered Jo scornfully.

Why does Laurie pretend that he is proposing to Meg?

"Don't say my John, it isn't proper or true," but Meg's voice lingered over the words as if they sounded pleasant to her. "Please don't plague me, Jo. I've told you I don't care much about him, and we are all to be friendly, and go on as before."

"We can't, for Laurie's mischief has spoiled you for me. You are not like your old self a bit and seem ever so far away from me. I don't mean to plague you, but I do wish it was all settled. I hate to wait, so if you mean ever to do it, make haste and have it over quickly," said Jo nervously.

"I can't say anything till he speaks, and he won't because Father said I was too young," began Meg, with a queer little smile, which suggested that she did not quite agree.

"If he did speak, you wouldn't know what to say, but would cry or blush, or let him have his own way, instead of giving a good, decided 'no.'"

"Not at all. I should say, quite calmly and decidedly, 'Thank you, Mr. Brooke, you are very kind, but I agree with Father that I am too young to enter into any engagement at present, so please say no more, but let us be friends as we were.'"

"Hum, that's stiff and cool enough! I don't believe you'll ever say it, and I know he won't be satisfied if you do. You'll give in, rather than hurt his feelings."

"No, I won't. I shall tell him I've made up my mind and shall walk out of the room with dignity."

Meg rose and was just going to rehearse the dignified exit, when a step in the hall made her fly into her seat and begin to sew as fast as if her life depended on finishing that particular seam. Jo smothered a laugh and opened the door with a grim aspect which was anything but hospitable.

"Good afternoon. I came to get my umbrella, that is, to see how your father finds himself today," said Mr. Brooke, getting a trifle confused as his eyes went from one telltale face to the other.

"It's very well, he's in the rack. I'll get him, and tell it you are here." And having jumbled her father and the umbrella together in her reply, Jo slipped out of the room to give Meg a chance to make her speech and air her dignity. But the instant she vanished, Meg began to **sidle** toward the door, murmuring . . .

"Mother will like to see you. Pray sit down, I'll call her."

"Don't go. Are you afraid of me, Margaret?" said Mr. Brooke looking hurt. Meg blushed up to the little curls on her forehead, for he had never called her Margaret before, and she was surprised to find how natural and sweet it seemed to hear him say it. Anxious to appear friendly and at her ease, she put out her hand with a confiding gesture, and said gratefully . . .

> **Vocabulary in Place**
>
> **sidle,** *v.* To move sideways or stealthily

Sidebar notes:
- What might Mr. Brooke ask Meg? What does Meg plan to tell him?
- What might Mr. Brooke see in the girls' "telltale" faces?
- Why does Jo "jumble" her words?

"How can I be afraid when you have been so kind to Father? I only wish I could thank you for it."

"Shall I tell you how?" asked Mr. Brooke, holding the small hand fast in both his own, and looking down at Meg with so much love in the brown eyes that her heart began to flutter.

"Oh no, please don't, I'd rather not," she said, trying to withdraw her hand and looking frightened.

"I won't trouble you. I only want to know if you care for me a little, Meg. I love you so much, dear," added Mr. Brooke tenderly.

This was the moment for the calm, proper speech, but Meg didn't make it. She forgot every word of it, hung her head, and answered, "I don't know," so softly that John had to stoop down to catch the foolish little reply.

What happened to Meg's carefully planned speech?

He smiled to himself as if quite satisfied and said in his most persuasive tone, "Will you try and find out? I want to know so much, for I can't go to work with any heart until I learn whether I am to have my reward in the end or not."

"I'm too young," faltered Meg, wondering why she was so flustered, yet rather enjoying it.

"I'll wait, and in the meantime, you could be learning to like me. Would it be a very hard lesson, dear?"

"Not if I chose to learn it, but . . ."

"Please choose to learn, Meg. I love to teach, and this is easier than German," broke in John, taking her other hand, so that she had no way of hiding her face as he bent to look into it.

Meg stole a shy look at him and saw that his eyes were merry as well as tender, and that he wore the satisfied smile of one who had no doubt of his success. This **nettled** her, and the love of power, which sleeps in the bosoms of the best of little women, woke up all of a sudden and took possession of her. She felt excited and strange, and

---

Vocabulary in Place

nettle, *v.* To annoy or irritate

not knowing what else to do, withdrew her hands, saying **petulantly,** "I don't choose. Please go away and let me be!"

Poor Mr. Brooke looked as if his lovely castle in the air was tumbling about his ears.

"Do you really mean that?" he asked anxiously, following her as she walked away.

"Yes, I do. I don't want to be worried about such things. Father says I needn't, it's too soon, and I'd rather not."

"Mayn't I hope you'll change your mind by-and-by? I'll wait and say nothing till you have had more time. Don't play with me, Meg. I didn't think that of you."

"Don't think of me at all. I'd rather you wouldn't," said Meg, taking a naughty satisfaction in trying her lover's patience and her own power.

He was grave and pale now, and stood looking at her so wishfully, so tenderly, that she found her heart relenting in spite of herself. What would have happened next I cannot say, if Aunt March had not come hobbling in at this interesting minute.

The old lady couldn't resist her longing to see her nephew, for she had met Laurie as she took her airing and hearing of Mr. March's arrival, drove straight out to see him. The family were all busy in the back part of the house, and she had made her way quietly in, hoping to surprise them. She did surprise two of them so much that Meg started as if she had seen a ghost, and Mr. Brooke vanished into the study.

"Bless me, what's all this?" cried the old lady with a rap of her cane as she glanced from the pale young gentleman to the scarlet young lady.

"It's Father's friend. I'm so surprised to see you!" stammered Meg, feeling that she was in for a lecture now.

Vocabulary in Place

petulantly, *v.* In an unreasonably ill-tempered or irritable way

"That's **evident**," returned Aunt March, sitting down. "But what is Father's friend saying to make you look like a peony?¹ There's mischief going on, and I insist upon knowing what it is," she said with another rap.

"We were only talking. Mr. Brooke came for his umbrella," began Meg, wishing that Mr. Brooke and the umbrella were safely out of the house.

"Brooke? That boy's tutor? Ah! I understand now. I know all about it. Jo **blundered** into a wrong message in one of your Father's letters, and I made her tell me. You haven't gone and accepted him, child?" cried Aunt March, looking scandalized.

"Hush! He'll hear. Shan't I call Mother?" said Meg, much troubled.

"Not yet. I've something to say to you, and I must free my mind at once. Tell me, do you mean to marry this Cook? If you do, not one penny of my money ever goes to you. Remember that, and be a sensible girl," said the old lady impressively.

Now Aunt March was able to rouse the spirit of opposition in the gentlest of people and enjoyed doing it. If the old lady had begged Meg to accept John Brooke, she would probably have declared she couldn't think of it, but as she was ordered not to like him, she immediately made up her mind that she would. And being already much excited, Meg opposed the old lady with unusual spirit.

"I shall marry whom I please, Aunt March, and you can leave your money to anyone you like," she said, nodding her head with a resolute air.

"Highty-tighty! Is that the way you take my advice, Miss? You'll be sorry for it by-and-by, when you've tried love in a cottage and found it a failure."

---

¹ **peony.** A bush with large colorful flowers

Vocabulary in Place
evident, *adj.* Obvious
blunder, *v.* To move unsteadily or make a careless mistake

Why does Aunt March get so mad when she walks in on Meg and Mr. Brooke?

What threat does Aunt March make?

Does Meg change her mind about Brooke based on what Aunt March said? Do you think this was Aunt March's intention?

"It can't be a worse one than some people find in big houses," retorted Meg.

Aunt March put on her glasses and took a look at the girl, for she did not know her in this new mood. Meg hardly knew herself, she felt so brave and independent, so glad to defend John and her right to love him, if she liked. Aunt March saw that she had begun wrong, and after a little pause, made a fresh start, saying as mildly as she could,

"Now, Meg, my dear, be reasonable and take my advice. I mean it kindly, and don't want you to spoil your whole life by making a mistake at the beginning. You ought to marry well. It's your duty to make a rich match and help your family."

> *What is Meg's duty when it comes to choosing a husband?*

"Father and Mother don't think so. They like John though he is poor."

Aunt March took no notice, but went on with her lecture. "This Rook hasn't got any rich relations, has he?"

"No, but he has many warm friends."

> *Why does Aunt March keep mispronouncing Brooke's name?*

"You can't live on friends; try it and see how cool they'll grow. He hasn't any business, has he?"

"Not yet."

"So you intend to marry a man without money, position, or business, and go on working harder than you do now, when you might be comfortable all your days by minding me and doing better? I thought you had more sense, Meg."

"I couldn't do better if I waited half my life! John is good and wise, he's got heaps of talent, he's willing to work and sure to get on, he's so energetic and brave. Everyone likes and respects him, and I'm proud to think he cares for me, though I'm so poor and young and silly," said Meg, looking prettier than ever in her **earnestness.**

"He knows you have got rich relations, child. That's the secret of his liking, I suspect."

"Aunt March, how dare you say such a thing? John is above such meanness, and I won't listen to you a minute if you talk so," cried

---

Vocabulary in Place

earnestness, *n.* A person's state that shows depth and sincerity of feeling

Meg indignantly. "My John wouldn't marry for money, any more than I would. We are willing to work, and we mean to wait. I'm not afraid of being poor, for I've been happy so far, and I know I shall be with him because he loves me, and I . . ."

Meg stopped there, remembering all of a sudden that she hadn't made up her mind, that she had told "her John" to go away, and that he might be overhearing her **inconsistent** remarks.

Why does Meg stop in the middle of her speech?

Aunt March was very angry, for she had set her heart on having her pretty niece make a fine match, and something in the girl's happy young face made the lonely old woman feel both sad and sour.

"Well, I wash my hands of the whole affair! You are a willful child. I'm disappointed in you and haven't spirits to see your father now. Don't expect anything from me when you are married. Your Mr. Booke's friends must take care of you. I'm done with you forever."

And Aunt March stormed off, slamming the door in Meg's face. Meg stood for a moment, undecided whether to laugh or cry. Before she could make up her mind, she was taken possession of by Mr. Brooke, who said all in one breath, "I couldn't help hearing, Meg. Thank you for defending me, and Aunt March for proving that you do care for me a little bit."

"I didn't know how much till she abused you," began Meg.

"And I needn't go away, but may stay and be happy, may I, dear?"

Here was another fine chance to make the crushing speech and the stately exit, but Meg never thought of doing either, and meekly whispered,

"Yes, John," hiding her face on Mr. Brooke's waistcoat.

Fifteen minutes after Aunt March's departure, Jo came softly downstairs, paused an instant at the parlor door, and hearing no sound within, nodded and smiled with a satisfied expression, saying to herself, "She has seen him away as we planned, and that affair is settled. I'll go and hear the fun, and have a good laugh over it."

Vocabulary in Place

inconsistent, *adj.* Contradictory; the opposite of what one just said or did

But poor Jo never got her laugh, for she was **transfixed** upon the threshold by a spectacle which held her there, staring with her mouth nearly as wide open as her eyes. Her formerly strong-minded sister sat enthroned upon her lover's knee, wearing an expression of the most **abject** submission. Jo gave a sort of gasp, as if a cold shower bath had suddenly fallen upon her, for such an unexpected turning of the tables actually took her breath away. At the odd sound the lovers turned and saw her. Meg jumped up, looking both proud and shy, but "that man," as Jo called him, actually laughed and said coolly, as he kissed the astonished newcomer, "Sister Jo, congratulate us!"

That was altogether too much, and making some wild demonstration with her hands, Jo vanished without a word. Rushing upstairs, she burst into the invalids' room exclaiming tragically, "Somebody go down quick! John Brooke is acting dreadfully, and Meg likes it!"

Mr. and Mrs. March left the room with speed, and casting herself upon the bed, Jo cried.

Nobody ever knew what went on in the parlor that afternoon, but a great deal of talking was done, and quiet Mr. Brooke astonished his friends by the spirit with which he pleaded his suit, told his plans, and persuaded them to arrange everything just as he wanted it. The tea bell rang before he had finished describing the paradise which he meant to earn for Meg, and he proudly took her in to supper, both looking so happy that Jo hadn't the heart to be jealous or dismal. Amy was very much impressed by John's devotion and Meg's dignity, Beth beamed at them from a distance, while Mr. and Mrs. March surveyed the young couple with tender satisfaction. No one ate much, but everyone looked very happy, and the old room seemed to brighten up amazingly with the first romance of the family.

How do Amy and Beth react to Meg's new romance?

Vocabulary in Place

transfixed, *past part.* Motionless, as with terror or awe

abject, *adj.* Hopeless or wretched

"You can't say nothing pleasant ever happens now, can you, Meg?" said Amy, trying to decide how she would group the lovers in a sketch she was planning to make.

"No, I'm sure I can't. How much has happened since I said that! It seems a year ago," answered Meg, who was in a blissful dream.

"Hope the next year will end better," muttered Jo, who found it very hard to see Meg absorbed in a stranger.

"I hope the third year from this will end better. I mean it shall, if I live to work out my plans," said Mr. Brooke, smiling at Meg, as if everything had become possible to him now.

"Doesn't it seem very long to wait?" asked Amy, who was in a hurry for the wedding.

"I've got so much to learn before I shall be ready, it seems a short time to me," answered Meg, with a sweet gravity in her face never seen there before.

"You have only to wait, I am to do the work," said John, with an expression which caused Jo to shake her head.

As the front door banged, Jo said to herself with an air of relief, "Here comes Laurie. Now we shall have some sensible conversation."

But Jo was mistaken, for Laurie came prancing in, overflowing with good spirits, bearing a great bridal-looking bouquet for "Mrs. John Brooke."

"I knew Brooke would have it all his own way, he always does, for when he makes up his mind to accomplish anything, it's done though the sky falls," said Laurie, when he had presented his offering and his congratulations.

As the little party adjourned to the parlor to greet Mr. Laurence, Laurie followed Jo into a corner. "You don't look festive, ma'am, what's the matter?" he asked.

"I don't approve of the match, but I shall not say a word against it," said Jo solemnly. "You can't know how hard it is for me to give up Meg," she continued with a little quiver in her voice. "I've lost my dearest friend."

Why is Jo having such a difficult time?

"You've got me, anyhow. I'm not good for much, I know, but I'll stand by you, Jo, all the days of my life. Upon my word I will!" And Laurie meant what he said.

"I know you will. You are always a great comfort to me, Teddy," returned Jo, gratefully shaking hands.

"Well, now, don't be dismal, there's a good fellow. It's all right you see. We'll have capital times after Meg in her own little house, for I shall be through college before long, and then we'll go abroad on some nice trip or other. Wouldn't that console you?"

"I rather think it would, but there's no knowing what may happen in three years," said Jo thoughtfully.

"That's true. Don't you wish you could take a look forward and see where we shall all be then? I do," returned Laurie.

"I think not, for I might see something sad, and everyone looks so happy now, I don't believe they could be much improved." And Jo's eyes went slowly round the room, brightening as they looked, for the **prospect** was a pleasant one.

Father and Mother sat together, quietly reliving the first chapter of the romance, which for them began some twenty years ago. Amy was drawing the lovers, who sat apart in a beautiful world of their own, the light of which touched their faces with a grace the little artist could not copy. Beth lay on her sofa, talking cheerily with her old friend, who held her little hand as if he felt that it possessed the power to lead him along the peaceful way she walked. Jo lounged in her favorite low seat, with the grave quiet look which best became her, and Laurie, leaning on the back of her chair, his chin on a level with her curly head, smiled with his friendliest aspect, and nodded at her in the long glass which reflected them both.

So the curtain falls upon Meg, Jo, Beth, and Amy. Whether it ever rises again, depends upon the reception given the first act of the domestic drama called *Little Women*.

Vocabulary in Place

prospect, *n.* Something that is awaited or expected

Creative Writing

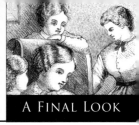

A FINAL LOOK

You Decide. Louisa May Alcott's *Little Women* was an instant commercial success, but it led to a flood of fanmail from readers who were eager to know what happened to the characters after the neat, though rather uneventful, ending. Alcott later wrote the following sequels to her bestseller: *Good Wives* (1869), *Little Men* (1871), and *Jo's Boys* (1886). Before you rush to find these titles in your bookstore or library, try inventing a sequel of your own in the form of a short story that involves one of the March sisters. Choose your favorite character and write a short story about what life is like a few years after the end of the book. Your treatment of the character in your story should reflect your understanding of that character's personality and how it developed over the course of the book. Your story should be believable. Where does this sister live now? Where are the other sisters, Laurie, and Mr. and Mrs. March now? What sorts of new "bundles" does this sister have to deal with, and how did her upbringing affect the way she handles problems in adulthood? When you have finished, read *Good Wives* (or a good synopsis), and find out what really became of Alcott's little women.

Speak Up! The girls form the Pickwick Club in order to practice their reading and writing, but public speaking is also an important function for the group. Speechwriting differs from writing essays because speeches depend heavily on the oral presentation of the work. Often, writers will include repetition, parallelism, and vivid images in order to more effectively capture the audience's attention, particularly if the speech is meant to persuade audience members to a certain point of view. Write your own 3-minute persuasive speech to be addressed to the Pickwick Club. Pretend that you are trying to gain admittance for a friend, just as Jo argues in favor of the addition of Laurie. You should list ways in which your friend would contribute to the club and make your argument both compelling and entertaining. Practice giving your speech in front of your classmates and friends.

A FINAL LOOK

Critical Writing

Novel Teaching. Sometimes *Little Women* is called a **didactic** novel, meaning that the author's intent was to teach moral lessons about how to behave or how to fulfill one's duties toward one's self, one's family, or one's community. Through her characters, Alcott illustrates why certain moral values are important, as well as why it can be so challenging for people to uphold their duties and remain true to a strict moral code. By the book's end, each of the March sisters has overcome her personal "bundle," or at least learned to deal with it. Write an explanatory essay in which you describe, using specific examples from the text, each sister's major bundle and at least one important moral lesson that the author intended for us to learn through that character. Use your knowledge of the Victorian era and refer to your character charts in order to determine what the author intended for readers to learn through this book and how she used her characters as teaching tools.

Film Critic. Over time, producers and directors have put together many stage and film adaptations of *Little Women.* The most recent film remake of the book is a 1994 production starring Winona Ryder. Watch a copy of this film or one of the older versions. It is often hard for directors to translate a novel directly into a script that can be acted out. Pay attention to some of the variations that occur between the movie script and the events in the novel. Write a review of the film in which you explain whether the director and actors were true to the original storyline or whether they took too many liberties in order to satisfy modern theatergoers. You might want to watch the recent version and an older version and compare the way in which different directors and screenwriters treat the same material. After you watch, pretend that you are the director of a new *Little Women* movie. Write an essay explaining how you might stage the actors differently from the movie that you just watched. Mention any scenes that you might take out or add. Would you change the details of the script? Develop some of your own ideas that might make your movie better than the previous versions while being true to the original plot.

Revision Checklist

RESOURCES

Audience and Purpose

- ☑ Is the piece appropriate to the intended audience?
- ☑ Does the piece have the appropriate level of formality or informality?
- ☑ Have you included the background information necessary for your audience to follow what you are saying?
- ☑ Does the piece accomplish the purpose for which it was written?

Style and Voice

- ☑ Does the piece contain vivid verbs and concrete, precise nouns?
- ☑ Are your word choices appropriate throughout? Can they be improved upon?
- ☑ Have you varied the types and lengths of sentences used in the piece?
- ☑ Will the piece be interesting to your reader?

Structure and Organization

- ☑ Does the introduction capture the attention of the reader?
- ☑ Where appropriate, do your paragraphs have topic sentences? Note: An introductory paragraph in a piece of expository writing may lack a topic sentence. Paragraphs in pieces of fictional writing typically do not have topic sentences. Body paragraphs in a piece of expository writing should have a topic sentence or, at the very least, a main idea.
- ☑ Do the body sentences in those paragraphs with topic sentences support the topic sentences?
- ☑ Do ideas follow one another logically throughout the piece?
- ☑ Have you used transitions to tie your ideas together?

Focus and Elaboration

- ☑ Are your main ideas supported with evidence, specific details, or examples?
- ☑ Have you included any material that is unnecessary or irrelevant to your topic or to the ideas and/or emotions that you are trying to convey?

Revision Checklist

Questions to Ask about an Essay

- ☑ Does the essay have a clear introduction, body, and conclusion?
- ☑ Does the introduction present a thesis statement, or main idea of the essay as a whole?
- ☑ Does each body paragraph present a main idea, in a topic sentence, that supports the thesis statement?
- ☑ Does the conclusion provide a satisfying ending for the essay? Does it restate or summarize the argument of the essay, make the main point again in another way, call upon the reader to take some action, or otherwise provide a sense of an ending?

Proofreading Checklist

RESOURCES

Manuscript Form

- ☑ Is each paragraph indented?
- ☑ Have you left standard margins (usually one inch) on all sides?
- ☑ If the piece is handwritten, is the writing legible?
- ☑ Does your piece have a title? Is the title written correctly, using uppercase and lowercase letters?
- ☑ Does your name and other information required by your teacher appear on the page in the appropriate place (generally in the upper, right-hand portion of the paper)?

Grammar and Usage

- ☑ Does each verb agree with its subject?
- ☑ Does each pronoun have a clear antecedent and agree with it?
- ☑ Are commonly confused pronouns such as *I* and *me* and *who* and *whom* used correctly?
- ☑ Have you avoided sentence fragments and run-ons?
- ☑ Are commonly confused words such as *lie* and *lay* and *effect* and *affect* used correctly?
- ☑ Have you avoided using double negatives?
- ☑ Have you used active sentences, instead of passive ones, whenever possible?

RESOURCES

Proofreading Checklist

Mechanics (punctuation and capitalization)
- ☑ Does every sentence begin with a capital letter?
- ☑ Does every sentence end with an end mark (a period, question mark, or exclamation mark)?
- ☑ Are commas, semicolons, and other punctuation marks used correctly?
- ☑ Are all direct quotations enclosed in quotation marks or, in the case of quotations longer than three lines, set off and indented from either side?
- ☑ Do all proper nouns and proper adjectives, including the names of people and places, use initial capitals?

Spelling
- ☑ Are all words used in the paper spelled correctly?
- ☑ Have you checked the spellings of any names of people or places that you have used?

Vocabulary from the Text

GLOSSARY

abashed, *past part.* Taken aback, as from embarrassment

abject, *adj.* Hopeless or wretched

abominable, *adj.* Truly awful

affable, *adj.* Gentle and gracious; approachable

affected, *adj.* Speaking or acting in an artificial way in order to make an impression

affliction, *n.* A cause of pain, stress, or suffering

agitated, *adj.* Upset or stirred up by something

air, *n.* Outward appearance; aura

alight, *v.* To step down from

allusion, *n.* Reference to something else; a vague or indirect mention of something

aloof, *adj.* Off by oneself; not friendly or approachable

ambitious, *adj.* Full of high hopes or big dreams of success

amiable, *adj.* Friendly, good-natured

amicable, *adj.* Friendly

amiss, *adj.* Out of place

appease, *v.* To soothe or quiet down

aristocratic, *adj.* Characteristic of the ruling class or nobility

artfully, *adv.* With skill and subtlety; not in an obvious way

assuage, *v.* To calm or pacify

bashful, *adj.* Shy

beckon, *v.* To call over or invite, usually with a hand motion

becoming, *adj.* Appropriately attractive

behold, *v.* To see or view something

benefactor, *n.* A person who helps another person

bind, *v.* To make a definite, lasting commitment or promise

blunder, *v.* To move unsteadily or make a careless mistake

blunt, *adj.* Abrupt and often embarassingly frank in speech

breach, *n.* An opening or tear; a disruption of friendly relations

bridle, *v.* To show anger; to take offense

brood, *v.* To focus attention on; protect; worry over

bulletin, *n.* A brief report or update of current news

calamity, *n.* Disaster

capitally, *adv.* Agreeable; excellently

265

Vocabulary from the Text

GLOSSARY

cavalier, *adj.* Carefree and nonchalant; casual

cease, *v.* To stop

chagrin, *n.* Annoyance or disappointment

chide, *v.* To scold

coax, *v.* Trick someone into revealing or doing something

complacently, *adv.* With satisfaction; contentedly

compose, *v.* To make oneself calm

conceited, *adj.* Arrogant; vain

condescension, *n.* The act of descending to the level of an inferior or looking down upon someone

confidant, *n.* A trusted friend with whom one shares secrets

confide, *v.* To tell something private

conscience, *n.* Sense of right and wrong; moral or spiritual guide

consign, *v.* To set apart for a special use or purpose

consolingly, *adv.* Soothingly, with encouragement and support; in a manner meant to make someone feel better

contempt, *n.* Scorn, disgust

contentedly, *adv.* With a calm, quiet feeling of comfort or satisfaction

contraband, *adj.* Prohibited from being imported or exported

contrary, *adj.* Opposed or opposite

contrite, *adj.* Genuinely sorry and sincere

cordial, *adj.* Warm and friendly

countenance, *n.* Appearance, especially the expression of the face

counteract, *v.* To attempt to improve, relieve, or replace, often by providing a better option

covet, *v.* To desire; to wish to possess

culinary, *adj.* Of or relating to the kitchen

culprit, *n.* The one guilty of wrongdoing; criminal

cunning, *adj.* Clever

daunted, *adj.* Intimidated or discouraged

dawdle, *v.* To poke along or waste time

delectable, *adj.* Extremely tasty; also highly pleasing or delightful

demeanor, *n.* Way of behaving or carrying oneself

demonstrative, *adj.* Marked by the open expression of emotions

Vocabulary from the Text

ined, *adj.* Sm

:ess, *n.* An ind

rvade, *v.* To s

GLOSSARY

denounce, *v.* To criticize sharply or condemn

despairing, *adj.* Without any hope

despondent, *adj.* Hopeless or very depressed

dexterity, *n.* Coordination, efficiency, and skill, especially involving use of the hands

dignified, *adj.* Formal and proper; concerned with appearances

dignity, *n.* The respect and honor associated with an important position

discontented, *adj.* Unhappy or dissatisfied

discretion, *n.* Restraint or judgment, especially in handling a secret or delicate matter

disheveled, *adj.* Untidy or sloppy; out of order

dismally, *adv.* Hopelessly; with despair

dismay, *n.* A feeling of disappointment or alarm

diversion, *n.* A game or pastime; leisure activity

docile, *adj.* Easy to get along with; easily tamed

dote, *v.* To be very kind and generous to

dowdy, *adj.* Lacking style or shabby

earnest, *adj.* Sincere; openly honest and direct

earnestness, *n.* A person's state that shows depth and sincerity of feeling

effectually, *adv.* Adequately; producing the desired effect

elated, *adj.* Thrilled, very happy and excited

eloquent, *adj.* Expressive; conveying thoughts vividly in speech

enchant, *v.* To cast a spell over; to attract or delight

ennui, *n.* Boredom; dissatisfaction resulting from lack of interest

enticement, *n.* A lure or attraction; a bribe or hint of future reward

estimable, *adj.* Worthy of praise, esteem, or admiration

evident, *adj.* Obvious

exertion, *n.* The act of putting great effort into something

exile, *n.* Forced removal from one's home

expectancy, *n.* Expectation; eager awaiting of something

exploit, *n.* Adventure, usually involving bravery or daring

Vocabulary from the Text

GLOSSARY

exultation, *n.* The act of rejoicing greatly; celebration

falter, *v.* To be unsteady in action or speak hesitantly from lack of confidence

feeble, *adj.* Weak

flourish, *v.* To wave about

frivolous, *adj.* Trivial; of little meaning or importance

gallant, *adj.* Courteous, very polite; flirtatious

gallivant, *v.* To roam about in search of a good time

glower, *v.* To look angrily

gravely, *adv.* Very seriously

grope, *v.* To feel one's way, especially in the dark; also to reach out for support

hospitality, *n.* Welcome

idle, *adj.* Lacking substance, value, or basis

idol, *n.* An image used as an object of worship

immense, *adj.* Enormous; of very large size or extent

impertinent, *adj.* Rude in speech; fresh

imploringly, *adv.* Pleadingly; with begging

impromptu, *adj.* Not planned in advance

incoherent, *adj.* Impossible to understand; not making sense

inconsistent, *adj.* Contradictory; the opposite of what one just said or did

indifferent, *adj.* Without care or concern

indignant, *adj.* Angry, especially anger brought on by something unjust or mean

industrious, *adj.* Hardworking

infringe, *v.* To violate or break the rules

inquiry, *n.* A question about something or someone

irascible, *adj.* Crabby; difficult to get along with

issue, *v.* To come out

keen, *adj.* Sharp or intent

kindle, *v.* To flame or become very bright; to catch on fire

lame, *adj.* Disabled so that movement, especially walking, is difficult or impossible

Vocabulary from the Text

lament, *n.* Expression of sorrow or grief

languid, *adj.* Showing little spirit or energy; weak

lark, *v.* To engage in spirited fun or pranks

leave, *n.* Permission

libel, *v.* To make a false written or spoken statement that damages someone's reputation

lisp, *v.* To speak imperfectly, like a child

literal, *adj.* Focused on exactly what is said, word for word

lumber, *v.* To be heavy on one's feet, not graceful or effortless

maneuver, *n.* A skillful or strategic movement, sometimes a bit tricky

martial, *v.* Relating to an army or to military life

meddle, *v.* To interfere

melodramatic, *adj.* Elaborate or exaggerated; overly emotional

modestly, *adv.* With a moderate opinion of ones own talent and abilities

mortification, *n.* A feeling of shame, humiliation

mystify, *v.* To confuse or puzzle, to make mysterious

nettle, *v.* To annoy or irritate

nimble, *adj.* Skilled in movement or action

notion, *n.* Impulse, whim; a spur-of-the-moment idea or decision

novelty, *n.* Something new or unusual

obligingly, *adv.* Agreeably; without complaining

omen, *n.* Sign of the outcome of future events

pacify, *v.* To calm down

pallor, *n.* Extreme or unnatural paleness

patronizing, *adj.* Belittling or condescending, as if one is better than others, even if well-meant

penitent, *adj.* Very sorry, apologetic

pensive, *adj.* Deeply, dreamily thoughtful

perplexed, *adj.* Confused or puzzled

perturbed, *adj.* Troubled or upset

pervade, *v.* To spread into every corner

petulantly, *adv.* With a pout; in an unreasonably irritated manner

petulantly, *v.* In an unreasonably ill-tempered or irritable way

Vocabulary from the Text

Glossary

pious, *adj.* Deeply religious; devout

pique, *n.* Slight temper tantrum or feeling of resentment or wounded pride, often in response to something that seems like a slight

piteous, *adj.* Worthy of pity; pathetic

prevail, *v.* To use persuasion. Often used with *on*, *upon*, or *with*.

prim, *adj.* Very precise and proper; straight-laced

procession, *n.* A group of people (or vehicles) moving along in an orderly fashion

procrastination, *n.* Putting things off or delaying them to an indefinite time in the future

prospect, *n.* Something that is awaited or expected

provoking, *adj.* Baiting or stirring up anger; aggravating or irritating

prudence, *n.* Self-discipline and carefulness

prudently, *adj.* With good judgement or common sense

quaver, *n.* Shaky or trembling sound; unsteadiness

queer, *adj.* Strange; odd

quench, *v.* To put a limit on

rapture, *n.* An experience of ecstasy; a feeling of being carried off

rapturous, *adj.* Ecstatic (very happy) and overcome with awe or surprise; thrilled

rash, *adj.* Reckless or done in a hurry, without much thought; impulsive or foolish

ravish, *v.* To seize and carry away by force

recess, *n.* An indentation or niche (in a wall or between furniture)

recline, *v.* To lie back, rest

recollect, *v.* To remember, recall

reconcile, *v.* To come to terms with; accept

refined, *adj.* Smooth and polished; improved through hard work and effort

refuge, *n.* Hideout or retreat; a safe, quiet place

relapse, *n.* Setback in the process of getting well

relent, *v.* To give in

relic, *n.* A treasure or leftover from the past

Vocabulary from the Text

reminisce, *v.* To share memories; to trade stories and recollections about the past

remorseful, *adj.* Full of regret for one's actions

render, *v.* To cause to become

renounce, *v.* To give up something, especially for good

reposeful, *adj.* Calm and peaceful

reprehensible, *adj.* Horrible, hateful; worthy of blame or criticism

reproachful, *adj.* Expressing criticism, disapproval or blame

reproving, *adj.* Disapproving

resentment, *n.* An angry feeling, often about something that is unfair or undeserved

resign, *v.* To accept as inevitable; to submit

resolve, *v.* To make a commitment to do something

retort, *v.* To reply or make a counter argument

revel, *v.* To thoroughly enjoy or immerse oneself in

roguish, *adj.* Naughty or mischievous

rummage, *v.* To search through a pile or layer of things

satirical, *adj.* Sarcastic; intentionally insulting or humiliating another publicly

savage, *adj.* Very angry; on the verge of being violent

scornfully, *adv.* Showing disgust or contempt

seldom, *adv.* Not often; rarely

self-possessed, *adj.* Cool and calm in a crisis; poised, not flustered

self-reproachful, *adj.* Full of blame for oneself

sentimental, *adj.* Characterized or influenced by emotion as opposed to reason

sidle, *v.* To move sideways or stealthily

skirmish, *n.* A small conflict or battle

smitten, *past part.* Affected sharply with great feeling, afflicted. (From *smite*, to strike down.)

sober, *adj.* Serious

sociable, *adj.* Friendly; eager to make friends

solace, *n.* Source of comfort, especially in difficult circumstances

solemnity, *n.* The quality or condition of being serious and sober

Vocabulary from the Text

Glossary

stamina, *n.* Strength to resist illness or hardships; endurance

start, *v.* To move suddenly or jump when startled

stratagem, *n.* Clever plan or scheme

subdue, *v.* To suppress or fight down; to overcome

submissive, *adj.* Willing to acknowledge or give in to someone else's authority or control

tact, *n.* Polite sense of restraint; ability to say and do the right thing at the right time

tempest, *n.* A violent storm; also, turmoil, uproar, commotion

tranquility, *n.* A state of being calm, peaceful, and unruffled; not easily disturbed

transfixed, *past part.* Motionless, as with terror or awe

treacherous, *adj.* Very dangerous

trifle, *adv.* A small amount

triumphant, *adj.* Proud and victorious

tyrannize, *v.* To bully or rule over without question

unworldly, *adj.* More concerned with other things besides money or material possessions

vain, *adj.* Excessively proud of one's appearance or accomplishments

vex, *v.* To annoy or upset; aggravate

vigil, *n.* A watch kept during normal sleeping hours

voraciously, *adv.* With great appetite

vulgar, *adj.* Rude or offensive

will, *n.* The part of the mind by which one deliberately chooses a course of action; determination

wistful, *adj.* Tinged with sadness or regret

wits, *n. pl.* Intelligence and resourcefulness

wrought, *adj.* Put together, created